Also by Merrie Destefano

LOST GIRLS

MERRIE DESTEFANO

Entangled Publishing, LLC
2614 South Timberline Road
Suite 105, PMB 159
Fort Collins, CO 80525
rights@entangledpublishing.com

Entangled Teen is an imprint of Entangled Publishing, LLC.

Visit our website at www.entangledpublishing.com.

Edited by Heather Howland
Cover design by LJ Anderson, Mayhem Cover Creations
Cover images by
Kesu01/depositphotos
everlite/iStock
Interior design by Toni Kerr and Heather Howland

ISBN 978-1-64063-426-8
Ebook ISBN 978-1-64063-425-1

Manufactured in the United States of America
First Edition December 2018

10 9 8 7 6 5 4 3 2 1

entangled teen
an imprint of Entangled Publishing LLC

For Jesse.
I would save the world for you.

"Whosoever saves a single life, saves an entire universe."

Mishnah, Sanhedrin 4:5

Part 1: Jumpers

2037 A.D.

PROLOGUE

The invasion started as soon as the sun went down.

It was the best day of our lives. For the first time in years, we finally had hope. We weren't worried about the drought or the Depression or the fact that space solar power hadn't solved our energy crisis. Our parties stretched as far as the eye could see. From one end of the United States to the other, there were fireworks and dancing and politicians giving speeches.

People lucky enough to have jobs took the day off work. All my friends and I met after school.

A group of us hung out down in the street where we could see the shadows and smog of Los Angeles in the distance. Natalie sneaked some beer from her mom's fridge; I had a handful of joints from my parents' stash. My little brother, Gabe, was goofing off with Justin and Billy. We were all daring Justin to lift cars and, being the abnormally strong, easygoing Genetic that he was, he laughed and raised the front end of a Caddy off the ground. Genetics like Justin were bred for war in a government program that had been abandoned long ago.

Nobody believed we'd ever go to war again.

They were wrong.

My little brother's eyes glistened with excitement when the *Valiant* launched.

Even though the launch was actually all the way in the San Gabriel Mountains, we saw it up close and personal when our skin sites flashed images inside our minds.

All around us, people *ooh*ed and *aah*ed, glad to have their addiction to skin site programs temporarily soothed.

It felt like we were all standing at the base of the rocket as it ascended, up and up into the heavens, heading toward Titan. This was the one event that was going to change everything. We were sending a mining expedition to another planet, and since we were all investors in this publically funded program, we were going to get rich and climb out of the horrible Second Depression.

We'd be able to buy food and clothes and new tech.

We had hope. So much hope.

I think Justin may have given me a hug; I may have leaned into it longer than I ever had before. I may have wondered why we were only friends when he was drop-dead gorgeous—

But that was as far as I got. It's as far as I ever get.

Because that's when the invasion started.

As soon as the *Valiant* disappeared, flying out of our sight and out of Earth's orbit, everything changed.

There was a bright flash of light, almost like a thousand mirrors were swiveling and turning all around us. The ground tilted, and I almost fell, one hand grabbing onto the same car that Justin had lifted a minute ago. And then, so many things happened at once that I can never remember which one was first.

An army of silver aliens appeared, walking out of the mirror doors, their skin sparkling like stardust in the dim light.

Gabe stumbled back. "What the—"

I didn't stop to think. I grabbed his hand and jerked him toward me. "Stay with me," I told him. I had no idea what was going to happen next, but I knew that my fourteen-year-old brother rarely made the right decisions.

None of us knew what was going to happen, but Justin's Genetic training kicked in. He braced his legs and took a defensive stance in front of all of us. "Sara, go!"

I didn't go. I couldn't make myself move. Natalie grabbed my other hand. Billy just stood and stared.

The silvery aliens surveyed our street, still filled with people who'd been laughing and dancing only moments ago, but now ran and screamed or stood frozen in place like us, their mouths hanging open in shock.

That was the worst decision they could have made.

Justin looked at me again, his blue eyes pleading and resolute all at once. "Get them out of here now!"

I don't know how he knew that the aliens wanted to kill us, but he did. It was like he had a sixth sense that none of us knew about.

In an instant, the alien creatures morphed from flesh into smoke and hurtled toward the people still in the street.

It happened so fast.

Justin was faster. He didn't run. He yanked the bumper off the Caddy he'd just lifted and swung it at the few aliens who were still flesh and blood. It was a slaughter. Their bright, shining blood sprayed through the night air until he was covered with it, until he was as bright and shining as they were.

It all happened in a fraction of a second. A blink of an eye.

The plumes of alien smoke dove into the open mouths of everyone who'd been gaping or screaming. Billy was one of them. He twisted and fell to the ground, choking as an alien pushed its way down his throat. I dropped to my knees, shaking him, trying to save him but not sure what to do.

Justin pulled me to my feet, his face blotched and glowing, sorrow in his eyes. "You can't save him. Go. Keep your mouth closed and run."

I didn't want to leave him behind, but instinct and self-preservation kicked in. Less than a heartbeat or two had passed, and now half the people in my neighborhood were flopping around on the ground, just like Billy.

Natalie and Gabe and I ran, not knowing where to go. We ran as fast and as long as we could, around parked cars and past abandoned buildings, down an alley, and through some backyards, doing our best to keep to the shadows. Every street was crowded, full of panicked, choking people.

I recognized some of the people we ran past. They were my neighbors, they were the local gang members, they were kids I knew from school. Twisting, flinching, choking, and then—climbing back to their feet, eyes glazed, jaws hanging loose, muscles tense. That was the part I didn't want to remember because it was so horrible. But I had to remember it. I had to believe it.

Life on planet Earth depended on me remembering and believing.

My neighbors started to attack one another. Those who had been choking were different now, like they were possessed. They started to kill people who were still normal.

People like me. And Gabe. And Natalie.

"Holy crap, girl, run! Come on, Gabe!" Natalie shouted. She was a take-charge girl and she was doing just that. She'd broken away from me and was leading the way, charging ahead of us down the street, through another alley, and then running across Bristol Street. I think she may have been heading toward her house or maybe the high school. There was some point of reference in her head—that's how she was—and she was heading toward it.

But she forgot the simplest of things.

She didn't look when she ran across the street.

She didn't know that Mrs. Thornton, the old lady who dug through my trash on a regular basis and lived on her dead husband's pension, was possessed. She didn't know that Mrs. Thornton was racing her SUV down Bristol Street, looking for people to run over.

Or that she'd already gotten two dogs and a little boy.

"Natalie!" I screamed.

"Stop!" Gabe shouted.

Natalie glanced back at us but not in time.

The grill of Mrs. Thornton's SUV hit Natalie square in the chest. She bounced backward, then her head hit the pavement with a dull *crack*, then the SUV ran over her and finished the job.

So fast. I didn't know someone could die that fast.

I couldn't breathe. I couldn't run. I couldn't think.

Until Mrs. Thornton backed up her car and aimed it at Gabe.

We ran.

We hid.

We waited.

Maybe everything would have been different if I'd come up with a better plan. Maybe. But I still hadn't figured out what that better plan was.

Gabe retched and shivered. I wept.

But we didn't say anything. We huddled together in silence, beneath a flattened cardboard box that a homeless guy used to live in. We weren't too far from our apartment, which was probably one of my biggest mistakes. I just never expected that anyone would be looking for us.

At least, not anyone who wanted to kill us.

I thought maybe I'd see Mom or Dad from this vantage point. Maybe one of them would have a plan. Or maybe Justin would still be out there, and he'd come to help us.

All of Santa Ana was in chaos, houses burning, cars crashing, people screaming. A jet that was heading toward John Wayne Airport took a sudden nosedive and crashed beside the 405 Freeway. We saw it go down, felt the ground shake when it hit, saw the spray of metal, the explosion, the fire that wouldn't go out. The whole freeway was as bright as day for miles. Then it was like someone realized what a great idea that had been. About twenty minutes passed, then every plane heading for the airport fell from the sky, causing huge explosions that started to take out chunks of Santa Ana, Costa Mesa, Fountain Valley, and Irvine.

Gabe hid his face, and I held him in my arms.

This was an alien invasion. But we were the ones killing one another.

People ran up and down the street, sometimes crying out in fear, sometimes in joy when they found a loved one. From my vantage point, I couldn't see their faces, only their feet. A pair of white Converse high-tops raced back and forth, and a tiny alarm went off in my head. Somebody I knew wore shoes like that, but my brain wasn't working right. I couldn't remember who. Mud on the soles, splatters of blood on the canvas, dots of something that glowed in the dark.

Alien blood.

My heart slowed, and my eyes narrowed.

Justin fighting those aliens, swinging that Caddy bumper.

But these weren't Justin's shoes.

It was as if my thoughts gave off an audible signal,

something that said, *Here, they're over here, hurry before they get away—*

The shoes stopped running, turned toward me, started walking in my direction.

I inched backward, pulling my brother with me.

"Gabe?" a voice called. "Hey, buddy, are you in there?"

It was Billy. But he was possessed, wasn't he? Or had he found a way to break free?

I didn't need to say anything; Gabe could tell something wasn't right. I nodded at him, giving him the signal to run. I gestured which way to go. My little brother was going to veer to the left, while I was going to run straight at Billy. I was planning to knock him down, giving Gabe and me time to escape.

But two things happened at once.

At exactly the same instant.

Gabe and I jumped out of the box, but before either one of us could run, Billy raised a gun and shot my brother. Right in the chest. Game over.

My brother crumpled to the ground, his eyes staring forward, his final breath coming out in a gurgle of blood.

No! No! The shock of his death ran through me like ice. My whole body went numb, and I didn't even have time to feel the pain or the sorrow or the anger.

Because the second thing happened. Right then.

Mirror doors opened; fire and light poured into the street, as bright as one of those plane crashes. The ground slipped beneath my feet. Billy's head spun around, and we both stared as another glowing alien stepped out from the mirror doors.

"Shit!" Billy said and suddenly, he went into a panic, like he didn't have enough time to do what he had to do. He swung back toward me, lifting his gun, aiming it at me.

But before he could fire, a blast of scorching white

light shot toward him from the street. It hit him in the back, knocked him a step forward, and his body caught on fire. He opened his mouth and screamed while his body dissolved in a pile of smoldering ash and flame. That alien inside him tried to escape but failed.

"Sara, come with me," the alien from the mirror door said, its timbre hollow, its accent foreign. It walked toward me, one hand outstretched. "I want to help."

I didn't stop to think. I was still in survival mode and, because of it, I almost destroyed every chance the human race had. I knelt, grabbed Billy's gun from the pile of ash, stood, and held the weapon with both hands.

I had no idea how to shoot it, but still I aimed it at the alien.

"Stay away from me!" I said, my hands shaking.

"Do you want to save your brother? Your friend Natalie?" the creature asked as it continued to approach me. "What about your parents?" It paused. "Justin?"

"It's too late to save Gabe or Natalie. And how do you know us?"

"I know you because I've been trying to save your world for a very long time."

I shook my head, not believing him.

"Help me save Gabe. He always dies today, but if you help me, we can change that." The alien tilted its head, studying me. "I've met you before. I hope you say yes this time."

"*This* time?"

"I'm a time traveler, Sara. You can be one, too."

My hands tightened on the gun. My heartbeat thundered in my ears. None of what it was saying made sense. "What does Gabe have to do with any of this? Why my brother?"

In the distance, a crowd of people screamed as yet another jet plummeted from the skies. The alien glanced over its shoulder at the growing carnage. "We don't have long. Maybe a minute or two before my brothers learn where you are. You're the target now. The next plane crash will be right here. Just nod your head."

I don't know why I did it. I had so many questions. But some part of me knew I was out of options. I was all alone. I wasn't going to live long—I could feel it, like some part of me was already gone.

I nodded.

That alien was Aerithin, part of an alien resistance, a rebel who didn't want to slaughter every race his kind—the Xua—targeted. He was different. Later, he explained his plan to save us, although he would never give me very many details. But he did tell me that he'd been trying to save Gabe for a long time and, as a result, Aerithin was getting weaker. Time travel breaks down alien DNA.

Gabe was the key to human survival. If I could get him through the night and through the initial invasion, Earth would be saved.

Save my brother, save the world.

That was all I knew.

Aerithin grabbed my hand and pulled me toward an alien beast that waited for us in the street. Tall as an elephant and made of long liquid strands of fire, it watched me as I approached. I took a cautious step nearer, wondering if I'd get burned. The fire-beast leaned its head down so I could touch it. I ran my fingers through its fur—it felt smooth and slippery, like threads of warm light, and I felt a deep vibration, like it was purring.

It looked terrifying, but it acted like it already knew me, bending down for me to climb up onto its back, waiting until both Aerithin and I were aboard before letting out a mighty roar. The mirror doors opened, and I saw reflections of myself, a thousand different Saras, a hundred different lives, countless endings to my story.

A *crack* sounded, like the universe had split in two, as we raced through the doors. I glanced backward and saw my neighborhood consumed in an explosion as a 747 jet crashed, right where I had been standing moments earlier.

Death was behind me, so I leaned into the future, a loop of time travel that would let me relive this horrible day, always hoping for a better ending. One where I somehow saved the world.

1

Traveling through time is kind of like dying.

It's terrifying. You never know when it's going to happen. When it does happen, it hurts so bad you don't want to survive.

Gabe just burned to death in a car wreck, Natalie was shot, I don't know where Justin is, and Billy was just possessed by a Xua. Usually Aerithin is here by now, but he's late, and I'm running.

The Xua are right behind me.

I've failed. Again. For the fourteenth time.

Back in the beginning, I didn't know who had attacked us or why. Aerithin tried to explain things to me, or at least as much as he thought I needed to know. The problem was I didn't always believe him, especially when he was talking about "cascading events." I thought he was talking about some weird alien religion, not a scientific anomaly.

Apparently, there are certain things that can never be changed, no matter what you do or how hard you try. Cascading events are like destiny. These are the events that set other things in motion. The launch of the *Valiant*, my meeting Aerithin, my supposedly meeting some guy named Noah in the future—according to Aerithin, those are all unchangeable.

I can't change them no matter how hard I try.

I know, because I didn't believe him. Not at first.

My first three jumps through time, I tried to stop the *Valiant* launch. I thought it was the pivotal event that needed to change in order to save our world, because the launch always led to Gabe's death. Save Gabe, save the world, right? It made sense to me, but the cascading-events thing always got in the way.

Normal people live and learn. Not me. I watch everyone I love die and I learn.

In the distance, a skyscraper tumbles to the ground, dust and debris flying into the sky, shadowing the city of Los Angeles. The sky darkens, and I can feel the end, can taste it on my tongue.

Right when I think I'm toast, Aerithin appears. He calls to me, and I jump onto his steed, that fiery lionlike beast, and together the three of us gallop away. There's only one place to go—back.

In an instant, we're racing through the Corridor of Time that separates the future from the past, and I think we're safe.

Then I glance over Aerithin's shoulder behind us and see that the army of Xua is chasing us, all of them running as fast as the beast we travel upon. Some are running faster.

All the breath leaves my chest. *No.* They've never done this before. They've never been able to follow into the Corridor.

And then I realize—

The Xua have learned, too.

"Faster!" I yell, leaning forward, my hands gripping the beast's long fiery fur.

It cries back with a thunderous roar.

The faster Xua are gaining ground, and I don't think we're going to make it, but we have to. If we don't, it's all over for everyone on Earth. The Xua will win, and everyone I know will be dead.

The door to my past opens up ahead of us. Just a little bit farther and I'll be there.

But the fastest Xua have already climbed onto Aerithin's fire-beast. One of them wrestles with Aerithin, trying to dislodge him, while the other Xua grabs at me. Its long fingers latch and snarl into my hair. I scream, turn, and bite its hand. Its glowing blood sprays on my face.

I'm not going to make it; I know it. They're going to kill us both.

"Jump, now!" Aerithin yells. His steed slams to a halt, and I fly off, tumbling toward the open doorway ahead of us. I roll, then hit the ground running. Another version of myself stares back at me through the mirror and, for an instant, I feel like Alice in Wonderland staring through a magical looking glass.

Behind me, Aerithin howls in pain, a horrific sound that makes me shake. I can tell by his soul-wrenching cry that he's in torment. They've caught him and they're probably killing him and I can't stop it. I have to escape. If Aerithin dies, I'm the last chance for my world—

I stretch one hand toward my reflection, and as soon as my hand touches hers, we merge. It feels like I've been slammed against a wall, like my bones are poking through my skin, and I'm being turned inside out. But I have no choice. It's this or we all die.

I'm in the past.

I'm crammed back inside my own skin.

For a few brief moments, I can still hear Aerithin screaming. Then it's quiet, except for my breathing and my heartbeat, except for the panic that surges through me.

My hands tremble.

I made it.

But they got Aerithin. Nobody yells like that unless…

Please, don't let him be dead, I beg, even though I fear it's already too late. *If he's dead, this is my last life, my last chance to save my brother, my last chance to save everyone.*

Instinctively, I listen for the low growl of enemy ships circling through the skies overhead. The Xua have never come to Earth before the launch, but I don't know what to expect. None of this has happened before. They've never followed us through the Corridor of Time. They've never caught Aerithin.

Have they finally learned how to change destiny?

So many things I've gotten wrong, so many times I've failed. If this is my last chance to get it right, I'm screwed, because the Xua are already a step ahead of me.

2

he first time I saw one of the aliens—the Xua—I thought they were all the same. They look alike with their long arms and yellow eyes and glowing silver skin, but they're *not*. Not at all. There are three types of Xua, and Aerithin made sure I understood the difference, because knowing exactly which type I was dealing with in a situation meant the difference between living and dying.

The first are the Jumpers. These aliens are the foot soldiers of the Xua army. Fast and determined, they're the first to turn into a vaporous smoke and enter a human host through the person's mouth. You'll know when a human is possessed by a Jumper—their muscles tense, their jaw hangs loose, and they hunch forward when they walk, like they're on a mission.

Jumpers can't hide what they are. There'd be no point anyway, because as far as they're concerned, they *will* possess you.

Second are the Hunters. They're the Xua's special-ops soldiers. Hunters are highly intelligent, methodical, and nearly impossible to evade. Unlike Jumpers, when they possess a human, they're skilled enough to manipulate their host's body. You'll never know there's an alien standing in front of you until it's too late. They can track a person for miles—that's their primary purpose, and they're extremely good at it.

A Hunter possessed Billy once. That's how he was able to find Gabe and me.

I need to avoid Hunters at all costs.

Finally, there are the Leaders. All Xua answer to them. These aliens are calculating and controlled, planning every attack and leading every battle. They don't care how many Xua they lose in a skirmish, as long as they win. A Leader led that first attack on my neighborhood.

Like Hunters, you'll never know a human is possessed by a Leader unless they want you to, though in my experience, they don't seem to care whether I know. And why would they? They're just as deadly as Hunters, *and* they have an army of Xua at their backs.

The possession itself is horrible. Being taken over by a Xua is like being possessed by a demon: you have no control over what you say or do. No matter which type you're dealing with, if a Xua takes full possession of a human, that human is dead. There's no saving them—a fact I learned that very first invasion. A Xua can leave a host's body and possess another person if it wants, but humans weren't built to withstand it. Our insides get ripped to shreds. Sometimes you can even see the claw marks on the body, torn apart from the inside out. Sometimes it's a full-body explosion.

Yeah, you can't come back from that.

I pull in a long breath and look around. It takes a moment for my surroundings to appear, for fog to give way to walls, for blotches of color to turn into furniture. I'm in my bedroom and, for a split second, I almost feel safe. There's a photo of Gabe and me from last Christmas on my nightstand, there's the vintage *Anne of Green Gables* book Grams gave me for my ninth birthday, there's the thrift-store stuffed bear Dad gave me when I started having panic attacks. He doesn't know they began when I first traveled through time. He doesn't know I travel through time, period.

Voices rise and fall in the kitchen. My parents. They're always arguing, and it's always a different topic.

I could almost relax into how normal it feels to be back home, for life to feel the same. But I know I can't.

First things first. There's one thing I have to do before I round up my crew and impress the urgency of the end of the world upon them. I have to check in on Gabe and make sure he's okay. Then I have to tell him the truth about all of this.

I've seen my little brother die fifteen times. He's drowned, burned to death, been shot, and stabbed. He's had his head chopped off, his eyes plucked out, and his skin flayed. He's died from a car crash and he's been poisoned.

Even though I know he won't believe me—heck, even I wouldn't believe what I have to say—he has to know how to fight. I wasted ten jumps trying to keep him in the dark and trying to protect him. On the eleventh jump, I lost it and told him everything. Ever since then, he's survived a little longer each invasion.

This time, I'm going to teach him how to fight. I didn't think he was ready before, or maybe I was just scared of letting him get too close to the Xua, but we're out of options.

I slip from my room as quietly as I can, but it doesn't matter. The volume of my parents' fight has escalated. Something just crashed in the living room—I think Mom threw a lamp or a beer bottle—so nobody is looking at me. I sneak down the hallway, past the shadows in the living room, a volatile moving-fighting performance, arms swinging, brows lowered, snippets of words spilling out.

"Our credit got shut down because of your gambling debts—"

"Maybe if you made more money—"

"Maybe if you didn't suck down all the profits—"

"What profits—"

I cringe, remembering a time when they didn't fight, back before all this started, before the Second Great Depression, before the invasion, before Gabe's first death. If I could pick a timeline to live in, that'd be the one I'd pick—the one where we were all a normal family, when nobody was pushing drugs, when Gabe was just a video-game-addicted boy, when I was a girl trying to graduate from high school and hold down a job at the same time.

When I was just a normal girl with a secret crush on a seventeen-year-old boy who's supposed to be my friend.

Justin.

There's never enough time to fall in love when you're trying to save the world.

The closer I get to Gabe's room, the tighter and smaller the hallway feels. The low hum of tech that's hooked up to SkyPower filters through the thin walls. I'm not sure if our low-income access to space solar power is a blessing or a curse with as many hours as my little brother spends playing video games.

My throat is dry as I open his door, not bothering to knock. There's no need to be polite when you've got the end of humanity hanging over your head.

My fourteen-year-old brother sits at his desk curved over his tablet, his thumbs flicking the controls as he plays one of his favorite video games. Headphones cover his ears, and he's lost in his own world, where he's in control and he can survive if he just practices hard enough.

I wish it were that easy.

"Hey," I say as I approach him.

He glances up, only slightly startled to see me.

"S'up?" he asks, dimples growing as his grin widens. He takes off his headphones and hangs them loosely around his neck.

Soft blue light flares from his screen and patterns from his game scroll across his face, revealing those brown eyes, the face that looks a lot like mine, the wild dark hair that neither one of us can ever keep under control, the cheekbones that look like Mom, the nose that looks like Dad.

Gabe stares at me, waiting for me to speak and, I swear, I want time to stop. I want to live forever in this moment where my brother is safe and happy and alive. Where we're just two kids from Santa Ana, not the only hope for our planet.

I grab his left hand and put something in his palm. It's a laser switchblade. My weapon of choice. It's old tech that can survive an EMP, a power outage, an earthquake, a flood, name your favorite disaster. Better yet, it's solar-powered and needs only about half an hour in the sun for two weeks of full-time use—handy when the government controls power consumption.

The most important thing? This baby can kill a Xua, even when it's in smoke mode and halfway down someone's throat.

"What the—" he begins, but then the geek boy he is stops to admire how cool this old-fashioned weapon is. He's fascinated by old tech and old sci-fi, two things that work in my favor. I look around his room, at his hand-drawn pictures of Superman and the X-Men, at the list of digital graphic novels he wants to check out from the library, and at the black-market photocopied poster of an old movie, *Zombie Brides From Outer Space*. A cardboard model of the Mars terraforming project rests on his nightstand, beside a partially painted, handmade clay model of the *Valiant*.

I wish, in at least one of these timelines, he wouldn't be so blasted enthusiastic about the pivotal event in our future that will kill him and change everything.

"Where'd you get this?" he asks, completely transfixed by the blade that glows with a short beam of red light when he snaps it open.

"It's a secret," I say.

He looks up at me, his eyes wide, excitement in his voice. "Whoa. Isn't this thing illegal? Any chance I can keep it?"

"Yup. I have one, too," I say.

He grins and turns it over in his hand. "Wicked."

"Let's go up on the roof, and I'll teach you how to use it."

"Seriously?"

"Yup. Come on."

Gabe and I practice for two hours. I make up a story that isn't a story. I explain that if someone's coming from another planet, maybe their physiology is different from ours. What if they're solid sometimes but a vapor other times?

"You mean like the monsters in *The Urban Alien Trash Kings*?" he asks.

"Uh, sure." I haven't seen that movie or read that graphic novel. I've never even heard of it, but if it gives him a point of reference, then we'll use it. "If they're in vapor form or, let's say they're like smoke—"

"Smoke! That's cool!"

I frown. "It's not cool. It's creepy. Anyway, if they're smoke and they're flying through the air, swing your laser like this." I sweep my blade up and to the left. "If you cut through their vapor trail—or whatever the heck you want to call it—they'll die."

Gabe does a couple of practice swings. I watch to make sure he gets it right. Before long, he's got more enthusiasm and each strike looks killer.

"And let's say this *Urban Alien Trash King* monster is flying toward you. It probably wants to get inside you and possess you—"

"Holy crap, that's so wicked. You should be writing graphic novels!"

"Gabe, pay attention!"

"Sorry. It's just, that was a great idea."

I sigh, then continue. "It will probably want to get inside you through your mouth, so keep it closed! Don't yell, don't talk, don't frigging sneeze when one of these things is nearby—"

"So much great detail, we should be writing this down. Seriously, this is better than the *Trash Kings* or *Body Snatchers* or *The 5th Wave*—"

I kick his leg. "Mouth closed or you're dead! Now, fight!"

He obeys, mouth clamped shut, chin jutting out, right arm swinging, red laser blade glowing. Then he surprises me. He begins to advance, one bold step at a time, like he's taking down an entire enemy army. He swivels at the hips to get an imaginary Xua to his left, whips back around to get one behind him, moves forward two steps and then takes down two more—one to the right, one in front of him.

My little brother is a frigging natural.

Now is the time to tell him. He won't believe me—not at first, anyway. He never does. Still, he has to know. I give him my best Big Sister stare, the one that always makes him freeze in place.

"There really is an alien invasion coming," I tell him.

He snorts. "Yeah, right."

"The day of the launch, they're coming to kill us."

He rolls his eyes.

"All our friends are going to die, Gabe. Even Mom and Dad—"

His face turns pale, his eyes widen, and I swear I can hear his heartbeat speeding up. "You're starting to freak me out."

"Good. Because, if we're not really, really careful, you're going to die, too."

It's as if he knows this is true, as if he can feel his life getting shorter, like he's going to stop breathing any second. I hate this part. I know what it feels like to struggle with anxiety, and I just gave my little brother a panic attack.

"Shit, Sara, why are you saying all this?" His voice comes out in a ragged whisper, a long space between each word.

"Because it's my job to keep you alive. I have to. *We* have to."

"Why do you have to keep *me* alive? And who is 'we'? Are you— Have you been hearing voices?" He pauses and focuses on my face, studying me. "Maybe we should get you to see a doctor?"

I shake my head. Trying to make Gabe believe me has been one of the hardest parts of the last few jumps. I take a deep breath. "Okay, I'll make you a deal. Until the launch, let's just pretend there really will be an invasion. Once that rocket goes up in the sky, you need to be with me and you have to stay with me, got it? We stay together until the sun comes up. Then I'll go see a doctor. Deal?"

I hold out my hand, waiting.

His eyes narrow; he chews on his lip. It feels like a century passes. Finally, he extends his hand and shakes mine. This is something we've done since he was a little kid, and it was usually when I was promising not to tell Mom or Dad something he had done wrong. I covered for him so many times and took the blame, because our parents didn't have much patience for a boy like him. A boy who got beat up by local gangs, who forgot to do his homework, and who sometimes broke into their stash of drugs.

For now, he's safe.

"I gotta go, Gabe," I tell him. "See you at dinner, 'kay? Promise?"

"You're the weirdest sister in the world," he says.

I give him a hug.

Then I dash off to enlist the next member of my team, hoping that it goes smoother than this.

3

Natalie is my closest friend and the only person I can really confide in. She knows all my deepest, darkest secrets.

Including how I really feel about Justin.

But whenever I tell her about the Xua, she looks for the plot flaw in my story. Really, what sane person would believe that aliens are coming to take over our world and that apparently the key to stopping it all is to keep my brother alive?

I still go to her, though, jump after jump. I can't do this without her. Besides being a hacker supreme, she has the best ideas, and she thinks so far outside the box that you forget you're even in a box. I know I have to head over to her first, even though there's someone I want to see even more.

Justin.

He's in my thoughts when I call Natalie on my skin sites—a series of wetware transmitters we had installed back when I was ten when they were the latest techno rage. Pretty much everyone born within the last hundred years now has to listen to an endless stream of government-approved music and news.

It's why half the people in L.A. are addicts. What we call "Addies."

I jog down the stairs, out the front door, and down the street, until finally my call goes through and I hear her voice.

"What's up, Sara?" she asks. "You don't sound right. Is something wrong?"

Well, there's the part about how we only have a few days to do something that really takes about a year, and oh yeah, the last time we did this, you died, right in my frigging arms, your blood pouring out onto the ground, and then I was gone, traveling through time again, with your blood still on my hands—

I hate telling her that part.

"Yeah, can we hang out?" I ask, my voice shaking. "Like, now?"

"Sure. Where are you?"

"I'm almost there." I sprint around a corner, past a cluster of First Street Dragons in the midst of a drug deal, and I see her, standing on her front porch, one hand on her ear as she tries to block out other noises so she can hear me better.

I wish Justin were here, too. And Gabe. And Billy. Unfortunately, it never goes well if I try to tell them all at once. Either Billy or Gabe will think it's all a joke, and it ends up taking days to convince them.

I don't have days. I have hours.

That's why I always have to see Natalie first.

She usually dies right before Gabe.

"You look like crap. You aren't taking that Syn-Op your parents are trying to sell, are you?" Natalie asks. She hands me one of her ReCyc drinks, something she makes out of homegrown ginseng and recycled water. At this point, I'm so out of breath that I gulp it down without complaining about the taste. We pass the kitchen along the way, where her mom is making dinner, and the smell of sweet potatoes, soy sauce, and synthetic beef makes my mouth water.

By the time we reach Natalie's bedroom, her mom has given me a bowl of *japchae* and I'm almost ready to give my practiced speech. I've learned this is what I have to say to everyone on my team, to convince them there really is a Big Bad Apocalypse of the Alien Variety hanging over our heads.

Everyone except Justin.

All I have to do is look at him, my eyes reflecting the torment of my recent journey through time, the pain of having just lost my brother and Natalie and Billy and sometimes him, too. One look and he *knows* something horrible is going on. Just being with him makes me feel better, like somehow we're going to make it.

But this isn't about me feeling better, so I'll go see him later.

Later.

Later is a mantra I repeat to myself over and over, like when I want to go to a concert or find a dress for prom or sleep late on a Saturday morning like every other seventeen-year-old girl. There's plenty of time for normal girl stuff. Later.

I have to do this *now*.

Or there won't be a later.

We sit next to each other on Nat's bed as I talk, and I try not to look at all the math and science trophies she's got lining her bookcase. I try not to think about the fact that she'd be the perfect candidate to intern at JPL-NASA next year or that she's already been accepted at Columbia and Cornell, if she wants to go to either of those universities. I hate seeing the perfect future that is waiting for her because, so far, all I've done is fail to save that future.

I focus on the day of the launch.

Natalie stares at me, her mouth hanging open, which isn't like her—it's not like her at all. She's the calm one in our group of five, this group that has stood together to protect Gabe the last fourteen jumps. Maybe some part of her knows that the Xua always kill her, too, even though I haven't mentioned that yet. Maybe she feels a shiver racing up her spine and maybe she really wants to say, *No, I'm not down for this, not this time.*

But she just watches me as I ramble on, giving her my speech, the one that breaks hearts and delivers nightmares, the one I've practiced over and over. She doesn't remember, but she's the one who helped me put this talk together, and she convinced me that I have to repeat it to her right away.

I need to know who the monsters are. That was what she said four lifetimes ago, right before she died.

Best friend, meet the monsters.

So I tell her about all the different kinds of Xua, from the Jumpers to the Leaders. I stutter, my hands shake, and I stare at the floor while I talk. I don't look at her until I've finished telling her about the aliens.

She's staring past me, almost like she can see a Xua standing in the distance.

"Gabe isn't the only one who dies, is he?" she asks. She licks her lips and struggles to swallow, but she still won't look at me.

"No," I say.

Her gaze slides toward me, and it's as if she's seeing me

for the first time, that she finally recognizes me as a harbinger of death instead of a best friend. I don't want to keep talking, but I have to.

"Sometimes Billy dies. Sometimes Justin does, too," I say, then pause. When I speak again, my voice cracks. "But Gabe dies every time. And so do you."

"How do I die?"

"It's different—every time, it's a different way." A tear slides down my cheek and my lips tremble because, in my mind, I can see her dead already. She's a ghost who haunts me.

Her brow furrows. She's beginning to believe all of this is real. I can see the anger building inside her. It's only a small flame right now, but Natalie never does anything as a slow burn. She's an inferno. She's either all in or not at all.

I wait for her to answer, to say she'll help me.

She has to say yes; she just has to. I can't do it without her. Aerithin acts like I'm the one who will save the world, but he's never been here and seen Natalie in action.

She blinks and then swallows again, as if what she wants to say won't come out.

"Natalie. Please, I need you," I say. If I have to beg, I will.

I think I see a glisten of tears in the corners of her eyes, but she's not the type to cry. WTF is going on?

If she says no, I'm lost—

She straightens, forces a smile, and puts one hand on top of mine.

"You know I'm there for you." Her voice sounds hoarse. She knows I think this is our last chance—I had to tell her that part, too.

I nod, and we hug each other.

Natalie's not the type to cry, but I am. I try to hold it in, but I can't. I really suck at this end-of-the-world crap.

4

I meet him in the park on the corner of Segerstrom and Douglas, halfway between his house and mine. The sun hovers on the horizon, turning the whole world orange and red, setting all the rusted playground equipment ablaze. The slide looks like it's made out of rubies, the merry-go-round looks like it's made from layers of gold, and the swing set…well, it looks like it was created for this moment when it would hold a minor god.

Justin is human perfection—literally—because he's a Genetic, part of a military experiment that went awry more than a decade ago and had to be shut down. Before he was born, his parents won a government lottery to be part of an experimental program for Genetic Embryo In Vitro Enhancement.

Every kid in the GEIVE program got a different genetic cocktail, but all those records have either been destroyed or are top secret, so no one knows exactly what Genetics can do. Justin made it out alive when most of the other kids didn't. And even though almost everyone else is either repulsed by or scared of him—because of his height, his bulk, his speed and intelligence—to me, he's only Justin.

When we're together, I'm only Sara.

He's not a Genetic boy, and I'm not a girl who's supposed to save the world.

He's one of my closest friends, and he hangs out with my little brother almost as often as he hangs out with me, and the sight of him takes my breath away.

I walk toward him at a normal pace even though I want to run.

He's studying me, noting my posture, my expression. I want to tell him everything, that the last time I saw him, an army of Xua was chasing him and I couldn't fight them off. I tried, but that was when Aerithin came back for me.

Guilt washes over me.

Everyone I care about dies.

I'm the worst friend in the world.

He could change his mind this time. He could say, "Hey, you're like poison ivy, girl, stay away…"

But he won't. He's been the one constant in my life.

He's the person who always makes me feel safe.

He flashes me one of his heart-stopping grins and holds the swing next to him for me. I know other girls get weak in the knees looking at his muscles, even though they won't admit it, and, yes, that body of his is pretty sweet. But the thing about him that always gets me is his smile. I swear, it's brighter than the sun and it gives off the same amount of heat.

As soon as I sit down, he knows. Not everything—there's no way in the world he could know everything. He might be a Genetic, but he's not psychic.

His blue eyes study me; his dark hair is tucked behind his ears, a few strands hanging loose.

"What is it?" he asks. He hasn't let go of my swing yet.

"There's some bad stuff going on," I say, and I force my lips not to tremble. I don't want to cry, not now. "And I need to tell you about it."

"Yeah? You know I'm here for you. Doesn't matter what it is."

He gives me a look that's so innocent and full of concern. He doesn't even know what I'm going to ask and yet he's still willing to do it.

I wish more than anything that we could talk about something else.

Instead, I give him the same speech I gave to Natalie.

He blinks and nods, quiet. He doesn't even flinch when I tell him that I've seen him die. The only part that gets him is when I tell him that sometimes we get separated and I don't know where he is. His face darkens and his brow lowers and he stares at the ground, almost as if he remembers.

"I've never hurt you, have I?" he asks. "Because I can't do this if I might hurt you."

"No, you've never hurt me, I promise." I take his hand in mine. "You try to save me."

Then I give him a laser switchblade. "Keep it with you at all times, even when you're sleeping," I say. After that, I teach him how to fight the Xua, just like I did with Natalie and Gabe, and like I will with Billy tomorrow.

It doesn't take long. Genetics were bred for war. That much we know.

By the time we're finished, the sun has disappeared, and a handful of stars are glistening overhead. I have to get home. I give Justin an awkward hug, wrapping my arms around his waist and leaning into him.

"It's going to be okay this time," he says.

Then he does something he's never done before, and I know I shouldn't read anything into it, but I can't help it. He kisses me on the top of my head. It's such a perfect moment, I wish it could last forever. It's hard to say goodbye to Justin.

I'll only see him a few more times before the end of the world.

There's never enough time to tell someone you might be falling in love with them.

No way. You guys are totally making this up. Who's filming this? Is it that homeless guy over by the dumpster? He's been watching us the entire time—"

Billy's rant goes on and on, and I honestly don't think he's ever been this hard to convince before.

Usually all he needs to know is that Natalie will be there.

Those two have never admitted how they feel about each other.

Billy looks a lot like me except his hair is bleached blond, always tangled and always hanging in his eyes. Average height, average build, he's got just enough tats to fit in with the ride crowd and hair long enough to fit in with the slacker crowd. He's wealthy enough to fit in with the rich crowd, and he's smart enough to fit in with the geek crowd. He fits in everywhere, makes friends easily, and can convince people that if they hang out with him, he'll show them a good time— which is why he's one of the most valuable members of my crew.

We argue for another half an hour before he drops the prank theory, grabs the laser blade from me, and starts asking real questions.

"So this Aerithin person," he says, turning the weapon over in his hands. "He told you if we keep Gabe alive, the invasion ends?"

Not exactly, but I've got to believe saving the world includes the Xua leaving. "Something like that."

He stares at me. "What if he's wrong?"

"Then we move on to plan B," I say, hoping my panic over the idea doesn't bleed through my words. I don't have a plan B—Aerithin didn't give me any other options—but I really need Billy on board if we have any shot at pulling this off. "Are you in or not?"

Billy's jaw ticks, and his eyes harden. "What, exactly, is plan B?"

Crap. "I haven't figured that out yet, but I will."

Beside me, Natalie glares at him, her hands on her hips and her teeth gritted. Billy's one step away from getting the Wrath of Natalie, which nobody likes. I wince, waiting for it to hit the fan. Justin glances at me, his eyebrows raised. I'm just about to step in when Natalie suddenly takes a completely different approach.

She moves to stand behind Billy and takes his right hand—the hand holding the blade—in hers, then puts her left hand on his waist, holding him in place. "Use it like this," she says. Natalie lifts Billy's arm up and then swings it down in a swift motion. "We need you," she says gently as she moves in front of him. "We're going to do this. All of us. Together. Okay?"

Billy blinks down at her, and his expression says it all. I don't even have to ask.

He's totally with us now.

Just like every lifetime before this. It only took a little convincing from Natalie.

I just hope it doesn't come down to a plan B.

5

Morning comes too soon.

All night long, sirens wailed, fireworks exploded, and people celebrated an event that hasn't happened yet. They can't wait for the *Valiant* to launch.

A sick feeling settles in the base of my stomach.

Today is the day everything changes.

I don't want to do this. I don't want to live through today again.

I push out of bed and wrap my arms around myself as I pace my room, panic setting in. This isn't going to work. Even if we save Gabe, even if we stop the invasion, so many people are still going to die, and I doubt that I have any do-overs left. This is probably the last life I have, and I keep seeing the faces of the people who are going to die tonight. My neighbors, kids from school, Gabe's friends, my parents—

I've always had the security of knowing I could come back and try again. But I have to believe that Aerithin's screams mean that security net is gone.

This is it. My last chance.

Billy's questions have my brain spinning. I have to do something different or I'm going to fail, just like all the other times.

I flip on my skin sites and call Natalie.

Get up, get up, get up.

"Sara? What's going on?" she says.

"We can't keep doing the same thing over and over," I tell her. "Meet me at the park in fifteen. Bring your camera and laptop."

I stop at the kitchen faucet on my way out, wanting a glass of water, but a quick glance at the meter tells me we've already exceeded our daily allowance, and it's not even five a.m. yet. Great.

This drought's lasted for two years—during that time, 85 percent of the world's crops have failed, all the genetically engineered seeds sold by U.S. companies have proven they're not drought resistant, farmers in the U.S. have lost their property, our recession has turned into a full-blown Depression, and the northern states have claimed that they have barely enough water for themselves.

Chalk up another win for modern science.

Everyone thinks the *Valiant* will solve our problems. That sending a rocket to mine natural resources on another planet is going to restore our economy. They think it's going to create new jobs and, as a result, everyone's going to have more money to spend. They think that money will save us all and make the U.S. a world power again.

They have no idea what's about to happen today.

I jog to the park, the sky still dark. Traffic is moving slow, and I pass a line of people getting tickets for the tram. The longest line is always the Barter Line, where people trade SkyPower credits or food vouchers or lottery tickets—anything they've got so they can make it to work. The end of the month is always the worst, so people get in line before the sun even comes up. We run out of money, gas, food, water, and we turn into beggars and thieves.

Everyone's struggling to survive, and I'm fighting to give us another chance.

Natalie waits for me up ahead, standing under a solar-streetlight that bathes her in intermittent pale-green beams. Once upon a time, space solar power was going to save us. Then it was recycled water, then it was urban gardens, then it was free WiFi and free health care and—

And now it's me. I'm going to save the world, flawed as it is.

"Up until now, I've basically been doing the same things over and over," I tell Natalie. "But they've never worked, so why should they work this time? Maybe if we weren't all alone, maybe if there were more people fighting and distracting the Xua, we'd have a chance."

Natalie studies me. "You want to warn everyone."

"Yes," I say.

"I thought that was against the rules. Part of the whole inevitable thing."

Technically, the launch and meeting Aerithin were the only inevitable things. Well, that and my meeting some guy named Noah. There's no way the government would shut down the *Valiant* based on what a seventeen-year-old girl had to say, so warning as many people as I can won't stop the launch. Still, if enough people believe me…

"Videos," I say. "We have to shoot some videos. If people know what's coming and they know how to fight, maybe that will slow down the Xua enough that we can win."

She nods and gets her equipment out of her backpack. "Let me know when you're ready."

I don't know what happens in the rest of the world—there was never enough time to pay attention to anything beside

Gabe—but I know how the Xua attack L.A. I can only assume they do the same things, or even worse, in other places.

She holds a video camera, red light blinking, and I begin to talk, a faceless silhouette, the streetlight behind me. My hands tremble and my voice wavers, but I get through it.

I should have done this before. Natalie's got her own site on the dark web, and her stuff has gone viral lots of times. She doesn't talk about it much, but every now and then I've seen people at school watching conspiracy theory videos and Natalie would give me a sly wink.

But I'm not like her, and I'm definitely not used to public speaking, so my narration for our video sounds rough. We have to shoot my part over and over. It's basically the same spiel I give my team when I first get back from the future.

In the first video, I tell them who the Xua are. I explain how the aliens can turn into vaporous smoke and possess a human. And once they do, that human is dead.

I tell them the aliens will invade right after the *Valiant* launches, so they have to be ready. I warn them to stay away from mass transit. Don't even think about getting on an airplane.

Natalie and I watch the first video, make a few changes, and then shoot two more. Each video ends with me demonstrating how to kill a Xua. The sun is rising by the time we've got three videos put together. She uses a voice-scrambling program to hide my identity, and I kept my face in the shadows, just in case.

Doing this, going public, even as secretive as we're being, breaks all Aerithin's rules, but I don't care. He's not coming back, so I'm making the decisions from now on.

I watch the second video again—after all her changes—and listen to myself warning how to protect yourself from the Xua, what weapons to have on hand, what supplies you'll need to survive.

"There's going to be a war," I hear myself say. "You won't know who your enemy is, so you need to form core groups. Three or four people you know you can trust."

At the end, I take a can of orange paint and spray a large *V* on a stucco wall behind me.

"This sign is how you will know who you can trust. Everyone else will think this *V* stands for *Valiant*. But it really stands for Victory," I say. "Paint this in places you know are safe, so other people will know who they can trust and where they can find shelter. Just remember—never, ever give up, no matter what."

I swallow, my throat dry.

It's only a matter of hours before the Xua show up.

6

Natalie's videos went viral, even better than we hoped.
The Century Unified High School lunchroom is buzzing with a mix of excited chatter, laughter, and panicked conspiracy theories. Some students have on T-shirts with bright-orange *V*s. Girls are watching my videos on their tablets, then practicing that killer upward swing. Boys are nodding and challenging each other, using plastic knives instead of laser switchblades. They might not all believe what I said, might even think it's a big joke, but when the invasion starts, at least they'll know how to fight. That's more than we had going for us before, and I have to believe it'll make a difference.

In front of me, students are lining up for the free Syn-Lunch, which today looks like fake tofu in a muddy brown sauce. Across the room, some students huddle in small groups, guarding their food from their stronger, hungrier classmates.

Half the student body is dressed in rival gang colors and sporting full face tats, while the other half is trying their best not to get noticed. Nothing unites this crowd. Not hunger strikes, water rationing, or pestilence control. Not even the gossip about our videos. Except for my team and Gabe, every single one of them is wearing an orange bandanna tied around his or her left arm to support the launch. Almost all of our parents, teachers, and government officials have bought stock in the Titan mission.

Some of these people will live.

It's almost enough to give me hope.

Almost.

I find my crew. We sit together and we put our lunches on the table, then divvy it all up. Soy milk, synthetic tofu, power bars, peanut butter, bottles of ReCyc. This might be our last meal for a long time, so we do our best to cram in the calories.

Natalie grins and raises one eyebrow, lifting her tablet to show us one of my videos. "Two million hits, girl," she says, then she snatches a chocolate power bar right as Billy was reaching for it.

"Whoa," I say. Viral was one thing. I never imagined we'd get that many views.

She shrugs, talking with her mouth full. "I have mad skills."

"When did you make those?" Justin asks as he passes out chunks of a peanut butter sandwich.

"Early this morning. Hey, Billy, would you grab my brother before he pisses off one of the Blood Lords? I told him to quit bragging about his team winning the World Cup—"

"On it." Billy jumps up and jogs across the room. He latches onto Gabe's collar, points him toward me, then stops to chat with the gang members until they're all laughing. Meanwhile, Gabe sulks back to our table in pure fourteen-year-old-boy form.

I give him a sandwich and some carrots. "I own you until tomorrow morning, remember?" I say. "Stay where I can see you."

He slaps a torn piece of paper on the table in front of me. It's got a skin site number scrawled on it. "The doctor you're going to see tomorrow," he says.

I nod and put the paper in my pocket.

"Doctor?" Natalie asks with a frown.

"Just a promise I made to my brother." Panic rises in my throat, but I push it down. I have a list in my other pocket, one Gabe doesn't know about. All the ways he's died in the past, what time and where. Who was with me. Who was already dead or possessed by a Xua.

Logically, I know the list won't matter. It never happens the same way twice.

I hate cascading events. I hate the *Valiant.*

I hate today.

Gabe rests a hand on my shoulder and smiles. "I'll stay with you. Okay? All day and all night. Tomorrow and the next day, however long you need. Don't worry."

My little brother has one of those smiles that can break your heart, and damn if mine isn't ripped in half right now. And then—when I'm made out of broken bones and fragile glass and don't know how I'm going to survive the rest of this day, much less keep anyone else alive—Justin reaches for my hand under the table. It's like he's a SkyPower panel and my batteries are powering up.

"We're going to make it," Justin says.

I'd have gone insane if I didn't have him with me through all of this.

I look at him and, for a moment, I get lost in his eyes. They're bluer than the sky with tiny flecks of green, and they're like an instant trip to the ocean. He gives me a slow smile, and every part of my body catches on fire.

I want to kiss him. I want to be more than friends. I've wanted that for as long as I can remember. But if we cross this line, I might not be able to stay focused. And we'll all die if Justin is distracted.

So I take a deep breath and look away from him.

He squeezes my hand. "Is there anything I can do?"

I shake my head. "Just be at my place half an hour before the launch."

Then lunch period ends with a bell tone that sings in the skin sites that run along the base of my jaw, a tingle that makes my tongue quiver. Like little soldiers, we all stand at attention and head out of the room, single file.

I know the *Valiant* will ultimately destroy our world. But right now there's nothing I can do about it.

So, like everyone else in Century Unified, I head off to my first afternoon class.

7

"Are you sure you can trust him?"

Natalie's a step ahead of me as we walk toward the tram stop. I mean to warn her about the upcoming crack in the sidewalk. She always stumbles and skins her knee—right here, right now—but before I can say anything, she takes a quick step to the left. It surprises me, and that makes me catch my breath. As a result, I forget to answer her question, so she swings her head around and asks the same thing again.

"Are you sure you can trust him? I mean, he's an alien, so that makes him one of the bad guys. Right?"

She's talking about Aerithin.

She always brings this up whenever we get close to the launch. I don't know why, but she's never accepted that Aerithin is on our side. I hunch my shoulders against the wind, shove my hands deep inside my pockets.

I don't want to talk about it. Especially not today.

Clouds pass over the sun, darkening the street.

"He's an alien," Natalie repeats. "That doesn't worry you?"

"Aerithin hates the Xua just as much as we do," I say. "He's part of a secret resistance team."

We're almost at the tram stop, so we can't talk about this anymore. That doesn't stop me from thinking about it, though, especially about the Xua. Natalie and I push our way onto the tram, squeezing through one car after another until we find two seats where we can sit together. As soon as the tram wheezes away from the stop, I notice a new bracelet sparkling on her wrist, jade mixed with gold beads. She hasn't mentioned it. That's how I know it must be a birthday present from her father. She catches me looking at it and tucks it back inside her sleeve.

She doesn't like to talk about her dad or how much she misses him or that he lives in Seoul, away from her and her mother, so she tries to divert my attention. She leans closer and whispers to me behind her hand. "You have to admit, there is one *amazing* thing in your life," she says. "Justin."

I blush, and my eyes go wide.

"Natalie!"

"I'm just saying. He's pretty hot."

I hope she doesn't say more.

No such luck.

"I really don't know why the two of you never hooked up," she continues, staring out the window. Then she holds her fist on her lap and starts flicking her fingers up one by one. "First, there was that time in eighth grade when we all went to the beach. You were goofing around with Alexander, and Justin pretended not to notice, but girl, he was staring at you all day."

"No, he wasn't."

"And back in grade school, remember how his Gen traits hadn't kicked in yet? Back before everyone knew he was a Jenny—"

"I wish you wouldn't call him that."

She shrugs. "He doesn't care. He'd tell me if he did. Anyway, all the girls in our class thought he was so cute—I mean, he *is*, but he always wanted to sit by *you*."

I'd forgotten about that.

"And this whole time-traveling thing. You have to convince Billy and me, but Justin always believes you, doesn't he? Right from the beginning. I'm telling you, there's something there. I know you like him, but I seriously think he likes you, too. A lot."

"I don't know," I say, but I can't help wondering if maybe she's right. But I never have told him my biggest secret—that the Xua go after everyone I love. My brother, my parents, my cousins. Even Natalie. It's horrible what those aliens do to the people I care about. I have no idea how they figure out who I'm closest to, but it's like they measure their torture based on how much I love someone.

I can't bear to see what they might do to Justin if they knew how I really feel about him. Better that they think he's just part of the group.

Maybe this time he'll make it out alive.

8

The sun sets in the west, shimmering through the smog as it heads toward the Pacific Ocean. In the distance, L.A. skyscrapers turn into tall, spindly silhouettes and, even up here on the roof, the ceaseless thrum of freeway traffic keeps us connected to the heart of the city.

At least a hundred people have crowded onto my apartment building roof for a *Valiant* launch party. Three people have dyed their hair orange, and one guy has orange face tats. Everyone mingles about, awkward and excited, a strange mixture of ages and races, chattering to one another as if they've been friends for years, when in reality, they religiously avoid one another.

The launch is the only thing that could've brought them together, that brittle hope of something good on the horizon, as if the shadow of the *Valiant* can stretch across valleys and freeways all the way to Santa Ana. You can hear that hope in the pitch of people's voices, see it in the way they carry themselves. Despite the fact that today is the end of the month and most everyone has already spent their paychecks on bills, drugs, and gambling debts. Despite the fact that the Second Great Depression has lasted longer than we expected, and those of us in Southern California have been hit harder than most.

I nod at my downstairs neighbors, trying to remember their names, then I wave at the couple who just moved into 4B. A playlist of classical music thuds through my skin sites as I lean against a perimeter wall, chewing my fingernails, watching the crowd, waiting for Justin and Natalie. Normally they'd be here by now, but I gave them a list of things to do after our last class.

Every person on my team has a different function, and right now, Billy's job is to make sure my brother stays where I can see him. They're about five feet away, and Gabe is chatting with a group of his friends.

A cheer echoes across the roof. Gabe either forgets what's going to happen or he never believed me about the invasion, because he whoops and yells along with everyone else. It sends a shiver of dread through my bones. Billy and I lock eyes, and he nods. He leans closer to Gabe and whispers something. The expression on my little brother's face changes, like he just remembered a nightmare, and he frowns.

I'm the nightmare.

He can't help the fact that he's loved airplanes and rockets and space travel since he was a little kid. When he's not reading about the Mars terraforming project or the moon colony, he's reading biographies of famous astronauts like John Glenn and Neil Armstrong. In every single lifetime, my brother has looked forward to this event like it was Christmas.

I, on the other hand, have looked forward to it like it was Armageddon.

I see my dad, walking around a few minutes earlier than usual, and I mentally go over the list of things I'm going to do differently this time. I've already tried running away with Gabe, heading up into the mountains. Once I even convinced him to go with me as far as Arizona. It doesn't make a difference how *far* I run—they always catch us.

Gabe survives longest if we hide in a crowd, so this time I'm going to use this party to our advantage.

"Where are you guys?" I say, speaking into the private com channel set up for my crew. I haven't heard from Justin or Natalie in the past thirty minutes, and I'm beginning to wonder if this is the mistake that's going to wreck everything. I never know when I do something different if it's going to make things better or worse. This time, it'll be too late by the time I find out.

"Almost there," Justin says.

"We're on our way up," Natalie says. "I had to do quite a bit of hacking to get all the stuff you wanted."

I'm craning my neck, looking for them, knowing that fourteen flights is a long way to walk and it sucks that my elevator is still broken, but they should be here any second, and we only have about fifteen minutes before the launch.

Fifteen minutes before the end of the world.

I panic. "I know you're on your way up, but don't stay here after the launch, okay?" I say. I wasn't going to mention this until a minute or two before the rocket took off. Aerithin always said that I have to keep my plans secret, since someone could be watching or listening to me. But I can't let my crew die just because those alien monsters are after Gabe and me. Not this time.

"Got it."

"Okay."

"Yup."

Gabe's staring at me with his head cocked. He knows Billy and I have been talking to each other. He frowns, then he gestures to a red-haired girl standing beside him.

Her, too, he mouths.

WTF. My brother suddenly has a girlfriend he wants to save? When did he get a girlfriend? But before I can react, Mom and Dad begin weaving through the crowd, passing out samples.

Twenty or thirty years ago, my parents would have been called pushers. They'd have been arrested and put in jail while Gabe and I would have gone into foster homes.

Instead, today, Mom and Dad are the stars of our neighborhood, the hosts of monthly pharm parties where they dole out samples of the latest legal drugs. Marijuana is always a free giveaway at the door, and I already have my sample joint stuffed in my jacket pocket. But the VIP of tonight's party is the sweetheart of the century, the new release everyone has been waiting three years for: Syn-Op.

My mom's walking a few steps ahead of Dad through the crowd, spinning her sales pitch as she hands out free samples.

"This synthetic opioid guarantees to deliver all the traditional morphine-like benefits with none of the downsides," she says with a wide grin, her lips painted bright red. "Nonaddictive. No side effects. This is what's gonna get us through the rest of this Depression with a smile on our faces."

A soft laugh spills out as she places a tiny blue pill into each outstretched palm. Dad follows behind her, handing out marijuana samples.

The smells of marijuana, incense, and cheap cologne mingle, then waft my way.

This is the real reason why my parents staged this party, not to celebrate the launch of the *Valiant*. They just need to make more money so they can pay off our latest tax bill. Our taxes have steadily increased, ever since California divided into two states and somehow Orange County ended up right in the middle.

T-minus ten minutes and counting.

Fireworks burst from nearby rooftops, gunshots ring out somewhere down the street, and sirens wail in the distance.

Justin and Natalie push their way through the crowd toward me. I hear whispers of "not another Jenny" and "who invited that thing here?" as Justin walks past people. Justin's reaction is so subtle most people wouldn't even notice it, but I can see it. His expression changes, just a fraction, and his muscles tense. Then he sees me, and there's that smile as bright as the sun.

I have no idea how he's able to ignore comments like that. I couldn't. I'd be smashing faces and breaking bones. In other words, I'd be in prison or juvie, which is where most Genetics end up.

Even my parents give him dirty looks when they see him.

The only person in this crowd who acts glad to see Justin is my brother.

"Hey, Justin's here!" Gabe says. He latches onto Justin's arm and pulls him closer, introducing him to the red-haired girl. She looks scared at first, which is only natural if it's your first time meeting a Genetic, but I can see Gabe going on and on, probably telling her how awesome Justin is. The red-haired girl's face softens into a timid smile, and she shakes Justin's hand.

I don't know who this girl is, but I like her.

If she can run—and she looks like she can—then there's room on our team for one more.

9

The crowd thickens and grows as another hundred people pour up the stairs and join the party. Good. There will be plenty of places to hide when the invasion starts. It'll be scary once the Xua get here and people are possessed, but I just need to make sure we're gone before our advantage becomes a disadvantage.

Yes. A crowd is good.

Except this crowd is getting bigger than I expected.

I spin around and realize I can't see Gabe or Justin anymore.

My mouth is dry, and sudden panic surges through me.

"Hey, where are you guys?" I say into my skin sites.

"Here!" Natalie says. And I see a hand stretching above the crowd. It must be Justin. He's the only one tall enough to reach that high. The crowd shifts and pushes my team about twenty feet away from me.

"Don't move; I'll come to you," I tell them.

"We're all gonna be rich soon," a woman standing beside me says, stating the common belief of every *Valiant* shareholder. She lifts a beer bottle to the heavens in a toast, clouds of MJ thick around her. Everyone near me is coughing, laughing, shouting, cheering, so loud I can't hear what Justin and Billy are saying. I know they're talking to me; I can feel the rumble of their transmission, vibrating through my jawbone.

I have to get to them and quick.

I shove my way through a tangle of overexcited, overmedicated techs, all of them rambling on about the possibilities of cyber-connecting with Titan, of taking the internet beyond global, all the way to universal. Then I'm surrounded by laughter as I push through a group of tatted Blood Lord gang members. One of them, Manny, eyes me hungrily. This guy's had an unwelcome crush on me since he sat behind me in fourth grade. He might have been attractive once with his easy smile and deep-set black eyes, but that was before he joined the gang and covered his face with blue-black tats. The symmetrical patterns and words curve across his cheekbones, following the thrust of his jaw and circling his eyes.

He reaches out and grabs my arm. "Hey. Where ya goin' in such a hurry? You're not looking for your Jenny, are you?"

"You know I'm packing," I tell him, that fear inside me ratcheting up. "Let me go."

His hand slides down my arm and rests there a moment too long.

I pat my jacket pocket with my free hand, raising my eyebrows. My friends and I don't align ourselves with any of the Santa Ana gangs—not the Sin Nombre de los Muertos, not the First Street Dragons, and definitely not the Blood Lords.

Manny steps back with a shrug. His buddy Aleksei laughs and then takes another hit of MJ. Smoke swirls around his face, but I can still see the acne sprinkled across his facial tattoos.

"She ain't worth the trouble, bro," Aleksei says with a sneer. "Too skinny."

As if I need a reminder that I don't have much time left, another burst of fireworks blazes across the sky, leaving a message written in sparkling orange: *T-minus five minutes.*

And still counting.

I hurry away from the Blood Lords, trying to ignore Manny's hot gaze on my back.

To the west, the sun continues to sink. Already, half the rooftop is in shadow, faces darkening, arms, legs, and torsos merging until the crowd looks like a single entity. Soon the sun will disappear behind a forest of glittering skyscrapers, dusk will loom around us, and we'll run out of time.

Where are they? Where's Gabe? I have to find him before the launch starts.

Then the crowd parts like the Red Sea, some people are being shoved and some are just moving like they're terrified. There's a split second where I'm scared, too, worried that maybe the Xua are here already and I made a horrible mistake, but then I see *him*, pushing people out of the way. Justin. With one hand, he's shoving people aside so he can get to me, and with the other hand, he's pulling Gabe behind him.

Shoulders wide, jaw gritted shut, eyes narrow, he's a one-man rescue team.

He sees the fear in my eyes, and I can tell that for a heartbeat he's worried I might be afraid of him, but I've never been afraid of him. I shake my head and reach for his outstretched hand. He pulls me to his chest, and part of me melts. Sometimes I think the Genetics program went a step too far when they made this boy.

They were striving for perfection, and I think they got it.

I fit right into the curve of his chest, his left arm wraps around me, and the heat from his body sets me on fire. I want to stay here forever.

Right now, all five of us are still alive, and I swear Justin knows I want more from him, so much more than friendship. And he wants it, too.

"It's okay," he says, his voice a deep, soothing rumble that vibrates through my body. "We're together. We're all safe."

Natalie's a step behind him, a wide grin on her face, like she knows how I feel right now. She lets out a laugh, and I'm so glad she doesn't say anything.

But Billy and Gabe and Gabe's red-haired girlfriend are beside her, and they don't look happy at all.

"What's the game plan?" Billy demands. "This place is getting crazy, and the launch hasn't even happened yet. What are we doing after the launch?"

"How much time do we have?" I ask.

"Four minutes. No, three," Natalie says.

"Okay, everybody stay with me. Bandannas at the beginning of the launch—"

"What?" the red-haired girl asks. She latches onto Gabe's hand and looks like she wishes she were anywhere but here. "What's going on?"

"Do you have a *Valiant* bandanna?" I ask.

She nods. We all got one at school today.

"Wear it around your face like this." I do a quick demonstration. "Time?"

"Two minutes," Natalie says.

"This is what we're doing. First, bandannas. Second, stay with me, no matter what. We'll head toward the fire escape before the *Valiant* leaves orbit and then—"

Billy frowns. "Where's the frigging fire escape?"

I swallow, my mouth dry, and then more fireworks burst overhead, a dazzling display of violet and orange words written in the sky, but I don't have time to read them.

"To my left. And stay focused!" I say. "When I give the signal, you guys will start to head down to the alley below. The broadcast is about to begin, so make sure you stand where you can see me give the signal. You might not be able to hear me over the—"

Just then, we all get the news flash. Gov-Net sings through my skin sites, pictures jolt through my brain, and a government-approved newscaster begins to speak. Gabe turns his attention away from me, but fortunately Justin still has one hand clenched around my brother's wrist like a steel vise.

"The moment we've all been waiting for is finally here," a familiar male voice says. It's David Perez, one of the top newscasters. All sixty million of his subscribers on Insta-News rely on him to tell us what's going on in the world, and with his popularity, he's Gov-Net's favorite choice to narrate their broadcasts. "The *Valiant*'s just about ready to launch."

A pause follows, then we see David waving at the camera, all of us immersed in the holo-mind images Gov-Net projects directly into our heads, whether we want them to or not. Layered on top of those, we see David with his curly black hair, chiseled cheekbones, and neatly trimmed, signature beard so perfect it looks like it's painted on. "Okay, all the ship's five main engines are online, ready for ignition—this is exciting, isn't it?"

I cringe as the broadcast continues, and I start pushing my way toward the fire escape. The others follow me, all of us holding hands, Justin snarling a warning at anyone who gets in our way.

"The *Valiant* computers are now in control of the countdown," David continues. "What's that? Oh, the firing chain is armed and the sound suppression water system has been activated—"

An image of the rocket superimposes on top of David

Perez's grin, and the countdown begins.

The event that no one can change is about to take place.

"T-minus ten, nine, eight, seven, six, five, four—"

There's an explosion of sound and fire; thick clouds blast across the platform, and behind it, we all see a panoramic view of the San Gabriel Mountains in the background.

"Three, two, one, zero—"

Dark clouds envelop the rocket, fiery flames at the base. A collective gasp from the crowd sounds around me, and it seems like the last second stretches into infinity. Then, finally, a column of red-gold flame pushes the spacecraft up and up and up; thick, dark clouds grow, billowing until they rival the clouds in the sky; thundering, deafening, the craft shoots up farther, slicing through darkening skies, a radiant plume of fire broadening at its base.

My skin tingles and turns numb. The countdown is over. There's no turning back.

We're on a collision course with destiny.

Our destruction awaits us.

10

Onward and upward, the *Valiant* shoots until it's out of sight. David Perez continues to talk about how this is the dream that has united our country, despite the Depression and our overwhelming international debts, how this will replenish that which has been lost, how it will give everyone a new hope and a brilliant new future.

Gabe stands at my side, staring upward. "Wow," he murmurs.

We've made it to the edge of the roof. Natalie has one hand resting on the fire escape. Everyone on my team, all except Gabe, has their gaze fixed upon me, waiting for my signal to run.

It's at moments like this that I wonder why Aerithin chose me to help him stop the alien invasion. What made him think *I* could save the world?

The cameras inside the spaceship switch on, and we all see the view from the craft—earth below, a swirling ball of green and blue, covered with wisps of white.

This is when I realize how truly insignificant I am.

Meanwhile, our planet continues to grow smaller and

smaller, until it dwindles to the size of a basketball. Then the moon appears on the right, crater-dappled and covered with a network of experimental domed cities.

The image fades, superimposed with the words: *It's not too late to invest.* Valiant *stock just shot up 40 percent, but you can still take part in the future. Call now: a live operator is standing by, ready to make you the deal of a lifetime.*

My heart thumps a rapid beat in my chest. I raise my right hand, ready to give the signal to run, and force myself to wait. It's coming; I can feel it. Our planet is about to be invaded for what I fear is the last time —

The universe shifts. I can tell because I get an empty feeling in the pit of my stomach, and it's like the floor drops away beneath me, tilting at a sharp angle. Other people always think it's an earth tremor. We get enough of those in Southern California.

They're wrong. It's no tremor.

Somebody — or a lot of somebodies — is traveling through time.

All around me, people let out cheers, as if a potential earthquake is an extra party favor.

I struggle to breathe. My pulse races so fast it sounds like a war drum. Gabe stares at me, his mouth hanging open, his dark eyes telling me that he no longer thinks any part of this is cool.

Just to the left of us, the air shimmers. Most people would think it's just heat rising off the rooftop, but I know better. A nanosecond later, a series of mirrors appears from nowhere, spinning and reflecting. They disappear almost as quickly as they appear, before most people can see them.

Natalie notices them, though. She looks around, then pulls out her laser switchblade and powers it up.

"They're here," Justin says, his feet braced. He's ready to fight.

About ten feet away from us, the air ripples, outlining a

humanoid-looking creature. Slightly taller and more slender than the rest of us, it glitters like it's made out of starlight.

A Jumper.

Right on time.

"Put on your bandannas!" I shout. *"Quick!"*

Because it isn't just *one* Jumper. The whole rooftop begins to glow as one after another after another of these monsters appears. They'll be turning to smoke and possessing people soon. At that point, we won't know who to fight.

"Run!" I yell. "They're here! Get on the fire escape!" I give the signal and then grab my switchblade from my pocket.

Gabe and Natalie and Billy are already hopping over the perimeter wall, landing on the fire escape with a dull metallic *thud* and scrambling down the steps. Gabe's girlfriend is next, but Justin waits for me.

"Get out of here!" I yell as I pull my bandanna up.

He shakes his head. "Not without you."

I rush toward the fire escape. If I timed this wrong, we'll never make it down. A hundred other people will be trying to get down at the same time. And some of them will have Xua inside them. They could push us off the stairs to the alley fourteen stories below; they could kill my brother before he even makes it to the street—

Justin stares at me. For a second, one of my neighbors gets between us, but before I can slow my pace, Justin grabs the guy and pushes him away.

"Down the ladder now," he says to me.

"You were supposed to stay with Gabe!" I shout as I pass him. I hop the perimeter wall and jump down to the first landing, but I'm mad. "If anything happens to him—"

"Good, you're mad. That's better than scared." He leaps off the roof behind me, making the same move I did, skipping the ladder and falling to the fire escape landing. Together, we both start running down the stairs, as fast as we can, sometimes skipping over two or three steps at a time. Back up on the roof, people are already screaming, and even though my plan was always to leave as soon as the *Valiant* was out of orbit and the Xua arrived, I regret that decision.

My mom and dad are still up on the roof.

The Xua are there, too.

The fire escape sways precariously beneath us as we run, the metallic hum vibrating through us. I glance at the moorings. The connection joints are rusted, and some of the bolt heads that connect the stairway to the building are missing. This thing is unstable.

I strain to look below us, gauging how far away Gabe is. He's only one flight below us. I wish he were already on the ground. "Gabe, run faster!" I yell down to my brother. Then I look up and see the horror unfolding above us.

Either people are being thrown off the roof or they're starting to jump.

A chill floods my veins.

Bodies fall past us, some of them striking and bouncing off the stairway with a dull, wet *thud*. One woman screams when she passes me, her eyes wide, and she reaches out, trying to latch onto the stairway, but her fingers slice off when she grasps the metal railing, and her blood sprays across my face.

"Don't look at them," Justin says.

But I can't stop.

Because they're coming after us. People are climbing down the ladder from the roof, so many I can't count them. Some of them make it to the first landing, but others lose their purchase. They tumble and pinwheel downward, arms spinning. Some of the falling bodies burst apart in explosions of flesh and blood as the Xua inside flee.

"Hurry, hurry, hurry," I say. "Don't wait for me! You can

get to the bottom faster without me. You have to save Gabe. I'll catch up with you—" I can't stop talking, and I can't look away from what is happening.

"I'm not leaving you behind," Justin says.

A cloud of Xua smoke swirls around us. All the Xua that jumped off the roof and survived are trying to possess us. They beat against us, almost blinding me, there are so many. But Justin and I keep our mouths closed, and the aliens can't get past our bandannas.

"Sara! We're down!" Gabe calls up to me. "Hurry!"

But the fire escape can't hold all the people who are clamoring on. It teeters and sways and groans and it's going to fall any second now. We're going to die, and not even two minutes have passed since the *Valiant* left orbit.

No. Just no.

That's when Justin pulls me into his arms and he jumps.

With one leap, we're both over the edge of the stairway and plummeting downward. Even the Xua that were tormenting us can't keep up. We fall two stories, and I worry that we'll splat on the pavement like all the other bodies. Justin might be a Genetic, but I don't know if we'll be able to do this. Maybe if he were alone he could. Maybe if this were a normal day and we weren't being chased—

We land, awkward, crooked, his body taking the brunt of the impact and still, he never lets me go. We teeter and almost fall backward, but he manages to keep his balance, holding me in his arms, pressed against his chest the whole time. There's a part of me that's in awe and speechless.

The other part of me, the part that realizes we're still in danger, wins.

I turn my head toward the street and yell loud enough for everyone on my crew to hear. "Run! Get away from the building and the alley! Now!"

II

We hit the ground running, and the whole world is screaming.

Every human, every car, every airplane, and every building. Bodies continue to fall from the roof above, and every one of them is like a bomb that could kill us. The air fills with the crack of bones and the death cries of the falling people, and then the fire escape breaks free from my apartment building. It starts to topple and falls apart on the way, metal landings flying off, steps ringing, bolts shooting through the air like bullets—

Justin wraps an arm protectively around me as we run, trying to shield me, making sure my pace keeps up with his. Finally, we make it to the street.

I lift my gaze, searching for Gabe, but I can't find him.

Instead, I see chaos and destruction, cars crashing into other cars, silver aliens lining the street and then turning into smoke, mirror doors swinging open and even more Xua pouring out. A jet drops lower and lower in the sky, its descent much too rapid for it to make it to John Wayne Airport.

"Station One," I yell into my skin sites. "Answer me!"

"Station One," Billy replies.

But I can't see him or Natalie. Or my brother.

The jet crashes a few blocks away, missing the 405 freeway, and there's an explosion of blinding light. It lands much closer than in any of my other lifetimes, and buildings across the street topple to the ground from the impact. Before I can react, Justin tackles me and slams me to the pavement. Shrapnel from the plane and the buildings whistles past us, *thunk*ing into nearby cars and bystanders. More screams echo around us, and the ground rumbles as the jet erupts in yet another explosion.

"Gabe, where are you? Natalie, do you have eyes on him?" I scream, my face pressed against the ground, Justin still holding me down.

"Better than eyes. I'm holding his frigging hand," Natalie replies calmly.

"Where are you?"

"No descriptives, remember? Use the code, girl. Clear your mind. Five minutes from Station One."

My heart thunders, and I can't think.

"Answer her," Justin whispers in my ear. "You know what to say."

My mouth is dry, and panic makes me want to get up and run, but Justin is still holding me down. Where are we, what should I say, what is the next step... Finally it comes to me.

"Ten minutes from Station One. Keep him safe," I say. "If we're not there in fifteen, move to Station Eight."

"Eight?" she asks. There's a pause. We don't have a Station Eight. It's code for Do Whatever You Must to Stay Alive. "Got it. See you soon."

I glance at my watch. Ten minutes into the invasion and already I've lost my brother. I don't think it can get any worse.

But it does.

The space solar panels have always continued to provide power. They're one thing that the Xua have never tried to take down. Maybe they need them for some reason. Whatever the case, this is the first time the aliens use them to their own advantage.

We all get a Gov-Net transmission, a jolt of news, right in the face, ready or not.

"Station Eight!" I yell into my skin sites. I don't know what's coming, but now is not the time to follow protocol. We have to survive. We can regroup later.

"Got it," Natalie answers.

I wish my brother would say something. I want to hear his voice. I need to hear it. Instead, I hear David Perez. He stares at me—at all of us—his eyes wide, as he tries to appear calm. His normally perfect hair looks like he's been running his hands through it. The news must be bad, because when he finally speaks, he stutters. "T-Two cities have just been— They've—" He whispers to someone beside him, but it's still loud enough for us to hear. "I wasn't going to say *attacked*." Then he tries to smooth his hair and begins again. "Some sort of natural disaster or eco-anomaly has— It ripped through Sydney, Australia, and Auckland, New Zealand. Wait. Now I'm getting reports from—" His voice chokes as he palms his left ear to receive more information, and he shakes his head. "No—"

"What's going on?" Justin asks in my ear, his expression serious. "You must know something. Has this happened before?"

"No, they've never broadcast what's happening in other countries—"

Before I can finish my sentence, transparent images flash across our line of vision.

First we see a holo-mind image of a European city—it must be Rome—the morning streets dotted with tiny foreign cars, half of them smashed into one another, the other half crashed into buildings. Shopping bags filled with apples and oranges litter the sidewalks, a cappuccino cart is overturned, and the Colosseum is etched in the background. Countless bodies lay still and unmoving in the street.

"We don't know what to make of this yet," David continues, his voice cracking with emotion. "Whatever's going on, it appears to be happening all around the world..."

Then we see an apocalyptic montage, similar scenes, over and over again, each one set in a different city: trains off their tracks, freeways choked with unmoving cars, bicycles lying in the street. Hordes of dead bodies strewn about like cast-off dolls.

Several of the cities are still dark with only an occasional headlight, streetlight, or fire for illumination. Those images are the scariest, because you can see sparkling aliens moving in the shadows.

"It's the Xua," I whisper, in shock. I always wondered what was happening in other parts of the U.S. and in the rest of the world during the invasion, but I never knew. There were never any broadcasts until now. They've been attacking our entire planet, all at the same time. But this is the first time they let me know.

This is worse than seeing the aliens on my roof, worse than when they captured Aerithin.

It's the worst attack I've ever seen.

They want me scared.

It's frigging working.

"We need to get out of here," I tell Justin. "They're trying to distract us. Something is coming this way; I can feel it." Then I speak into our com system. "Gabe, if you can hear me, Station One in fifteen. If you're not there, I'm going to come find you. Don't make me do that," I say into my skin sites.

No answer.

I don't know if anybody on my team heard me.

Justin and I scramble to our feet, and we start to run, back the way we came, down the alley. It's like an obstacle course now, half-blocked by the fallen fire escape and littered with dead bodies. A few of the corpses are Xua, and their bright shining blood paints the ground and the buildings on both sides of the alley. It lights our way through the darkest night ever.

We run while David Perez continues to tell us about the worldwide invasion, flashing a continuous montage of images so visceral that they hit me in the gut. I have no idea how small children are handling this. I can barely stand it, and this is my fifteenth time.

"So far, we have reports of similar incidents occurring in Rome, Paris, Sydney, Beijing, Seoul, Auckland, and Kabul," David Perez says while familiar landscapes flash through my mind. "Wait. It's hit the United States, too. We now have video from New York City and Los Angeles."

The Statue of Liberty stands in the distance while the city of New York burns, the flames red and orange against a black sky. Then we see the Hollywood sign and a sweeping view of L.A. freeways, a snakeskin of metal cars, all heading toward some predetermined destination. But now, the cars are out of control, smashing into medians and plunging off overpasses. A jet crashes into the seventy-three-story U.S. Bank Tower—

I feel sick, but I don't stop running. I can't. Justin's fingers lace with mine, and we're finally at the end of the alley. Our city is being destroyed, and we have to get away from here.

I don't want to listen to the announcer, but I need to know what is going on.

I have to know how to fight, how to survive, how to win.

"Right now the death toll is too high to count," David Perez continues. "But early estimates put the numbers in the millions. And, while everything is still too chaotic to verify, apparently all the governments in Europe have gone dark. We're still in contact with Great Britain, Canada, and Mexico, but we aren't sure how long that will last—"

The images disappear as the Gov-Net transmission cuts off.

I stumble. I'm out of breath and confused.

To my left, a woman stands quietly weeping. An elderly man across the street starts to run away. An unnatural silence falls over all of us. I'm still trying to get my bearings when Natalie's voice comes over our com system. I'm not sure if she's talking to me or to someone else.

"Did he...did he say *Seoul*?" she asks.

"Station One," I say to her and anyone else in our group listening. "Stay alive. No matter what."

Station One is a parking garage just down the street. I can see it from here. We have some supplies stashed inside, and there's a stairwell that we locked and barricaded between the first and the second floor. Justin and I have to make it only a couple of blocks and we'll be there.

Then I see something—shadowy movement up ahead, a solar streetlight that still sends green beams down to a darkened street. Someone swings a laser switchblade, red beam lighting up his fourteen-year-old face, revealing the fear in his eyes.

"Oh no," I say, pulling away from Justin. I can't do anything about what already happened in those other cities, but I *can* do something about what's going on down the street. My legs don't work at first, then I'm running, faster than I knew I could.

Something is happening to my brother, right in front of the parking garage. My brother's life is in danger, and I almost missed it because of that Gov-Net transmission.

The Xua did this on purpose.

I thought they were trying to scare me, but it was more than that.

They wanted to get Gabe when I was distracted, when I couldn't protect him.

The Xua have definitely stepped up their game.

"Hurry!" I yell at Justin.

Then I pull out my switchblade and I flick it on, ready to fight.

12

I'm running toward Gabe, and Justin is at my side. My blood roars in my ears. My heart beats fast, then faster; my legs pump hard, then harder.

Earth has just been invaded by the Xua.

But sometimes humans are more dangerous than aliens. You never know who you can trust. Or how much time you have.

"Leave my brother alone!" I yell, waving my switchblade above my head.

Two guys have my brother and Billy cornered and pinned down. One of them pummels a fist in Gabe's face. The other is going hand-to-hand with Billy. I can't see Natalie.

I hope she's following our plan for Station One, even though I gave the order to improvise a few minutes ago. Now is definitely the time to stick to the plan.

"Station One!" I yell into my skin sites, although I know everyone is too busy to answer me.

The blond guy beating my brother doesn't ask any questions. He's not demanding our food or any of our supplies.

He briefly glances up at me and probably figures I'm nobody to worry about, then he pummels Gabe again, faster this time. Like he needs to finish off my little brother before I get there.

There's a dark glimmer of bloodlust in his eyes and a grin on his face.

Both these guys have shining weapons drawn. Knives.

My brother getting stabbed to death. One of the many ways he can die tonight.

These guys have to be possessed by Hunters.

"Let the boy go!" Justin shouts.

The first guy pulls himself up, stretches broad shoulders wide, blade in one hand, his other fist wrapped around Gabe's collar. His skin is covered with prison tats, and his blond hair hangs in long, greasy dreadlocks. I wonder if this Hunter is stupid or if he just doesn't know what's coming, because he's not intimidated by the obvious danger here—a Genetic who's about to roll over his sorry carcass.

And me. Nobody ever worries about me until it's too late.

Blood drips from my brother's nose, and there's a deep gash in his forehead. Blood on the cement, on Gabe's shirt. On this guy's fist.

"You are *so* dead," I say, leaping into the air, kicking my right foot out and slamming the blond creep in the jaw. He stumbles backward, his grip on my brother loosens, and his knife clatters to the ground. I kick it away. Natalie runs out of the parking garage shadows, looking like she's been in a battle of her own. There's a long scratch on her face and bloodstains on her shirt and jeans. I really hope it's not her blood, because there's a lot of it.

"Are you okay?" I ask her.

"Yeah, but the Xua-possessed jerks in the parking garage who tried to mess with me aren't," she says. Together, Natalie and I check out my little brother, and I don't like what I see.

He's got a wide gash on his forehead that looks like it needs stitches, but I can't remember if I packed a first aid kit for this station.

Meanwhile, Billy swings a brass-knuckled punch at the bald guy who was attacking him, then follows with a nightstick thud to the back of the head. The bald man crumples to the ground and lays there, still. Billy knocked him out so fast, the Xua inside him didn't even have time to jump. A few steps behind me, Justin grabs the blond-haired Xua and, with a single punch, this guy is unconscious on the ground, too.

Justin glances back at me.

"Should I kill him?" he asks, his voice calm.

"We don't have time," I say. I'm still examining Gabe's injuries when a siren wails in the distance, distracting me. "Are we ready to leave?" I ask.

"Yup," Natalie answers, and she jogs back inside the garage. "I'll be right back."

"Where's that girl, the one with the red hair? And what's her name?" I ask.

"Ella," Gabe says. He pushes me away, wobbles to his feet, and looks back toward the garage. "You okay?"

Ella emerges slowly from the shadows, step by cautious step. She looks terrified, her eyes dark, her hands trembling. She's covered with blood, too, even more than Natalie, and I wonder what happened. Ella opens her mouth to speak, but nothing comes out.

"You're going to be all right," I tell her, hoping my words are true. But I know we all have to get out of here, now. I stare down into the face of that blond thug with the dreadlocks, glad he's still unconscious. I think I see a tooth missing, no doubt from my running kick.

Just then, a 1960 Chevy pulls out of the garage.

It screeches to a rugged halt, Natalie behind the wheel.

Good job, she found something vintage that can't be remote controlled by anyone else. It's just what we need, although there's only one person in our group who can really drive this thing.

Billy.

His eyes widen; his jaw drops open.

Nobody but Natalie and me knew that we would be stealing a car at Station One.

"Hurry up, everyone. Get in the car. Billy, you're driving." I sprint into the garage as I talk. I'm looking for our stash of supplies, hoping those Hunters didn't touch the overflowing trash Justin set up earlier. I'm looking for smelly black trash bags, but instead I stumble over something. "We have to get out of here before the Xua crash another jet nearby or more Hunters show up—"

I look down and see that I tripped over a dead body. No. Holy crap, I think there might be *two* dead bodies half-hidden in the shadows.

There's so much blood and carnage that I'm fighting a gag reflex.

Justin grabs me by the arm. "Don't look," he says. "I'll get the bags. Ella, you too, come on, get inside the car."

It sounds like he's coaxing a baby deer out of the woods, and that's how she looks when she walks haltingly toward the Chevy, stepping carefully over the bodies on the way. Two men, I think, although I'm not sure. It's hard to tell from what's left over. Ripped open from throat to gut, skin and bones shredded from the inside out, these two were definitely possessed by Xua.

I can almost feel the claw marks, like I'm the one who got shredded.

Every time I see what these creatures can do to us, it hurts more.

"Come on!" Natalie calls to me. She scoots over to the passenger seat, Ella beside her. Billy settles into the driver's seat. "They're dead. I got all of them, even the Xua that were inside the humans."

"Did they send out a warning before they died?" I ask, hoping that more aren't on the way here. Ours didn't have a chance, but I wasn't here when Natalie took down these two. I push Gabe in the backseat with me and start digging through the black plastic bag that Justin tossed in a second ago.

"Nope. Here." Natalie hands me a zippered pouch. "Found this in my backpack."

I open it and see a tube of skin glue and some antibiotic cream. But that will have to wait. I have to do something else first. I push the plastic bag toward my brother. "Grab something else to wear," I tell him. "Strip down to skin and change your clothes—"

"Are you kidding me? This stuff smells like piss!" he says.

"That's the idea. Take a left and drive past Station Three," I tell Billy. "But don't let anyone there see us."

With a wild scream of burning tires and roaring engine, the Chevy almost flies down the street, weaving past human and Xua obstacles, and all the while, Billy grins. It's like he's been waiting his entire life for this moment, when he could drive a vintage car through an apocalyptic landscape—one with no stoplights or stop signs or police cars with blaring sirens.

If there are any cops out and about tonight, we're the last ones they'll be chasing.

Ella starts to whimper and shake. "Can I go home?"

"Maybe later," Natalie tells her. "You're safer with us right now."

I'm not sure if that's true, but we definitely don't have time to swing by her house and tuck her in. If anything, we'd lead the monsters right to her doorstep. As soon as we left her at home, there'd be a slaughter, one that would wipe out her entire family.

We're not the safe port in a storm.

We *are* the storm.

Justin's playing the role of enforcer, making sure Gabe strips down, and when each article of clothing comes off, it gets tossed out the window. Getting my brother to take off his clothes was hard enough, but now it's taking both Justin and me to dress Gabe in the clothes I got from the garbage. I'm pretty sure some homeless guy was using that dumpster as a toilet. But it's what we need to survive.

Up ahead is the proof.

Every station was taken care of in a different manner, with precise instructions.

The supplies stashed at Station Three were very specific. Justin took some of Gabe's dirty clothes—his soccer jersey and shoes and socks—and hid them inside Taco Mesa, a local restaurant. I've been trying to figure out how Hunters always find my little brother. If we drive past and the restaurant is deserted, the Hunters aren't tracking him by smell and I'll need to adjust my strategy.

Then Taco Mesa comes into view, one wall painted with a bright combination of graffiti and street art, and I can't breathe. I don't know if I wanted to be right or wrong, but I never expected to see this horror movie come to life.

The entire restaurant has been ravaged, windows cracked, trash cans overturned, chairs broken, and over it all, there's a haze of black smoke. But it's not from a fire. It's a frigging cloud of Xua, looking for bodies to inhabit. They're in a frenzy.

Holy, holy, holy crap.

"Turn, quick, get us the eff out of here *now*!" I say, and I push my brother down so no one outside the car can see him. Justin clamps a hand over Gabe's mouth, just in case he was going to yelp a complaint. Natalie does a similar floor dive with Ella.

The Chevy swerves and turns left fast, Billy slams his foot on the gas pedal, and I hope we look like a car being driven by normal humans — normal humans who are terrified of the Xua.

I close my eyes and grit my teeth and pray.

Don't let them know that the one person they really want to kill is inside this car, please, please, please... Don't let them catch the scent of my brother's skin, let his disguise work, let us escape this part of the invasion...

And then when we are five blocks away from Station Three, aka Taco Mesa, eight blocks away from Station Four, we ditch the car. Because maybe they figured it out, maybe they smelled my brother, maybe they smelled me. Maybe they can hear and recognize the beat of his heart. Maybe it's his voice or his aura or his brain waves —

Whatever *maybe* is true doesn't matter.

We're running and hiding, while people all around us are getting slaughtered. We try not to look when people are being possessed or killed. We can't, not now. We head for the Santa Ana River, which is really just a concrete flood-control channel, and it's a place where smart people my age never, ever go.

13

Every city has a horrible secret, a place so dark that cops won't go there and news reporters refuse to cover what happens there. In most cities, it's either the tumbledown ghettos or the historic, falling-apart inner city. Here in Southern California, it's the man-made system of rivers, built to help channel runoff during winter rains, a Hail Mary effort to prevent floods. Tent cities first formed along the edges of the Santa Ana River back before 2020, but since our drought, the cities have spread down into the belly of the river. It wasn't long before every form of corruption followed.

Today, the flood-control system is a river of evil.

And it's called Snake City.

It's both a meeting place and a home for drug dealers, gang members, skin dealers, metal shops, Genetics for hire, back-alley surgeons, the homeless, and the mentally ill. It's secretly run by local politicians and policed by thugs enhanced with metal implants.

There's a pain in my chest as I remember the first time I stumbled across a man with fists lined with metal spikes. I was walking through downtown Santa Ana with Justin, and it was one of those times when I thought, *He's totally going to kiss me tonight.* It was back before I began traveling through time, before I found out just how dark the world could be. We were laughing and heading toward a frozen yogurt shop, and he slid his arm around my waist.

It might have been the first time I thought, *This guy is it; he's the one I could fall for.* I knew he was a Genetic and that nobody wanted us to be together. But I didn't care. He was sunshine on a dark night. He was heat when the cold winds blew.

I put my head on his shoulder.

It was only natural.

It was exactly right.

Then I saw the metal man, his brow furrowed as if his heart held all the anger in the world. He was chaos and destruction and he was walking toward us, eyes like fire, like he wanted to kill us both.

Maybe he was looking at Justin. Metal men hate Genetics, because in a real battle, Genetics win. It doesn't matter how much metal you've grafted onto your skin or bones—it might make you stronger, but you're slower, too. Nobody can match the speed and natural strength of a Genetic. So this guy might have been looking at Justin and challenging him, but it felt like I was going to be collateral damage.

One swing of his spike-covered fist and I'd be dead.

But I didn't have to worry about it for long, because Justin pushed me behind him. I couldn't see his face, but I could see the metal man. Doubt flickered in his eyes; he paused and glanced to the side. He was probably looking for a way out.

Justin took a step forward, his hands curled in fists. When he spoke, his voice came out like thunder, a loud, low growl that rumbled through my spine.

"Don't even think about it," Justin said. "Take one more step and I'll rip out your metal implants, one by one. They hurt going in, so you better believe it'll be a mother when I pull them out."

He paused to laugh, but I'd never heard him laugh like that before. It was chilling, like he was a different person. He continued to warn the metal man. "Especially when I twist those implants sideways and the roots tear off chunks of your flesh."

The metal man narrowed his eyes, and there was a split second when I thought he was going to tackle Justin.

Maybe he would have.

But he didn't get a chance. It was like Justin knew the metal man's plan, like it was an open football playbook. Justin rushed him, grabbed the guy around the waist, and slammed him against the brick wall of a local tattoo parlor. It took the wind out of the metal man's lungs, and he was temporarily stunned. Justin could have slugged him; he could have broken the guy's arms; he could have killed him.

All he did was lean close enough to whisper in the guy's ear.

Then Justin stepped back and let the thug slide to the sidewalk in a heap. The metal man caught his breath, his eyes flickered, and he glanced up at us. Then he floundered to his hands and knees and crawled away as fast as he could. By the time he got to his feet, we were surrounded by a Friday-night club crowd, most of them drunk and all of them laughing at the metal man as he ran away.

Justin didn't even hit the guy.

Sometimes you can win by intimidation alone.

So, do I melt every time I see this boy, who was willing to fight to protect me?

You better believe it.

Unfortunately, this time, he's got more than just me to protect as we head closer and closer to the nightmarish pulse of Santa Ana. He's got a team of six, all of us wary as we approach the guardians of this Snake City.

Right in the middle of us is my brother, Gabe. If he dies, this alien apocalypse will turn into hell on Earth.

None of us will get out of it alive.

And I really doubt that intimidation is going to save us this time.

"Are you sure?" Billy whispers.

We're standing on an overpass, looking down into Snake City, where occasional lights flicker and the air is filled with laughter and screams. The Xua haven't made it here yet, so the screams are just an everyday occurrence.

I swallow, running my fingers over my laser switchblade. It's perfect for fighting the Xua. But metal men, Genetic mercenaries, and gang members? Not so much.

"What weapons do we have?" I ask. I need to know what our arsenal is, all of it. "Besides your laser switchblades."

"Nightstick, brass knuckles—"

"Bowie knife—"

"Regular switchblade and a gun—"

I didn't expect Justin or Ella to have a weapon, and they don't. But my brother having a bowie knife and Natalie having a gun were both surprises.

"I—um— Okay. Well, I wouldn't want to mess with us," I say, giving them a weak smile. "Let's head down. Gabe and Ella, you guys stay in the center of us as we walk. And let me do the talking. If there *is* any talking."

Another plane nosedives in the distance, somewhere in

Irvine, and I close my eyes when it thunders and splinters into a bank of high-rise condos. Natalie takes my hand, and I hear the jingle of that gold and jade bracelet on her wrist. Her last gift from her father who may or may not still be alive.

We don't talk about the things that break our hearts.

But it doesn't mean our hearts aren't broken.

I open my eyes, catch a glimpse of the distant skyline on fire, hear the catcalls and shouts from down below as if all of this is a fireworks display for their enjoyment. The darkest souls of the city are below, their tents and booths and beds covering the river bottom, as far as the eye can see.

It's the place we shouldn't go.

It's the place we have to go.

So we begin our long descent.

14

We only have to make it until morning. No one we know would ever think to look for us here. It's possible that even the Xua are terrified of the people in Snake City.

Aerithin never would have approached me if he didn't think I could do this.

I tell myself all of this and more as I run down the overpass stairs, and then begin weaving my way through the tents that stand up at the top of the river embankment, Justin at my side. The rest of my team is a step or two behind us. I could turn around and grab my little brother if I had to; I could take his hand and we could run; I could tackle him and shield him if someone attacked us...

I'll do whatever I have to, even go through the gates of Snake City and come back out alive. I can do this. I can.

And then we hear the screeching of tires and metal as cars crash into one another back up on the overpass, where we stood only a few moments ago. I glance over my shoulder and see a haze of smoke above the cars. The Xua must be here.

My heart skips a beat.

Maybe soaking Gabe's clothes in piss wasn't enough. Maybe they can still smell him.

Ella lets out a terrified cry, but Billy clamps a hand over her mouth.

"Quiet," he says. "We can't look afraid. Not now."

"Hurry, guys," Natalie says. "Don't look behind us. I'll take care of anything that comes from that direction."

We're running even faster now, through the tents and the growing crowds of people who've crawled to the uppermost edge of the river. They're all craning their necks to watch the aftermath of the car crash, laughing and taking bets on what will happen next.

"A fiver on the guy in the SUV."

"Two fivers on the woman in the Fiat. If she survives, we should invite her to join us!"

I don't know what their currency is here, but I know I've got something they'll want. Six bags of Syn-Op that I stole from my parents' stash. It's not even on the street yet. So far, my crew has slipped past, unnoticed by the adults who are thriving on the chaos caused by the invasion.

That's when we meet our match.

A rugged gang of people about my age has spotted us, and they're headed our way, climbing up the sides of the river toward us.

This group looks even scarier than the adults, all of them wearing black-and-gray camouflage, their faces painted to match, and their hair black and spiked. Some are Genetics like Justin, which surprises me at first. I've never seen this many together in one place, but really, where else do they have to go? The Genetics almost fit in here, with their metal spikes and their skin covered in tats. I note that these are juvie tats, which are just as bad as prison tats.

It's easy to tell which one is the leader. She's a Genetic

with metal enhancements, and her black hair has light-blond roots.

She sizes Justin up as she approaches. "Traitor," she says to him with a sneer.

He pulls his shoulders back. She's not as tall as he is, nor as broad, and with her metal I bet she's slower than he is. But she's got a bigger, badder crew than he does.

She shoves Justin on the shoulder, almost pushing him backward. But he stands his ground. And thankfully, he doesn't take the challenge.

"Why didn't you come when we sent out the call?" she asks him.

He glances at me before answering. "I'm not for hire."

"Sure looks like you are. Is this your girl or is she your master?"

"We're partners," I say, taking a step forward. I'll be mincemeat if she swings a punch at me, but it's a risk I have to take. We need to get down into the belly of that river, into the midst of the booths and tents and mayhem that make up Snake City.

The girl nods at me. "Well, your *partner* is welcome to join us. The rest of you better be on your way or you'll regret coming here."

"Maybe we should leave," Gabe says from behind me.

I don't want to do this, but I have to prove I'm in charge.

"Shut up!" I yell, and I turn around and backhand him across the face, hard. He flinches and stumbles backward, a look of betrayal in his eyes. I want to cry and apologize, but I don't dare. Instead, I turn around and glare at the Genetic girl, my brother's blood on my hand. I narrow my eyes. "All of us or none of us. One night only. Down there, not up here on the embankment." I point toward the concrete river.

She crosses her arms, while the gang behind her murmurs

threats at us. I try to count how many there are, but it's almost impossible in the darkness. They're like an army of shadows.

"What do you have to trade? And don't offer me any of your weapons. The junk you guys are carrying isn't worth my time."

"I have two things: information and this." I pull out one baggie filled with tiny blue pills. "You might not recognize it because it's not on the street yet—"

"Syn-Op," she says, the word coming out like a sigh. "This right here will do it. I don't need your information. You don't know anything we didn't know last week."

I hand her the baggie of pills. Then I grab her wrist and pull her closer.

"You don't know this," I tell her. "The attack today is just the beginning. You have to keep your mouth closed when they come here. They look like shining silver men, but they can turn into smoke in the blink of an eye. Their goal is to get inside you, through your open mouth. And once that happens, they're in charge. You can't come back from that."

She does her best to show me her brave face, but her lip is trembling. "Where did you hear that crap?"

"I've seen it. Firsthand. I've lost people I love. You've got your own army. Let us teach you how to fight. Protect and shelter us for the night and we'll make sure you survive, too."

She lets out a hollow laugh. "Your crew can stay with me tonight and tonight only. We're down with the military vets. See the flag there?" She points to an American flag flying upside down, then she hands me a red poker chip. "The general's out on a scouting missing, but you can tell the lieutenant that Carla let you in. And if anybody wants to hurt you, show them this. It's my marker. Don't lose it, no matter what." She pauses to examine me again, running her gaze over me. Then she gives me a measured smile. "You're tougher than you look, sweetie."

"Sara."

Carla laughs again, then says, "Don't forget: you're teaching us your fighting techniques tonight. It's part of the deal. There's still time for all of you to wish you'd never heard of Snake City."

15

We make our way down to the center of Snake City, while the city of Santa Ana burns and explodes and crumbles. Except for Taco Mesa and the overpass, the Xua haven't attacked this part of town yet. They're busy looking for a boy who smells like Gabe.

Meanwhile, my brother—who smells like piss and looks just as bad—sits on a worn-out blanket, as far away from me as he can get. There's a wound on his forehead from earlier tonight, his lip is swollen from my backhanded slap, and there's an ache in my chest that feels like a Xua warrior has crawled inside me. It burns and scrapes, and I can't think of anything except the fact that I hurt Gabe.

I've never hit my brother before, not in any lifetime.

I want to hug him and tell him I'm sorry, but I don't dare. Not when we're surrounded by Snakeskins—that's what this gang calls themselves. They come and go while we eat their dinner of beans and rice, and at this point, I think there are at least thirty of them. But the ex-military camp is so large that I can't count them. There are hundreds of men and women, all outcasts, ignored, left to fend for themselves after their time in the service was over, no matter what injuries they might have incurred along the way.

Carla's father is the general, so it makes perfect sense now. Why her gang wears camouflage, why she's in charge, why she recruits the toughest of the people my age who end up here.

We're all fighting our own wars.

And we need people on our team to help us survive.

Justin is talking to Carla. Bits of their conversation drift over to me, and I can tell he's trying to convince her that everything I said is true. Billy and Natalie are arguing about who's a better lead guitarist, Nantucket Blue from Maximum Death or some old dead guy from Led Zeppelin, while Ella stares down at her plate, not eating.

Gabe sits beside her, his jaw clenched.

He looks like he might start crying.

I bite my lip, remembering our first time in this alien apocalypse, how almost everyone we know died. How he didn't make it.

He never has.

None of us has ever made it this long.

I don't care about the Snakeskins. Let them think I'm soft. Maybe the soft side of me is the best part. Maybe it's the only part of me that's still human.

I set my plate down and stride across the campsite, then I sit between Gabe and Ella.

"Eat," I tell her.

She shakes her head. "I can't keep it down. I…I keep throwing it up."

I put one arm around her. "Then don't eat. Just drink your water. Slowly."

Gabe stares into the darkness, acting like I'm not here.

"I'm sorry," I say to him, and I don't lower my voice like

I normally would. "I shouldn't have done that. You know I love you." But my last words are more of a question than a statement.

He shrugs.

"I know I'm bossy."

"More than bossy," he says.

"I'm a bitch."

A small grin teases his lips. That's when I notice that he's got the beginnings of a black eye and his jaw is turning green and purple.

"You're the fifth person to slug me today," he says as he rubs his jaw. "At least you didn't pull a knife on me. Or a gun. Or try to run me over with an SUV."

"Did all that happen today?"

He nods. "My skin sites aren't working, either. Not since that jerk in front of our apartment building jumped me. Why is everyone after *me*? I still don't understand."

There's a raw angst in his voice that hits me like a knife in the chest. How often do I feel like the whole world is against me? Whenever I don't pass a test in school, whenever I realize I'm not as pretty as the school cheerleaders, whenever I realize my parents are basically drug dealers. I guess we all feel that way sometimes. Except with my little brother, it's real.

The whole world really *is* out to get him.

"I don't know exactly why everyone's after you, but you're not alone. Remember that, okay? Now, let me get a look at you." I pull a small flashlight from my backpack and shine it on his jawline. It's swollen, more than it should be from just a punch. "Natalie? Can you come here?"

A heartbeat later, she's studying Gabe's injuries, gently turning his head back and forth in her hand. I didn't ask her to join us, but Carla comes over, too.

"That looks bad," Carla says. "Is this your brother?"

Justin must have given her more information than I
expected. "Yup."

"His skin sites need to come out. They're broken, and his
jaw's getting infected," Natalie says, then she looks at Carla.
"Is there anyone here who can do that? Without making him
deaf?"

"Deaf? I might end up frigging *deaf*?" Gabe pulls away
from us and stands up, looking like he might run. That's when
I notice that Justin and Billy are behind him.

"It's okay, buddy," Justin says. "I think we can get you
something to take away the pain. And nobody's touching
you unless they know what they're doing. I got your back."

And just like always, knowing Justin is with us makes us
all calm down. Gabe's shoulders relax, and I let out a sigh.
That Syn-Op in my pocket will do the trick. It will definitely
take the edge off my brother's pain—if we can find a surgeon
somewhere in this black-market city. If the apocalypse can put
itself on hold long enough for my brother to get the medical
attention he needs.

Because he has to survive. No matter what.

"You really owe me now." Carla stands akimbo at the door
of the tent. "You better have some unbelievable fighting
skills to share with my gang or you'll be owing me more of
that Syn-Op. I'll be outside waiting until your little princess
wakes up."

"Did she just call me a princess?" Gabe mumbles.

"Yeah," I say with a laugh.

Despite all Carla's threats to turn us into mincemeat,
she's done nothing but help us since we got here. I might be
starting to like her. A little. A thin trail of blood snakes down

Gabe's neck, despite the cold cloth the doctor's pressing against the wound.

His skin sites are now sprawled out on this black-market surgeon's instrument tray, along with a pack of cotton swabs and a couple of hemostatic clamps and a pair of scissors. Speckles of blood, long plastic tendrils, a clump of Gabe's hair tangled in the mix. We won't be able to call each other anymore.

I snap my fingers next to his ear. "Did you hear that?"

He nods.

Then the doctor hands me a bottle of antibiotics and moves on to the next person. Justin helps Gabe to his feet but basically has to carry him out. Natalie, Billy, Ella, and Carla stand just outside the tent doorway.

"Pay up, sweetie. I mean, *Sara*," Carla says. She motions with one hand, and four of her team members join us.

I glance at my watch. It's one o'clock in the morning and, so far, the Xua haven't invaded Snake City. Maybe we'll make it until morning.

Maybe.

But first, it's time to teach a gang of Snakeskins how to fight.

16

Billy and I swing and strike, our laser switchblades glowing bright red. Up until now, fires have been burning up in Santa Ana, Tustin, Irvine, and the rest of Los Angeles. People were screaming and cars crashing. But every now and then, there's a lull.

That's the scariest time of all.

The quiet makes my heart beat faster.

It makes me think they're looking for Gabe. They've stopped attacking because they know he's not wherever they've attacked. They're regrouping. A new Leader is giving them different instructions...

But I don't stop. "Like this," I say as I swing my blade up.

Carla's crew watches us, imitating our moves, puzzled. I know it doesn't make sense. If you haven't seen the Xua and how they attack, this looks ridiculous.

Then two Snake City residents stumble into camp and start telling stories about what they saw tonight, when they were "in the above." That's what they call the rest of the world. After that, rumors begin to ripple up and down the Santa Ana riverbed, tales of mysterious creatures murdering people, and everyone in Snake City stands at attention. Former soldiers, sailors, airmen, and Marines climb from their cots, Genetics prowl the edges of camp, all the lights dim, and Carla puts a hand on my shoulder.

"We got it," she says. "It's time to go dark."

She hands me a pair of night-vision goggles. Neither she nor Justin needs them to see in the dark, but I do. Darkness like I've never seen sweeps from one end of the riverbed to the other. All of Snake City is invisible and silent. The only thing glowing right now is Natalie's tablet. She's been studying something ever since I got back from Gabe's surgery. As soon as she realizes what's going on, she snaps her tablet off and gestures for me to join her.

I sit next to Natalie, while the rest of my crew joins us. Gabe blinks sleepily, trying his best to stay awake. If it wasn't for Justin propping him up, my brother would be asleep on the ground.

"I found some old diagrams of the river, then checked them against what the river looks like today," Natalie tells us. "There's a hidden space, like a long, narrow room, right over there." She points across the river. "From what I can tell, there's an alcove that was built maybe ten or fifteen years ago inside the concrete channel wall. It's possible nobody here even remembers it."

"What is it?" I ask.

"Maybe a storage area for stolen goods? The first people to live in Snake City were thieves and ex-cons. Maybe they even hid people inside there. I don't know. You've got night-vision goggles on. See how the slope of the western wall is different from the eastern wall?"

She's right.

"Look, I know you think hiding in a crowd is the best

way to ride out the night, but I'm having my doubts. It would only take two or three of these Genetics or metal men to be possessed by the Xua. They'd be able to get Gabe away from us. We're not strong enough to fight *everyone*."

"You guys are creeping me out," Gabe says.

"Shh," Ella whispers. Then she does something I don't expect. She quiets him with a kiss. It works. Neither one of them says anything. For a long time.

I don't mean to stare, but I can't help it. *That* has definitely never happened before. None of this has. I've never met Carla before or come to Snake City. And Gabe has never had a girlfriend.

Unless she was a secret.

Like how I have kept my feelings about Justin a secret. Even from him.

I glance up at Justin and Billy. Billy nods, then takes a protective stance beside my brother. Justin moves close enough that both Natalie and I can hear him when he speaks in a low voice.

"Where is the door?" he asks.

"I couldn't find a door," Natalie says.

He pauses long enough to study and compare the concrete slope of the eastern wall with the western wall of the river. "I'll find it and check it out. Will you be okay while I'm gone?"

I never feel okay when he's gone, but we're going to need the hiding place if everything goes south. "Sure."

He looks at me, like he's a soldier ready to go into battle but he's waiting for the command. I think he's reading my hesitation and interpreting it as a, *No, please stay*.

"Go," I tell him. "And hurry."

Then I sense something, like a tremor of fear, strong as a flood, moving our way.

I stand up and try to see over the crowds. Carla and her

team are positioned about twenty feet away, and they're picking up on it, too, all of them looking upriver. Whatever it is, it's still far away, on the northern edge of Snake City, somewhere beyond the bend in the river—I can't see it; I can't hear it. But I can feel it. Carla looks back at me.

I gesture for her and her team to join me. If we find a place to hide, her team can hide with us.

But she's been trained to guard this place, so I don't know if she'll like my plan. Her father, the general, is still gone and, even though the lieutenant is here, she might really be second-in-command. If so, she can't leave her post.

That means she might not survive.

"Any of you have a spare laser switchblade?" I ask my crew. Natalie digs through her backpack and pulls one out. That girl is always prepared for the worst scenario. I give her a hug, then take the weapon and run toward Carla.

Although, that could have been a big mistake.

Leaving my brother behind is never a good idea.

"We're getting out of here," I tell Carla when I reach her. "You can come with us."

She glances at me over her shoulder. All her attention is fixed on whatever is coming. I'm like a gnat, pestering her, distracting her. She doesn't have to answer me. I know she'll refuse. Instead, I put the laser switchblade in her palm.

"Stay alive," I tell her.

She swivels to face me. "You're the girl from those videos, aren't you? How did you know?"

"It's a long story."

"I told you any intel you might have would be old news here. But I didn't know about this," she says, glancing down at the switchblade. "Thanks." Then she pauses, as if she's got a secret, too, and she doesn't know if she should tell me. "I wish my dad was back. I think he'd want to talk to you."

"Maybe he'll be back soon—"

"Is there any chance you know a guy named Noah?"

Her words startle me, and I replay everything Aerithin has ever told me about how I'm supposed to meet a guy named Noah and that it's a cascading event. It's destiny. But before I can answer her, that horrible thing heading our way looms into view.

It sweeps around the bend in the river, a bright fog of light and chaos and destruction. Even though it's still far away, we can hear the screams. It's a frenzy of Xua, both in their sparkling silver shape and in a haze of smoke, moving like a rolling ball down the riverbed. Everything in their path disappears. Or gets absorbed. I can't tell what's happening from this distance.

I don't know if Justin has found that hidden alcove yet or if it can even protect us from this. All I know is that I have to get out of here and find my brother.

So, like almost everyone else in this man-made valley of concrete, I turn away from the approaching danger and run.

17

"Get Gabe into that alcove, or grab him and get the hell out of here, now!" I yell into my skin sites. More than anything, I wish Gabe's skin sites were still working. I need to talk to him and know he's okay. I'm running as fast as I can, but I'm getting pushed by thugs and human monsters three times my size. One of them slams me against the eastern wall, and it makes me lose my sense of direction. For a nanosecond, I forget which way I was heading.

Then I see that bright frenzy of Xua, rolling closer.

A glowing ball of death, plowing over every dark human monster.

"Natalie! Can you hear me?" I cry.

Her voice comes back like static, intermittent bursts of her low voice. "Inside…*crackle*…small space… Gabe isn't… *hiss*…"

"Gabe isn't what?!" I scream as I start running again. I'm heading south, toward the ocean, and I hope I don't go past the doorway that Justin was looking for. "Justin? I can't find you—"

"It's okay—I'll find you," he says, his voice so clear he could be standing next to me.

I lift my head, trying to see over the mass of bodies running and jumping and climbing over one another. They're fighting, swinging punches at anyone who gets in their way. This crowd is almost as bad as the Xua frenzy heading our way.

Why did I think it would be safe here?

Then I see Justin, moving toward me, carving a path like a butcher slaughtering his way through a herd. Bodies fall to the left and the right of him. He might be only seventeen years old, but he's a match and then some for anyone in this dark city. Another Genetic accidentally collides into him, and he almost punches her in the face because she slowed him down. He pulls his fist back, swings it forward, and then stops it a few inches away from her chin.

It's Carla.

I don't know where the rest of her team is, but that doesn't matter. Justin grabs her by the arm and pulls her alongside him, then he points at me. She nods, and they become a two-person destruction team, moving faster and more efficiently than before.

This is unlike anything I've ever seen. It's almost unholy, like a war machine built out of flesh and blood. I can't imagine them losing any battle, especially when they work together.

I shiver as I imagine an entire battlefield covered with warriors like this.

They'd win. Every single time.

Only top-level military leaders know why the GEIVE program was ended. Right now, it seems like the biggest mistake they ever made, because this is the only war that matters. Save Gabe, save the world. An army of Genetics could have helped make that happen.

I have to find my brother. He has to be safe.

But the frenzy is so close, I don't know if I'll have time to make it back across the riverbed.

Please be safe, Gabe. Wherever you are, hang on until morning comes.

Then Justin is beside me.

"Come on, hurry!" he says, and he takes my hand. Carla is beside us, and the three of us are pushing our way through the crowds. Someone knocks me backward, and those night-vision goggles go flying. I blink, touch my forehead, stagger.

I'm bleeding.

I don't care.

"Where is it? How far is the alcove?" I ask.

Justin elbows someone else, and the man falls to the ground. "There," he says, pointing, and I think I see it. A blank spot on the sloping concrete wall, where no algae grows, pale in the moonlight.

Carla punches a guy in the stomach, and he curls over, and then we're running and fighting and pushing our way through hordes of people who are all going in the wrong direction. They're crashing into us, buffeting us, and with every step I take, I worry that I'm going to fall to my knees.

I have to make it across the river.

But I might get trampled first.

Screams echo around me, and I realize that the Xua frenzy is rolling closer. A coppery smell fills the air, so thick I can barely breathe. Blood.

"Keep going, keep running, even if I fall, even if you lose me," I say. "Protect my brother, promise me—"

A metal man charges into me, his titanium spikes and thorns ripping my knapsack off my back and throwing me to the ground. I can't get up; I can't catch my breath. The metal man runs over me, one of his boots pressing against my chest, and I let out a scream.

Justin knocks the man away and scoops me up. "Sara!" he shouts, looking at me, needing me to answer him.

But I can't. I open my mouth, and nothing comes out.

"She's breathing," Carla says. "She's going to be okay."

Every slug of oxygen comes with superhuman effort. Justin clutches me to his chest so tightly that the only thing I can hear is his heartbeat. He's running, and I think we're heading toward the hidden alcove, but black spots are dancing in front of my eyes. I feel the wind on my skin, the thunder of his feet on pavement, the jostle of him kicking people out of our way.

He's in a war zone. This is what he was created to do, and even if I wanted to, I couldn't stop him now.

"You'll get to the alcove, I promise," he says, and I believe him.

I have to believe him, because I have to reach my brother. I have to make sure Gabe's okay, that he's safe.

But my skin is covered with pins and needles. I'm cold; I'm so cold.

Everything fades to black, and I try to focus, to stay conscious, but I can't.

And then even the black fades away to nothing...

18

My head hurts. My chest hurts.

It feels like someone has been beating me with a hammer.

I pull a shallow breath into my lungs and, holy eff, it hurts. There's a moment when I see yellow sparkles, and I flinch, thinking the Xua are here. I try to get away, to run, but I can't. Something is holding me in place, and except for that brief moment of light, everything is as dark as midnight.

Did they get me?

Did that frenzy strike us, and did I get possessed? Is this what it feels like to have a Xua inside you?

Trapped, stuck in darkness, unable to break free.

Oh Lord, no, no, please…

Then another thought thunders through my mind.

Gabe.

Where's my brother?

I pull in another shallow, painful breath and another. I swallow, and finally I think I might be able to speak. I don't have enough strength to scream, although that's what I really want to do. My words come out like a hoarse whisper.

"Gabe… Where is my brother? Is he safe?"

Something touches me, and I recoil.

"Sara, everything's okay; be quiet." It's Natalie. But this doesn't make sense. Are we both possessed? What's going on?

"Where's Gabe?"

"I'm over here," my brother says in a soft voice. "Now shut up—we're listening to what's going on outside."

"Outside… Am I in the alcove?" I ask.

"Shhh, yes. Quiet. They might be able to hear us," Billy says from somewhere farther away in the darkness.

Something touches me again, and I realize it's a hand. Someone is taking my hand in hers. I think it's Natalie.

"Where's Justin?" I ask.

But no one will answer me.

That's when I hear the frenzy outside. A muffled thumping and buzzing seeps into the alcove, combined with the horrific babble of people choking and crying. It sounds so hopeless. No one could survive this.

Panic surges through me.

Justin's out there. He must be. He's fighting to protect us.

Why can't both the boys I love be safe?

I know it then, just like I know that I'm trapped in here and there's nothing I can do to save myself.

I'm in love with Justin. I don't have a crush on him. I'm not "falling" for him like girls fall for a different guy every week at school. And I never had a good reason for not telling him how I feel. The Xua go after *everyone*, not just the people I care about.

They want every single human dead.

I might be locked behind a wall, and everyone might want me to stay quiet, but maybe he can hear me, even if his skin sites aren't working.

"You have to stay alive, Justin," I whisper. "No matter what. I love you."

I think I hear a pause in the fighting, as if all of heaven and earth stopped to listen to me. My heartbeat ratchets up a notch, and I hope that the Xua didn't hear me. But they must not have, because when the fighting starts again, it's fiercer, wilder, louder. I can't tell from my vantage point, but it almost sounds like we might be winning.

Morning comes in a breathless lull, like the entire world has grown tired of screaming and wailing. Like a baby after a long fitful tantrum, dragging one last breath into its lungs before letting out yet another earsplitting howl. Except that howl never comes.

The world is silent and still. Beams of sunlight spill under the door that I couldn't see until now. Shadows inside the alcove grow long and pale. I can see why I felt trapped last night—the space is so narrow. It's probably why Justin and Carla stayed outside.

They couldn't have fit in here.

There's been so much noise and chaos for so long that I don't recognize these sounds of silence. The metallic creak of a broken road sign swinging in the wind. The rushing whisper of leaves in the trees. The sound of my own heartbeat, steady and fast.

Wait.

I bolt upright.

It's morning.

I frantically scan the hidden chamber. Everyone is here: Natalie, Billy, Ella. All of them are staring at me. Only one of us has fallen asleep, probably because of that Syn-Op I gave him last night.

Gabe.

He's alive.

Did we win?

Every muscle in my body relaxes, joy floods my chest, and I can't wait to open the door. Justin has to be out there; he *has* to be safe. I pull myself to an awkward crouched position, the best I can do in this cramped space. My fingers trace the wall, searching for a handle or a knob or a latch of some sort that will open the door. But Natalie grabs my arm and holds me in place. She shakes her head, puts one finger to her lips.

"But Gabe's alive," I say. "It's morning."

She pulls me away from the door and shakes her head again.

I struggle to get away. This is what I've been trying to accomplish in all fifteen of my lifetimes—Gabe is alive!

"Let me go," I tell her.

She pulls me even farther away from the door.

I hear it then. Something is trying to get inside. It's digging, making a soft scraping sound against the door. I cock my head and lean forward, trying to figure out what it could be. Then I glance back at Natalie and Billy and Ella. Gabe is awake now, too.

We speak in the softest of whispers.

"What is it?" I ask them.

"I don't know," Billy answers. "The frenzy is gone. It left about half an hour ago. I think you fell asleep. Then, when the sun came up, this started."

"Whatever it is, it can't be the Xua," I say, no longer keeping my voice down. "Aerithin promised! We just had to keep Gabe alive until morning—"

The creature outside lets out a horrid scream, so loud it penetrates my bones, so strong I'm sure it can be heard for miles.

Icy dread washes over my body.

It's a Xua, and it's letting its brothers know where we are.

Panic grips me. But I can't allow fear to take over right now. I need to get my brother and my friends to safety.

"We have to go," I say. "Get ready to fight when I open the door."

We all pull out our laser switchblades and power them up. Natalie checks to make sure her gun is loaded. Billy brushes his hair out of his eyes with one hand, slips his backpack over his shoulder with his other. Ella stumbles to a crawling position, dark circles under her eyes and one hand clutching a car jack.

This girl is ready to rock and roll.

Gabe frowns at me. "But you said everything would be fine in the morning—"

"I was wrong," I say, fighting the despair that gnaws at me.

Natalie grabs her knapsack. "Maybe Aerithin meant later in the morning, like ten or eleven o'clock?" There's a glimmer of hope in her eyes as she asks the question we're all hoping is true.

Maybe Aerithin lied. Or maybe he was wrong. Maybe the Xua found a way to change destiny and nothing Aerithin said matters. A soul-crushing dread fills my chest, and I need all my strength to take the next step.

"As much as I want that to be true," I say, "we have to focus on the here and now. We have to fight our way out before more Xua arrive."

I find the door latch and get ready to push it open, worrying that the bright light will stun us, and the Xua will rush in, and there might be more of them than we can handle. This could be our last fight, our last few moments on Earth. I'm hoping Justin is out there somewhere, and that I'll get to see him one last time.

"Stay with me," I say. Then I swallow, tense my muscles, and get ready to swing my laser switchblade. I quietly unlatch the door.

"Three, two, one..."

I kick the door open, and I'm blinded by the morning sunshine that I've been waiting fifteen lifetimes to see.

19

The Xua come into focus one at a time, shadowy monsters that lunge at us, blocking out the sun, a dark silhouette of death.

We come out of the alcove, weapons swinging, arms punching, legs kicking. We fight, back to back, our mouths closed tight. There is no shouting of orders or skin-site communications. We don't dare open our mouths, not even to breathe. I clamp my teeth so tight my jaw hurts.

A quick sweep with my laser switchblade to finish the job and this guy won't ever bother me again. I kick him aside, still trying to figure out how many Xua have us surrounded.

Natalie fights like she's dancing, every movement precise and graceful, elbow to the throat, knee to the gut, blade to the center of the chest—where its heart lies—and we have two Xua down. Billy slams a nightstick against a Xua skull, and a dull *crack* follows. Then he twists the creature's head until its spine pops. Three Xua on the ground.

I can finally see now. A group of aliens must have stayed behind when the frenzy left, maybe to look for my brother.

They find Gabe, and for a moment I panic, but then I realize he's kicking their butt. My brother thrusts his bowie knife into a silver chest and slices a Xua from throat to gut, just like the smoky Xua cut us when they break free. This one will never possess another human. Or travel through time. Or try to kill Gabe.

Ella surprises me by tripping a Xua and then slamming it in the chest with her car jack. She doesn't kill it, but it's stunned long enough for me to finish it off. When I stand back up, I quickly scan our surroundings. Bodies, both human and Xua, are strewn all across the riverbed, tents are shredded, and the leftover bits of canvas flap in the morning breeze. I don't see anyone else alive, either north or south of us. There are only this group of Xua and the five of my team left.

Natalie takes on another monster, and it still looks more like a dance performance than an execution. Together, Billy and Gabe tackle two more Xua. Ella swings her car jack.

But where is Justin? Is he here somewhere? Have they taken him captive? Or has something even worse happened?

He can't be dead. He just can't be.

My heart bangs against my rib cage until I think my chest will explode, and I continue to scan the near horizon for anything, some clue that will tell me what happened—

A Xua grabs me around the throat and presses its hand tight against my windpipe. It's behind me, so I can't get ahold of it. If it keeps this up, I'll have to open my mouth. I'll instinctively start to gasp for air. Then the monster lets out a screech as someone pulls it away, breaking its bones and cracking its spine. I spin around, hoping to see Justin. *It has to be him; please let it be him.*

It's not.

Together, Billy and Gabe attack the alien, grabbing both of its arms until they split it into two pieces. Two very dead pieces. I should be glad that the Xua is gone and that I can breathe, but I can't stop worrying about Justin.

My lips tremble, and that ache in my chest won't go away.

"We need to get out of here," Natalie says. "If there are more nearby, they'll be here any minute."

My crew stands at attention, all of them holding their weapon of choice, all of them waiting for me to tell them what to do next. There's a smear of silver blood on Gabe's cheek, Billy's shirt is ripped, Ella has a fresh splash of red blood on her hands, and Natalie's arms have bruises where one of the Xua latched onto her.

"We really could use that plan B right about now," Billy says.

Natalie glares at him, but he's right. Unfortunately, I don't have a clue what to do. "Right now, plan B is to stay alive. When we get somewhere safe, we'll figure something out. Now hurry," I tell them. "Run up the eastern wall and head to Station Five. I'm right behind you."

Gabe, Ella, and Billy do exactly as I say. They're running and jumping over bodies, vaulting their way across the riverbed. Natalie doesn't move. She stares at me, her arms crossed.

"What are you doing?" she asks.

I don't answer. I cup my hands around my mouth and scream, switching my skin sites on at the same time.

"Justin! *Justin, where are you?*" I yell.

"Okay," Natalie says, then she joins me. "Justin! Come on, we have to go!" Then she pauses, narrows her eyes, and points toward the south. "Did you see that?"

"What?"

"Something over there."

She doesn't say any more, she just starts jogging away from me. I scramble to catch up with her, calling out Justin's name as I run. Every few steps I pause to yell in a different direction. He *has* to be here. I can't accept the alternative. I won't.

We've rounded a cluster of tents that are somehow still standing, ribbons of canvas shifting in the breeze, looking like they're alive, like they aren't just empty shells. And there I see what she saw. It's awful. And maybe it's hopeful at the same time.

Tears well up.

Natalie's already at work.

There's a pile of bodies, as tall and wide as an SUV, every color of skin peeking out. They look like trophy kills, like maybe the Xua frenzy paused long enough to take their photos beside this leftover heap of humanity. Here and there, a finger or a foot twitches. Maybe it's a death reflex, a muscle spasm. Or maybe someone is underneath the bodies.

And that person is alive.

Natalie's dragging bodies off the pile, I join in, and together we manage to pull off six bodies. All the while, I'm hoping that Gabe and Billy and Ella are safe, that they made it to Station Five, but then I realize that we've somehow managed to clear off about eleven bodies.

Gabe and Billy and Ella came back to help us.

I can't stop the tears that fall onto the bodies, a baptism of death. I can't stop because Justin might be here. He might be alive.

"Justin!" I call again. "We're here! We'll find you!"

The twelfth body slumps and rolls off the pile by itself.

Billy jumps back. Ella lets out a yelp.

Natalie and I look at each other. I want to smile, but I don't dare.

"Justin!" Gabe yells. "Come on, you can do it. I know you're okay!"

My little brother isn't startled, and he doesn't stop like the rest of us. He keeps pulling bodies off the stack; they slide to the left and the right until they're all around us, some of them staring up at us like they want to tell us their story—

I was trying to run away—

They came from nowhere—

What are those shiny monsters—

Pale skin, gray lips, eyes open and glazed, the dead tell us their deaths by their wounds—a sliced neck, a knife in the chest, a blow to the head.

More bodies slide off, the pile of cadavers begins to sway, limbs tremble, and it looks like they might meld into one large creature, like it will come to life with a vengeance and a groan.

Or with a smile like sunshine.

Justin pushes his way out, and we're helping him, prying away the last few corpses; we're laughing and chattering and telling him to hurry and asking how did this happen. Some of us, like me, are crying. And I don't care if he's half dead or if he has blood on his clothes or if he didn't hear me whisper *I love you* to him last night. Once he's set free and I know he's okay, I throw my arms around him.

He wraps me in his arms and pulls me close.

I can feel his heartbeat pressed against mine, the same thundering rhythm in both our chests.

It's not romantic. How could it be? We're in the midst of an apocalypse and he was almost dead, and we're surrounded by alien and human carcasses. I don't care.

"Don't do that again," I say into his chest. "Never do that again."

"You mean save you?"

I laugh. We all laugh.

"*No.* Don't let me think you're dead."

He grins down at me, and it's like the world shifts under

my feet, and not in a Xua-invasion kind of way.

In a million years, I never would have imagined this.

But you don't get to choose that moment when you die.

And you don't get to choose the moment you fall in love, either.

He cups my face in his huge hands. "I heard what you said last night," he whispers, so softly no one else can hear him. "I love you, too."

That ache in my heart disappears. Every problem in my life melts away. There's only gold and sunshine and hope. There's only this moment, right now, this horribly perfect moment in the midst of the end of the world.

"Are you okay?" he asks, gently touching my bottom lip with his thumb.

"I am now," I say.

I thought our first kiss would be when we were hanging out at the park or when we were standing outside the coffee shop or when we went to the beach. I'd have my hair combed and my makeup on. I would be showered. Clean.

Not this. Not in front of my friends, covered head to toe in blood, when more Xua could show up at any minute, when there are more dead bodies than I can count.

He gives me another smile, and I swear we're wrapped in a brilliant sunbeam, so bright I can't see anything but him. Then his lips touch mine, and his heat floods through me until I think I'm going to catch on fire. Together, we're either going to save the world or burn it down, and right now, I don't care which one. As long as he's alive, that's all that matters.

And so I add another item to my list.

Save Gabe.

Save the world.

Keep Justin alive.

20

We crouch in a patch of grass and bushes, catching our breath and staring at a building across the street, trying to decide if it's safe to approach or not. Justin lies on his back beside me, his eyes closed. If you didn't know better, you'd think he was asleep. He's not. It's more like he's recharging his batteries, like he's hooking up to a version of SkyPower for Genetics. I'd really like to stare at him, to spend the entire day thinking about what he said to me and the fact that we finally kissed, but I can't.

This is the happiest day of my life and the worst.

The boy I've fallen for is in love with me, too.

My brother is alive, but the alien I've trusted for fifteen lives lied to me.

The war isn't over. It's just getting started.

According to Justin, Carla might have survived the Xua attack back in Snake City. They got separated a few hours before sunrise when she got a call from her father. I totally understand why she had to leave us, why she had to take her gang and try to rescue her dad. No matter what, family and loved ones come first.

I would have done the same thing.

Then another wave of Gov-Net news comes on, and I wish I could close my eyes and block it out. It's as bad as what we saw back in Snake City, except it's everywhere. We're forced to watch the wreckage of London, Mexico City, and Ottawa — after those cities were attacked — bodies strewn throughout the streets, people running, children crying, and everywhere, silver bodies charging and turning into smoke.

Ella buries her head in the grass, weeping, and Gabe puts his arm around her. Billy slams his fist on the ground, over and over, and I don't know if he'll ever stop. Justin's eyes flicker open, and he stares into the sky above him, a tormented look on his face that breaks my heart.

"Can't we get these skin sites out?" I ask Natalie. "We need to be able to focus, but…" My voice cracks, and I can't say any more.

Natalie seems to be studying something, like she's taking notes on what's going on around the world. Her brow furrows and her lips move, as if she's talking to herself. "Huh? Um, yeah," she answers me finally. "But we'll lose our com system, too. And honestly, we'd need a surgeon. You saw how long the tendrils were on Gabe's skin sites, didn't you? They go deep inside your head and wrap around your — "

"If we can't take them out, can we turn them off?"

She nods. "I think so. I'll do some research, as soon as this news blast shuts off."

I force myself to concentrate, to stay focused on our next task. Regroup, enlist, restock. That was our purpose for coming to Station Five. We didn't get supplies before we left Snake City. I managed to find my backpack on the riverbed, but we're out of water and food, and we could use a few more weapons and a few more members on our team.

And we need to help any survivors, if we can.

I stare at the building across the street, a place both familiar and dangerous. Century Unified High School. Most Southern California schools have sprawling campuses with buildings spread out across acres of land. But Century Unified was built in the 1940s, so it doesn't look like other schools around here. It's a frigging fortress. Made from brick and stone and three stories tall, it looks like something out of a nineteenth-century Gothic novel. This thing should have gargoyles perched on the roof, that's how imposing it looks.

There are only two entrances, one in the front, one in the back.

That means it would be easy to guard, we'd have an escape route, we'd be able to see who is approaching from the upper-floor windows, and I'd bet a chocolate protein bar that the cafeteria is stocked with food and the water fountains still work.

On top of that, the front and side of the building are covered with new graffiti. Street art of the revolution kind. Most prominent is a large *V* scrawled across the front. I have no idea how anyone managed to make a *V* that big—the crazy thing stretches from the third floor to the ground floor.

V for victory. *V* for we're winning this war, you effing aliens. *V* for we might only be high schoolers, but we've got the skills to kick your butt across the universe and back again.

Other words have been painted with orange spray paint, too, and I realize that nobody knows how to spell Xua. These people only heard me say the name of the alien race on my videos, so they've written it phonetically, a bunch of different ways.

Death to the Zow!
The XOW suck!
Go home, you Zou jerks, before we destroy ALL OF YOU!

I shouldn't smile, but I can't help it. This might seem like the last place for us to regroup, but it could be the best place. If there are other kids our age still alive, they might be here.

"That makes six," Billy says.

"Seven," Natalie says. "Did you see the girl with blue hair? She went in—"

"I counted her."

"Then you missed one of the others."

If I measured relationships by heat, I'd give these two a score of Ten-and-Get-a-Room. Billy watches Natalie from the corner of his eye, probably hoping he'll see a smile or some sort of acknowledgment. She frowns. There might be a hookup in their future, but I kind of doubt it's going to be today.

Today we survive.

And take over Century Unified.

Plan B.

We've been watching the school for an hour. During that time, Natalie used her tablet to find out how to disable our skin sites, but she doesn't look happy about what she found. She signals me and writes something in the dirt.

Everybody should call Gabe by a different name from now on.

I frown. "Why?"

She puts a finger to her lips.

She writes, *Call him Alice or Sally.*

Oh, he's going to love this. I pull each member of our team over as quietly as possible and make them read what she has written.

"Are you frigging kidding me?" Gabe asks. He bends down and writes something in the dirt, then grins.

Handsome Boy.

Holy crap.

Billy cracks up, but then says, "Okay, Handsome Boy."

Meanwhile, the Xua have ramped up their attack in the south. Something exploded a few minutes ago, and I'd have to guess it was an eighteen-wheeler on the 405. The aliens are focusing on Costa Mesa and Newport Beach right now, so maybe they won't notice that we got away.

Maybe they don't care about Gabe anymore. That's not exactly saving the world, but if making it through the night means he's safe—well, as safe as any of us in an alien invasion can be—I'll take it.

"Okay, is everyone ready to go?" I ask.

"I've been ready for two hours," Billy says.

"We haven't even been here that long," Natalie counters.

Justin gives me a slow grin, one that sets me on fire. "You know I'm ready."

My heart skips a beat, and I try not to read anything else into his statement. He's talking about our mission, not *us*. He's not the type to tease. Or flirt.

Right?

His grin widens.

Whoa. This is probably why I never gave in to my feelings before.

Natalie jostles me with her elbow. "Hey," she whispers. "Are we ready to go or not, girl? Stay focused."

I swallow, clench my fists, and force myself to think about the few people who might be inside that school, looking for help.

"Go!" I say.

And we run.

21

We're an army of six, invading a building that never seemed safe, not in any of my lifetimes. School might be a great experience for some people my age, but it never was for me. I always wanted to be like all the other girls and, somehow, I never succeeded.

Fitting in is probably overrated.

Once we reach the front steps, I hold out my open palm, a signal that means, *Stop, wait.*

We slam to a halt.

"We can't all go inside. What if they're waiting for us?" I glance at Justin. "Keep Handsome Boy outside, okay? Keep him safe. I'll check back with you in fifteen."

Justin nods, and Gabe sulks.

I walk a little closer to him and take a whiff, then shake my head. "You don't smell like piss anymore. We're going to have to fix that before we leave."

"Seriously?" my brother says.

"We'll look for something," Justin says. He leads Gabe toward the field beside the school where some PE equipment got left out. Baseballs, bats, soccer balls, and basketballs lay strewn along the edge of the building. My brother's eyes light up, and I know he's looking at the soccer ball.

"You have fifteen minutes, but stay focused. We're looking for survivors. Got it?" I ask.

"Yup."

"Got it."

Then Natalie, Ella, Billy, and I jog up the stairs, ready to head into the building that used to be a place of dreams and rules and assignments. Weapons drawn, bandannas around our faces, we look more like Wild West bandits than students, and that's just fine with me.

The halls are dim, no lights are on, and the building is so quiet it's creepy. Our shoes squeak on the tile floors, and there's a smell of fresh paint in the air. Somebody must have tagged the inside of the school recently. But those six or seven people we saw earlier aren't in sight. Maybe they did a through and through—run in the front door and then go out the back. It's what you do when you're trying to ditch someone.

I hope they aren't afraid and hiding from us.

"Billy, you and Ella go to the cafeteria and get us some food. Anything you can carry. And if you find bottles of water, grab them, too," I say. "But hurry and meet us upstairs in about five minutes. We're going to do a quick sweep down here, then go up to the second floor."

He nods, and the two of them jog away. Ella's long red hair is the last thing I see before they disappear through the cafeteria door.

We haven't seen anyone else yet.

"Hey!" I call out. "Anybody here?"

Natalie flashes me a guarded look as we walk down the hallway. I shrug.

"We have to find them, right?" I ask her.

"Or not. I'm in the 'or not' camp."

We hear it then, a scurry of feet, a soft *whoosh* as a door closes, somewhere up on the second or the third floor. Natalie sighs.

"Whoever they are, you probably just scared them off. Can we at least get some water before we track them down?" she asks, pausing in front of a drinking fountain.

That's when we get yet another Gov-Net newscast, but the transmission on this one is sketchy, almost like it's breaking down. I stumble a couple of steps and grab hold of the wall for support.

It's a broadcast of a Xua attack—but this time they're in Washington, D.C., our effing capital.

My knees feel weak, and I can't understand what the announcer is saying.

Meanwhile, the Xua in the video are dissolving, turning into a dark cloud and heading for the White House. That's when the transmission stops.

It takes a minute for me to see the school hallway clearly. I rub my temples and blink.

Then we hear it again—shuffling sounds like there are other people somewhere on an upper floor. I nod toward the stairs, and the two of us jog in that direction.

"Hey," I say in a low voice. "What did you find out about turning off our skin sites?"

"I found an app on the dark web," Natalie says as we start up the stairs. "A lot of people use it to block out Gov-Net. It's not as good as having our skin sites removed, but it might help. The only thing is, some of the reviews were kind of freaky."

We pause on the landing between the first and second floor. She continues. "Some people think our skin sites have built-in tracking devices, like GPS markers—"

"What the—"

"Yeah, it gets worse," she says. "There are at least two cases where people think the Xua used our skin sites to find human targets. One was the president of France. He went underground as soon as the invasion hit, it was totally secret, but the aliens found him anyway and killed him—"

I hold up my hand for her to be quiet.

We're on the second floor now, and there are definitely people up here. It sounds like there's something going on downstairs, too. We jog toward the voices in a nearby classroom and both pull out our laser switchblades, just in case, all while my pulse is ratcheting up and I'm arguing with myself.

The Xua can't track Gabe. We took out his skin sites. So, why are we calling him Handsome Boy now?

"What else did you find out?" I ask her in a whisper.

"They might be listening in on our conversations. They might have hacked our skin sites and could even be listening right now. They might be searching for anyone who says you-know-who's name."

I freeze, trying to remember the last time I said his name. Was it back in Snake City, was it when we were on our way to Station Five, was it when we were crouched in the grass across the street?

I no longer want to find survivors. I only want to make sure Gabe is still okay. The fastest way to do that is to look out the windows from a second-story classroom. Billy and Ella just jogged out of the stairwell and are now right behind us.

"Follow me!" I say.

All four of us rush through the door of a nearby classroom, one that overlooks the field where we left Gabe and Justin.

Three girls are standing in front of the windows, and we startle them when we run in, our weapons drawn. These girls were our mission when we first got here, but not now.

Now it's all about Gabe.

"Move away from the windows!" I yell.

They were all staring outside at something, and I fight the fear that chews at my gut. I push a blue-haired girl out of my way so I can see down onto the field. For a moment, all the tension in my body dissipates. Gabe is okay. He's standing just below these windows, at the edge of the school building with Justin. Meanwhile, the group of people who'd been down on the field is talking to Justin. I think they might be sharing their food rations; I can't tell. They're all trying to keep to the shadows.

But then the universe shifts again, and it's like I'm tumbling through space, a swarm of butterflies spiraling in my gut.

No.

My skin prickles and burns. I grab onto the window ledge for support.

More Xua are coming.

I jerk back upright, panic flooding my veins. Everything happens so fast, I don't even have time to react.

For a split second, everything in the landscape has a mirror image, from the cars to the buildings to the people. What is and what might be. Now and in the future. Together in one moment.

Then the mirror doors open.

Long, slender silver bodies step from the future into our time. About thirty of them line the street and the field below. Their Leader makes a gesture with one hand, and the others get into position.

"Close the windows," Billy shouts. "Hurry!"

The Xua are about to turn from flesh-and-sparkling-blood into vapor. One by one, their bodies disappear as they transform.

Everyone on the field starts to run and shout, and I don't know what's going on. I push someone out of my way so I can see outside.

"Get away from the windows!" Natalie yells as she starts slamming the windows closed. But she slams one of them too hard, and the glass breaks. It shivers and falls in pieces to the floor.

One of the girls in the room begins to yell, really loud, so loud I can barely stand it. She won't shut up, and I start to get mad.

Then I realize the screaming girl is me.

Because my little brother is down on that field.

22

Only a heartbeat passes, but that's long enough for the Xua to turn into smoke.

Panicked, I scan the field for Gabe and Justin, but I don't see them. Maybe they're pressed up against the building, hoping to be invisible. Maybe they ran around the front of the school and they're racing up the stairs, trying to get to us.

Please let them be anywhere but down there.

The Xua fly at everyone on the field, diving toward their open mouths. One by one, everyone I can see falls to the ground, twisting and clawing at their throats, like they're being smothered and they're powerless to do anything. Their legs jerk; their eyes bulge.

It's awful.

I'm screaming, but I don't know if Gabe can hear me. I shouldn't say his name, but I have to; I can't help myself—

"Run, Gabe, run!" I scream out the broken window. "Close your mouth! Run!"

Just then, everyone on the grass below stops trying to fight the Xua. The possession is complete, and it's too late for them—they'll never be human again. As one creature, they all turn around and look toward the same spot, right where someone is trying to hide behind an equipment bin.

They've found Gabe.

Narrowed eyes, crooked grins, jaws hanging loose. They're Jumpers. Their shoulders hunch forward, their fists clench, and they all head toward my brother like they're trying to corner him.

"Run!" I scream. "Get the hell out of there!"

"Run!"

We're all shouting it now, a chorus of voices, male and female, all saying the same thing. Billy and Natalie stand beside me, frantically waving their arms as if that will make my brother hear us better. I still don't know where Justin is—I can't see him. Billy cups both hands around his mouth, creating a megaphone that carries his voice farther than any of ours.

Gabe takes off running as fast as he can, weaving across the field, trying to get to the street, but he can't. All the Xua-possessed people are after him like a band of evil demons.

I've got to get down there and help him.

Justin appears then, a few steps behind Gabe. He must have stopped long enough to grab a weapon, and now he's swinging a bat that had been left behind with the other athletic equipment.

"Leave him *alone!*" Justin yells. "You wanna fight? Come and get *me!*"

And then he runs toward the nearest possessed person, swings that bat, and breaks the guy's leg. Bellowing in pain, the guy falls to the ground in a twisted heap. Justin doesn't react; the Genetic soldier in him must have kicked in, because he's showing no emotion. He's in fighting mode, his muscles tensing as he races across the field, his mouth clamped shut.

He raises his arms over his head, both hands wrenched around the neck of that bat, and he swings again with dangerous precision. Kneecaps shatter, blood and bone spray out in a pulpy mist, voices howl in agony, and he doesn't stop.

But the Xua-possessed group doesn't stop, either.

They don't look back. They just keep charging after my brother.

Silver mirrors twist and spin, the ground slips out from beneath me, and ten more Xua soldiers appear on the field. All ten of them stand on the bloody field, looking up at me, at the broken window that beckons.

The one we were all screaming out of.

Oh, holy crap. I know what they're going to do.

Their bodies dissolve before I can react. Natalie pulls me away from the window.

Three columns of smoky vapor shoot upward, quicker than the wind. They fly across the field, higher and higher toward their destination.

Right toward our broken window.

23

I made a huge mistake. I know it now. In every life, there's a moment when I realize this is it, this is the mistake that's going to mess it all up. Sometimes it's a big thing; sometimes it's so small I don't even realize it was a turning point until much later—when I find Gabe sprawled in a pool of his own blood.

I should have kept Gabe with me, we shouldn't have come to the school, I shouldn't have tried to save anyone else. If I had just stayed focused on him, he would be safe. He'd be right beside me, complaining about the fact that he doesn't want to wear smelly clothes.

But I didn't keep him with me.

Plan B, hastily formed as it was, has already failed.

Ella grabs a backpack someone left in the classroom and tries to use it to block the window, but she's not fast enough. Ten columns of twisting smoke flow through that narrow opening, all of the aliens trying to get inside our classroom at once, they're so eager. Their vaporous bodies slide through the jagged opening of broken glass.

I swing my laser switchblade out and power up.

"Close your mouths!" Natalie yells.

The blue-haired girl starts to yell, while the blond girl dashes out of the room. Desks overturn, and chairs tumble through the air.

My lips press together tightly, and I slice up and to the right, red beam cutting through black smoke. Billy and Natalie do the same, all three of us with a red glow emanating from our hands; we become the brightest lights in a Xua-infested room.

But several Xua are after Ella. She runs backward, stumbles, hands over her head until she's backed into a corner. There's nowhere for her to run, she doesn't have a laser switchblade, and she's starting to panic.

"Help!" she cries out.

That's all it takes. A Xua swoops down and pushes into her open mouth.

I only have a couple of seconds to save her. The smoke has to get all the way inside or the bond won't take. I just don't know if I can get there in time.

I scramble across the room, push aside a desk, jump over a chair.

It's already halfway inside her, and she jerks left and right, her body flailing, arms waving, eyes wide, tears streaming down her cheeks. It looks like she's trying to cough, but in the process her arms swing out, punching me in the leg. This part is like trying to save a drowning person—they might take you down with them if you're not careful.

I'm in position, right beside her, that smoky alien plume about three-quarters of the way inside her. Her throat is distended, like she's a snake swallowing a mouse, and her chest swells up. She slugs me again, so I pin her left arm down with my foot. It's awkward because she's not holding still—this would be better as a two-person job—but I manage to swing my laser and slice through the Xua. It takes a split second before I know for sure whether it was a clean strike and if I cut through the alien or not.

The smoke lingering in the air turns red like fire. Then it dissolves.

Like it was never here.

The Xua is dead.

But Ella's not completely safe yet—she could choke on the part of the creature that's still inside her. She slumps to the ground, gagging, unable to breathe. I grab her by the arm and flip her over—this part is like CPR for alien invasions—then I slam my open palm against the middle of her back, praying. *Please work, please let her live, please.* She coughs, and more fiery red smoke pours out of her. I hit her on the back again and again, until finally she's breathing steadily and no more smoke comes out. She leans against the wall, legs splayed out beneath her.

"Get up! You have to get out of here!" I tell her. Then I turn around and try to figure out where the other Xua have gone.

Across the room, Natalie has a dark-haired girl pinned against a wall, and she's slicing through a Xua who's halfway inside the girl. Natalie's black hair sweeps across her face, almost hiding her gritted teeth, narrowed eyes, and the flush that colors her cheeks. She hasn't killed the beast yet, but it's obvious she's got everything under control.

Back in the corner, next to the hallway door, two more Xua chase the blue-haired girl, and Billy runs after them. There's no way to know for sure what's going to happen, but I know, between Billy and Natalie, all these aliens are headed for oblivion.

I have to get out of here. I have to get down to the field, before those monsters do something to Gabe or Justin. Right now I don't know which one of them I'm more worried about.

Less than a minute has passed since the Xua flew into the classroom, but it's a minute I'll never get back. Aerithin isn't coming to rescue me. I'm on my own. And the aliens are still going after my little brother.

I charge through the door and race down the hallway, my feet sliding when I get to the stairwell. I grab the railing with my right hand, leap over the first several stairs, and manage to land on the fourth step. At that point, I almost topple over and fall the rest of the way down, so I jump instead. It's a lot farther than I expect, and my landing isn't smooth. I fall forward, try to brace myself with my hands, but my shoulder slams the wall. Hard. Fortunately it's my left shoulder. I'll still be able to swing a weapon, even if it's only my fist.

Running down the rest of the stairs, I force myself to slow down even though I want to run faster than I've ever gone before.

My chest threatens to explode, shrapnel shooting out, all my fears turning into weapons of mass destruction. *He can't die, he can't be taken over by the Xua, he can't get hurt, not this time, no, that just can't happen—*

God, no. Not my baby brother. And not the guy I've fallen in love with, either.

I'm still running, out the front door and down the stairs, my shoulder burning like it's on fire and adrenaline flowing through my veins like a drug. I didn't notice my surroundings before. I was only looking at the possibility of a live threat. I wasn't looking at the dead.

I can't ignore them now.

The street is filled with cars that must have crashed into one another last night, bodies strewn on the pavement— women, men, children.

I didn't expect there to be little kids, and I can't look. I just can't.

I try to close my eyes as I pass a tiny body sprawled on the sidewalk, little fingers curved in fists, curls of blond hair smeared with dirt, a romper decorated with purple dinosaurs and blood. I want to block out the image, but I can't; I choke, my chest heaves, I curl over and stumble. Blood on the sidewalk. Blood on the hands of the woman who stands over the child, her eyes glazed, her head cocked as she watches me with curiosity.

Has she been here all night or did this just happen?

"Stay away from me or I'll kill you, I swear to God!" I yell as I pass her. She doesn't move; her hands hang at her sides, but I know at any moment she could swing into action and come charging after me.

I pause at the edge of the field, disoriented, trying to remember where Gabe was the last time I saw him from the second-floor window. Meanwhile, a Xua-possessed guy with a broken leg hobbles up and tries to grab me. I kick him back down. Two others are curled on the ground with injuries that should have them moaning—obviously they were struck by Justin and his bat—but they just watch me, quiet.

I scan the field again and note that both Justin and Gabe are gone, along with the rest of the kids who were here before.

I'm not sure which way they went, so I jog to the edge of the field.

There. At the end of the street. Six people are chasing someone weaving between houses and through backyards. I think I can hear them chanting, their words faint.

"Gabe—Gabe—Gabe—"

That's when I know for sure that at least one Hunter is leading the pack. It must have caught my brother's scent.

My laser switchblade is out now, and I'm chasing *them*, jumping off the curb, feet pounding cement.

24

I never catch up with the Xua-possessed group as I run through the suburbs, but it doesn't matter. I just follow the trail of bodies—an elderly man sprawled in the street, a girl facedown on the corner, a businessman still clutching his briefcase. They look like they were killed by Xua. I find several more people, all of them dead or seriously wounded, probably by Justin and his bat. As horrible as it is, I'm glad Justin's with my brother.

I know he'll do whatever it takes to protect Gabe.

I spot a cluster of cars on the ramp to the 405, their windshields busted, a woman standing beside an SUV, crying, blood on her dress. I don't look inside the cars. I've seen enough collateral damage today. These cars must have been here all night, and the woman must be in shock.

But I can't help her right now. I have to find Gabe.

And Justin.

The Santa Ana winds blow hot, whispering through the trees, ripping off leaves and loose branches. This is the kind of wind that starts fires that rage for days. My throat burns and my lips are cracked, but I don't dare open my mouth. I slow to a jog as I head down the freeway ramp, hesitant, wondering if Gabe panicked and ran onto the 405 or if he could be somewhere in the nearby suburb.

The slope of the entrance ramp lessens gradually until I stand beside a graveyard of cars. It was only yesterday that they were all zooming home on autopilot, everyone inside safe and oblivious, watching the *Valiant* launch on their tablets, probably excitedly chatting to one another through their skin sites.

Now, the freeway is choked with vehicles crashed into one another, cars that raced off the overpasses and tumbled down on the trapped sedans, SUVs, and buses below. The wreckage of cars is bad enough—there's still a lingering odor of burned rubber and spilled oil—but the human wreckage is even worse. Bodies are everywhere, inside cars, between the lanes, draped over the hoods and the concrete freeway median.

Over it all is the stench of burned flesh.

I fight a gag reflex and pull my bandanna over my nose. Maybe I can deal with it if I can block out the smell.

The Xua-possessed group swarms along the freeway shoulder about thirty feet away from me. Within a matter of minutes, this group has transformed from normal people to savages that look like they stepped out of *The Lord of the Flies*. They stand with feral postures, shoulders curved forward, legs bowed and ready to run, and a brutal expression in their eyes, a bestial gleam that sparks as their heads snap back and forth, surveying their surroundings. One of them licks his lips with darting lizard-like gestures, tongue sliding out then disappearing.

But they're not alone. Along the way, they've picked up more possessed people. New men and women push their way to the front of the group, all of them staring hungrily at the freeway.

Four of them break away from the pack and race after a girl who must have survived yesterday's car crash and is only now limping her way toward a freeway exit. Two other Jumpers rip out of their human bodies, killing their hosts. They change into smoke, and then fly toward a man and woman running across an overpass.

Those remaining on the freeway edge survey the wreckage hungrily.

I follow their gaze and see the carnage. The cars are a twisted tangle of metal. On top of that, bodies and pieces of bodies are strewn across all four lanes, dark stains on the pavement that must be blood.

My heart stops. I can't move; I can't think.

Gabe, please don't be out there in that mess.

I can't bear this. I close my eyes, trying to control the fear that surges through me. Finally I force myself to look—I have to if I want to find him. I lift my head and see Justin, standing atop a car in the second lane of the freeway.

He swings his bat and strikes a man who lunges toward him, knocking him backward. Another guy tries to climb the car, but Justin breaks that guy's hands, causing him to fall to the pavement. Then Justin leaps to the ground and races toward the rest of the Xua. Three of them burst into smoke, leaving their human skins behind like bloody shells. They swarm around Justin's head like bees, but he keeps his mouth closed and he's still able to fight the rest of the pack, taking them down one or two at a time.

He's definitely got this under control.

Where is Gabe?

I stand on my tiptoes to see all the way to the center of the freeway, past cars and bodies until I spot the concrete median. There he is. My little brother crouches low, trying to hide behind an overturned SUV, but it's him.

An extra dose of adrenaline floods through me.

He's safe! Both Justin and Gabe are still alive.

Without thinking, I climb over the nearest car, then I do the same thing again and again, like this is what I do every day. *I get up, I brush my hair, I get dressed, I race across a freeway covered with carnage to save my brother from aliens and possessed people.* As I'm running, I realize that Justin is only a step behind me.

Justin has his bat, and I have my switchblade, the red laser glowing like a beacon of death.

"Gabe, stay down!" I yell without looking behind me. "Get out your switchblade, just in case!"

No one is getting my brother. Not today.

Then the ground wavers unexpectedly beneath me. I stumble and fall, sliding off a car to the pavement as the universe shifts and a thousand silver mirrors surround us.

I push my way to my feet, and Justin is beside me.

"Gabe!" I cry out.

Reality changes, an alternate universe peeks in at us. A door to the future opens, and two Xua step out. Right in front of my brother.

"No!" Justin yells. "Gabe, get away from them!"

"Leave my brother alone!" I cry.

Justin and I clamber over another pile of cars, trying to get to Gabe. My hands keep slipping; my feet can't find purchase.

One of the aliens talks to Gabe, tilting its head as if speaking to a child who can't understand. Gabe looks back over his shoulder at me.

"Use your switchblade!" I yell as I make it to the top of the heap of cars. "Or your knife! *Kill them!*"

Gabe frowns, then he spins around, switchblade glowing and ready to slice the alien open.

That Xua must have known what Gabe was going to do, because it swerves to the side, then it knocks the blade out of his hand. Like it's done this a hundred times before and knows exactly how to win this fight. The blade clatters to the ground and skitters under a nearby car.

I'm running and sliding and climbing, Justin a few steps ahead of me.

We finally make it to the mcdian, but we're not fast enough.

The last thing I see is my brother's face when he turns back toward me one last time. He yells out my name, and I know he's scared. He did everything I told him; I kept him alive all night long, and none of it saved him.

The Xua grab my brother and pull him through the doorway.

Into the future. Into another world.

I have failed.

Part 2:
Hunters

25

Justin and I stand beneath a knot of freeway overpasses. Everything above and below is concrete, blue-gray in the half light of a late winter afternoon. Shadows fall across us—the shadows of technology, always moving forward, part of our continual race toward a better life, a race that includes our current space program.

Years ago, back before I can remember, the government ran our space program. Supposedly, it was part of our desire to "reach out to the universe and see if there's anyone else here besides us." Stupid idea. That original program failed, even though we still had a few probes wandering about through space.

Meanwhile, our central government slowly lost power. In its place, the individual states and a few mega-corporations rose up. Whoever had the most money gained control and, oddly enough, whoever had money always wanted more. So when our last experimental probes finally returned from Titan fifteen years ago, JPL-NASA was formed, and the first publicly funded space program began. We were promised jobs, a better economy, a decrease in crime—a whole list of promises went on and on—if we would only invest.

As a result, somewhere above us, the *Valiant* hurtles through the heavens, aimed like a bullet at Titan. Somewhere below us, the earth shudders at the mistake we've made.

My brother is gone, taken by the Xua, an enemy we'll encounter when we're mining on Titan. The aliens will come over a distant mountain range, drawn by the sound of our machines. They'll discover how easy it is to slip inside our bodies, and they'll add us to the ever-growing list of species they want to dominate and devour.

We'll find out there really is something else out there beside us.

And it's pure evil.

I curse, slamming my fist against the cement median. The Xua have something horrible in mind for Gabe. I just don't know what it is.

"I did everything he said!" I shout, not caring if I attract attention. Why bother? I've already failed. "We made it through the night and *it didn't work*!"

"Sara, it's not your fault."

Justin's behind me, trying to make me stop. He grabs my arm and holds it still.

"Why couldn't I fix it? Nothing I do changes anything!" And I'll never get another chance. I know for sure now. Aerithin would have come already if he were still alive.

Tears stream down my cheeks, and my throat aches. Justin drops the bat, then wraps both arms around me and pins my fists to my sides. I'm yelling again, but this time it's more like a primal scream. *"Why are we even still alive?!"*

"Calm down, dammit!" he says. "You're hurting yourself."

"I don't care!"

"I do."

He presses me up against the median and straddles me, arms on both sides of mine. For once, I hate the fact that he's so strong.

"Let me go," I say, my eyes narrowed.

"I can't handle this, Sara. You have to stop. Please!"

He has blood smeared across his cheek and his hair's wet with it. At first, I wonder if it's his blood. Then I remember that bat, how he was swinging it to protect my brother. *"Gabe."*

That one word comes out like a sob, rattling through my rib cage, taking all my breath and my strength. My legs sag, and if Justin hadn't been holding onto me, I would have collapsed on the ground.

His arms arc around me, his warmth seeping into my bones. Part of me wants to relax, to sink into him, but I can't. Instead, I let out a wail so loud it feels like it soars across the galaxy. It destroys asteroids, it explodes planets, it turns suns into black holes.

"Aerithin was wrong," Justin says. "He had to be."

I look at him, not understanding, my brow furrowing.

"Listen to me," he says. "Surviving the night may not have fixed everything—"

"It didn't fix *anything!*"

"I know. But that doesn't mean it's over." Justin pulls me closer. "Because it's definitely not over."

"That's easy to say, but it's not true."

Tears stream down my face. I worry that I'll never stop crying.

He lifts my chin gently with one hand, then leans in closer and kisses me.

"It's *not* easy to say," he says. "None of this is easy. My heart is breaking, too."

I lean my head on his shoulder, my eyes closed. I take in a long, shuddering breath.

Then he whispers words that give me hope.

"It's never over. Not for me. Not as long as you're alive."

For an instant, I forget that we're standing in the midst of a battle zone. This isn't the end of the world. It can't be.

His words echo in my heart, and one last tear slides down my cheek.

Maybe there is hope.

Maybe.

If he's here with me.

Then the world shakes harder than I've ever felt before. A jagged, sharp, soul-punching shift.

"What the—" Justin looks around. "That's not an earthquake, is it?"

I shake my head. Something really bad is about to happen, and we both know it. I can see it in his eyes, a panic, a cold, dangerous pit of terror, and we're both about to fall inside.

"We have to get out of here," I tell him.

Justin's fingers lace with mine; together we climb and vault our way back across the freeway, and I worry that I won't be able to keep up with him. But he doesn't leave me behind—he would never do that. He stays with me as we race across the first two lanes of cars and bodies.

We make it to the top of a car in the last lane.

"They're here," I say.

We both see it, a million mirrors reflecting us, a million Saras and a million Justins, a million cars that stretch out into infinity.

Justin puts his arm around my waist, and together we leap to the ground. It feels like we're falling through space, like we'll never land on earth again, like we'll just keep falling and falling past planets and asteroids and moons.

Then the reflections disappear.

We land on the pavement.

Now an army without number lines both sides of the 405 freeway—southbound and northbound, as far as I can see in either direction—Jumpers all ready to attack. Some of the aliens are probably Hunters, but I can't tell which are which. They all stand side by side, all facing the center of the freeway, thousands upon thousands of them, all focused on their Leader, who walks atop the median. One hand raised above its head, it's ready to give the signal.

Then a bank of clouds blocks the sun, and I see the Leader in mock twilight.

A chill rushes over me and I freeze, remembering the frenzy that rolled down the riverbed just last night in Snake City.

They're going to do it again.

"We can't stop," Justin says in a low voice.

He tugs at my hand, and we back away, slowly, trying not to be noticed. We step cautiously past the ripped bodies of the Xua-possessed people who had been chasing Gabe, all of them dead now.

Justin and I make it to the ramp, then start walking faster, past the cars with the broken windshields and the crying woman. Blood spatter stains her face and the sleeve of her blouse has been ripped off. Her hands tremble as she turns toward the freeway, her dark eyes mirroring what's happening out there.

"You have to get out of here!" I say as we jog past her.

But instead of running, the woman stares open-mouthed at the Xua army behind us. A frenzy is about to form, and it's going to start rolling through the suburbs. We have to get out of here, fast.

Justin grabs the woman by the wrist and pulls her with us.

Behind us, the skies darken as the host of Xua burst into smoky vapor.

My feet pound the pavement as we race through suburbs that used to be peaceful but are now peppered with dead bodies. Despite what's happening, no sirens wail in the distance. No one's coming to help us. We're all alone.

It's just the three of us.

But maybe, just maybe, the human race is going to survive somehow. Maybe we can still win this war. We have to, because I'm not giving up.

I can't give up, because I'm so in love with Justin that it hurts.

It's time to come up with plan C.

26

Downtown Santa Ana peers at us on the horizon. A skyscraper burns in the distance, flames licking the side of the building, thick clouds of smoke keeping us in an eerie, unending twilight.

We've been running for almost twenty minutes before I realize we've been going in circles. Fortunately for us, the Xua frenzy headed north of the freeway instead of south. Otherwise, we'd be dead.

Justin continues to lead the way, and I try to stay focused, but everything inside me is numb. All the streets here are two-lane blacktops, and every house either has a picket fence or a thick hedge. Everything looks completely normal, like in a dream. That's probably why I unintentionally guided us here. I wanted to pretend everything was better than before. Like maybe one of these houses belonged to me, and my parents were inside, waiting for Gabe and me to come home.

It's a dream I've had for many lifetimes, that one day my family would live in a little house like this, that my parents wouldn't sell drugs anymore, that Gabe would be safe, that

Justin would be my boyfriend…

But I'm not going to focus on dreams anymore. I need to focus on reality. And winning this war. I don't know how we'll do it yet, but I can't let Gabe die for nothing. I'll just have to find a way to save the world myself.

The woman who was with us breaks away, rubbing the skin sites on her jaw. "It's so quiet. I can't stand it," she says. "What happened to the music and why isn't my Raja yoga program on?"

I stare at her for a moment, before I realize that she's an Addy and her skin sites must be broken. She's not only in shock; she's probably going through withdrawals.

She gazes back at me, a look of torment in her eyes. I wonder if she remembers what happened on the freeway or how long she's been standing beside her car. Before I can ask if she's all right, she lopes away from us, mumbling something about her husband.

At least she remembers she had a husband.

It's important to remember the people we love.

I slow to a stop, one arm clutching my side, panting for breath. "We need to find Natalie and Billy."

Justin nods.

"I'll come up with a plan once we're together."

"I know you will."

If I didn't feel like my world had caved in on the 405, I'd smile at his faith in me.

I'm pretty sure I'll never smile again.

A few bodies litter the ground, but it's impossible to tell what happened here. No lights shine in nearby houses even though it's starting to get dark. We jog off at a slow pace, passing several car wrecks, bodies still curved over steering wheels or slumped against passenger-side doors. In two of the accidents, we discover a trail of bloody footprints that lead away from the cars, as if some of the people survived and walked away.

"Is that a fire truck?" Justin asks, a note of suspicion in his voice.

He points down the street, and we both stare at it for a moment, hesitant to move closer. The truck is a block away, flipped on its side like a discarded toy. Several bodies are strewn beside it on the ground, their limbs twisted and broken. This must have just happened—the wheels on the truck are still spinning.

The Xua who caused it could be nearby.

"We need to get out of sight," I whisper. We're heading into the shadows of a nearby alley when a police car rolls down the street, driving slowly. The officer at the wheel spots us.

"You kids better get home," he calls out. "We just put out a seven o'clock curfew for Orange County. Anybody caught out later than that's gonna get hauled in to jail."

A curfew? In the middle of the apocalypse? I glance at Justin, and he gives me an almost imperceptible shake of his head. This guy isn't a real policeman. Either he's a looter wearing a cop uniform or he's a Xua. I don't know which one is worse.

He stops his car and examines us, maybe noticing the blood on our clothes. "You need a ride?"

There's something in the backseat of the police car, but I can't tell what it is. A body, maybe. And there's a smear of blood on the back door. I shift closer to Justin. "No, we're almost home."

The man eyes us. "You two know anything about what happened over at Century Unified High today?"

A shiver floods through me as I remember that group of kids possessed by the Xua. Justin shakes his head. "Nope. Sorry, Officer."

He stares at us for a long moment. "Well, I'd stay away from that part of town," he eventually says. "There's been a lot of looting and vandalism over there. Go home and stay there, okay? Where did you say you live?"

"Fountain Valley," Justin lies, and he takes my hand. We're both ready to run if we have to.

The cop nods, then drives off. I wait until he's out of sight before I look at Justin. "It was almost like he knew exactly who we were. I think he was Xua."

Justin nods, wiping sweat from his forehead. "I was thinking the same thing. But if he was possessed, why would he let us live?"

I have no idea, but we need to get out of here just in case he changes his mind. I cup my left hand around my ear, trying to contact either Natalie or Billy. All I get is static. "We need to hook up with Natalie, Billy, Ella, and Gabe—"

I instinctively include Gabe in that list, and when I do, his name catches in my throat. I blink and turn my head away. I don't want to, but I start crying, deep sobs, and I can't catch my breath. I feel like I'm going to curl in a ball and it's taking all my strength to stand up.

Justin pulls me into the shadows of a nearby house, where no one can see us. Then he gently rests one hand on my shoulder. "Go ahead and cry," he says. "We're safe here."

I lean into him, my arms around his waist, my head on his shoulder, drawing strength from him. I need him more than anything right now.

Justin touches my chin with his hand, gently lifting my face until I can look at him. He wipes away my tears.

The look in his eyes breaks my heart. Losing Gabe was as hard on him as it was on me.

"I'm sorry," he says, his voice thickening, his words coming out slowly, like he's trying not to get too emotional. "I did everything I could."

"I know. This isn't your fault; I know it isn't."

"Isn't it?"

He pauses to flex his hand, stretching his fingers then clenching them in a fist, his skin speckled with drops of blood. A grimace settles on his face as he tries to scrape the blood off with his fingernails. "I did stuff—stuff I can't talk about." He pauses, and a long silence wraps around us. I remember that bat, the bloodstains on his shirt and his face, the bodies I saw lying on the ground between the school and the freeway.

"I'm supposed to be the 'hero,'" he says, tears forming in his eyes. "I mean, I'm the guy who's been genetically altered for things like this, and I just failed my most important mission ever. I love him, too."

Then he can't say any more. He leans forward and buries his face in my hair.

I close my eyes and try not to get swept away by the pain. It feels like my heart is cracking in two.

"We'll get through this," I say. "You've always been there for Gabe. And me." I pause to take a shaky breath. "I was so worried you would both get caught; I'd already lost Gabe, and I thought I was going to lose you, too. I can't... I just can't... I don't know what to do, not yet. But we'll figure it out. Together."

Justin holds me for a few minutes, both of us quiet, before he speaks.

"I was worried I would lose you, too," he confesses as he lifts his head. He cups my face in his right hand. "The Xua took your brother, but he might not be dead, Sara. You said those doorways go to different timelines, right? Maybe he's with Aerithin. Or maybe Aerithin will still come back—"

"No. I think he lied to me on purpose," I say, anger rising to the surface. "I don't know why. We can't count on him anymore."

He nods.

"We might not have anyone left, not my brother or our parents, but we have each other," I say.

He blinks. Maybe I shouldn't have mentioned our parents, not yet. But we have to face reality.

And we have to get through today.

One day at a time. That's how we'll win. By surviving.

Plan-frigging-C.

"I think we should head for Station Seven," I say. "Natalie and Billy might already be there, waiting for us. That was the plan if we got separated."

"Yeah."

"Come on."

It takes longer than I expect to get to Coffee, Tea, and Z. We hike through a commercial district—clothing stores, pharmacies, fast-food restaurants. We jog past a grocery store, its plate-glass window broken. There are people running down the aisles, loading up carts and then darting away without paying. Everyone is in survival mode.

The people we pass have manic expressions on their faces, their movements clumsy but not the same as if Jumpers were inside them. These people are just panicked. Probably in shock. A man rushes past us, leaving the grocery store. Eyes wide, he's muttering to himself and he can't hold onto the cans of food in his arms. They tumble away from him, one by one, until he races out of sight, dashing around a corner, empty-handed.

We finally make it to the coffee shop. Justin holds up his hand, and we come to a stop outside, staring at the broken door and a cracked window. The inside of the shop has already been ransacked. The streets around us are getting dark, and all the streetlights in this part of town are smashed and broken. We've got about another hour before it's completely black.

Where's Natalie? She knows we're supposed to meet here. She never forgets details like that. My heart ratchets up a notch at the very real possibility that something happened to her and Billy. I had to leave them with a flurry of Xua swarming in that classroom.

Is that another horrible mistake I made that I can't undo?

I grab Justin's hand, and when he looks at me, I can tell he's probably worrying the same thing.

"We need to go back," I say. "I need to find them. What if Natalie's trapped or hurt? What if Billy's—"

"No need to be dramatic," a familiar male voice says.

I whip around just as two figures materialize from the shadows on the side of the building. It's Natalie and Billy.

She runs over, throws her arms around me, and then she starts to ramble on, something she never does. "I was so worried when we couldn't contact you. I found a way to turn off our skin sites, but now I can't turn them back on and I know someone can still track us… Wait. Where's Gabe?"

I don't say anything, but she knows.

There's only one reason Gabe wouldn't be with me.

"What happened?" she asks.

"He… There were these… I tried to…" But I can't finish because the words catch in my throat.

"It's okay, it's okay," she says, even though we both know it isn't okay.

Speaking in a low voice, Justin tells them what happened, a few short sentences at a time. Neither one of us can talk about this without falling apart. His hands shake when he tells them how the Xua pulled Gabe through a mirror door.

Billy's eyebrows raise, and Natalie's mouth hangs open.

I move closer until I'm right beside Justin, watching Natalie and Billy, making sure neither one of them says anything that implies this is Justin's fault.

Nobody is going to say anything bad about Justin in front of me ever again.

They both seem to sense what's really going on, and it doesn't take long for them to remind me why they're on our team. Billy hands both Justin and me a bottle of water. Natalie gives us some pumpkin bread that she must have gotten in the coffee shop.

My mom used to make pumpkin bread when we had extra money.

I start to hyperventilate a little, but I fight it, biting my lip until I can calm down. She might still be alive. My mom and dad could still be human.

Maybe.

We can't sit around wishing to have our old lives back. We need to move forward.

"Aerithin was wrong," I say, staring down at the chunk of pumpkin bread in my palm. "Or maybe he flat-out lied. Whatever. The bottom line is, Gabe lived through the night, but the war didn't end." I swallow, my throat tight. "We have to find a way to save humanity on our own."

Natalie frowns, like she's waiting for me to say more.

"That's great, and not to be insensitive, but what does that mean?" Billy asks.

"It means we're not giving up. Before, our mission was to save Gabe." I pause because it's hard to say his name. It's like there's a hole in my heart that will never heal. "For now, our mission is to stay alive. We're going to take it one step at a time."

Justin nods. "I'm in."

"Me too," Natalie says.

Billy gives me a half smile. "Well, I wasn't going to ditch you guys. No matter what. Especially after what we've been through."

"Exactly," Natalie says. "Some really crazy stuff happened after you guys left the school. Military police drove up in these tank-car-things, and then guys in uniform were all over the school. You'll never guess who was with them—"

"Carla," Justin says in a matter-of-fact voice. So much has happened that I almost forgot about her.

"How'd you know?" Billy asks.

"I told her to meet us at the school if we got separated," Justin answers. "It was Station Five, so I figured we'd end up there eventually."

"Well, the really crazy part is they were looking for Sara," Natalie says, her brow furrowing.

"Me? Why me?" No one has ever been looking for me. They're always searching for my brother. I just happen to be there.

"They wouldn't say." Natalie shrugs. "They acted like everything was top secret and questioned Billy and me for an hour while we were just trying to get out of there and find you guys. They showed up right after we killed the last Xua that had flown into the classroom—"

"Wait—you guys were attacked by the Xua, too?" Justin asks.

"It's okay; they're all dead," Billy says like it was easy, but I remember how the Xua gave him a hard time, chasing that blue-haired girl. I bet Natalie killed most of the Xua in that room.

"How much did you tell Carla's dad?" I ask.

"Not much," Billy answers. "But we had to demonstrate how to kill a Xua when it tries to get inside a human. At that point, I thought they were going to take us back to their base camp. I thought they'd never let us go."

"Yeah." Natalie laughs. "We finally had to give them fake information before they released us—"

"Hey," Billy's tone turns serious as he looks at Justin and me. "You guys need to know there's been some serious stuff going on. I think the Xua have been knocking out the police and the fire department…"

I remember that overturned fire truck and all the dead bodies. That suspicious cop and the body in his backseat. I still don't understand how we got away.

"There's been some violent crap, and it's not all being done by the Xua," Billy continues. Natalie looks away from me, her lip trembling. "It's like everybody knows there's no one watching them, like there are no rules anymore. It's like the whole world is as bad as Snake City now."

"Wait." I look around. "Where's Ella?" I've been so focused on our core group that I forgot about her.

It hits me hard, like someone punched me in the chest.

Gabe would have wanted me to take care of her.

Natalie shakes her head. "I don't know. She ran off not long after you did. It was like she was in a wild panic. The other girl did the same thing after I cut that Xua out of her. It was like they weren't themselves afterward. Billy and I looked for Ella but couldn't find her, and then those military guys showed up. Maybe she went home—that's what she wanted, isn't it?"

I think Natalie's trying to give me some hope. I just nod.

It's never pretty after you cut a Xua out of someone. Almost anything can happen.

A large van turns down our street, music blaring, gnarly guys hanging out the windows. The vehicle's weaving back and forth, and the guys inside are laughing like they're drunk. Justin glances at the van, then he grabs both Natalie and me and pushes us back into the shadows of the alley.

There's been some serious stuff going on.

Natalie leans against me, her eyes wide. She pulls out her switchblade, tenses all her muscles like she's ready to fight to the death. I wonder what she and Billy have seen in the past couple of hours.

I can't even imagine what it would be like if the whole world was like Snake City.

The humans would be as bad as the Xua.

The van screeches to a halt in front of the coffee shop. One of the guys stares at Billy, the only one of us still standing at the curb.

"Anything left inside?" the guy in the van asks, gesturing toward the Coffee, Tea, and Z.

"No credits, but there's a few bottles of chai tea. And in the back room, they've got about five cases of Z," Billy says with a sly grin, as if the high-priced chocolate-raspberry caffeinated beverage is worth its weight in titanium. He's already figured out how to divert attention away from Natalie, Justin, and me. He always knows how to get out of a difficult situation.

"Awesome. Thanks."

The van doors slam open, and two guys jump out, then head into the shop. I crouch down in the shadows, hoping they don't decide to check out the alley, too.

"You know where I can score some motorbikes?" Billy asks.

"Maybe. Why?" The driver watches Billy suspiciously.

"Mass transit is down—that's the first thing the aliens strike. That's their pattern. First, they take down mass transit, then communication. The military will be next, if it hasn't happened already."

He's right. It probably took only a handful of Hunters to infiltrate all the mega-corporations that run our country. They probably already cut off our access to food and medical supplies, too. The Xua won't have to worry about taking us all out. Anyone left behind will starve to death, die of disease, or kill one another trying to survive.

A look of fear crosses the driver's face. "What're you talkin' about?" His words slur together like he's trying to sober up, fast.

"I'm giving you some secret intel. You're not gonna hear it on Gov-Net."

"Thanks, man. And the bikes—I'd check the used car lot on Main and Seventeenth. People been looting there, but they ain't taken no motorcycles yet. They're taking stupid stuff like SUVs and Mercedes, stuff that ain't gonna work if we run out of gas. Idiots should be stockpiling food."

"Yeah, get food and water," Billy says. Then he adds, "And if you run into any aliens, keep your mouth closed. That's how they take over humans."

"Dude, you're freaking me out," the guy answers. "Hey, Ben, hurry up!"

The two guys come out of the shop lugging five cases of Z between them. Billy joins them, takes one of the top boxes. "Let me help," he offers, and he sets the case inside the van. "Liquor store down the street was looted about an hour ago, but they've still got some stuff in their back room. I used to work there. I can show you, if you want."

"Sure, get in," the driver says with a grin.

"After that, maybe you could give me a ride to that shop up on Main, the one with the bikes."

"No problem. Let's go."

Billy hops in, and the door slides shut behind him. Then the van pulls away in a cloud of exhaust that would get them about fifteen citations.

Those guys never even knew we all were hiding in the shadows.

27

Billy's gone for almost an hour. The clock is ticking, and I really don't want to get stuck here for the night. While we're waiting for him to get back, Natalie shows us where she and Billy stashed some supplies from the coffee shop.

"We were supposed to get supplies back at Century Unified," Natalie grumbles as she grabs a pair of scissors from the counter and cuts through some thick plastic packaging. Inside is a shipment of food that must have arrived recently and never got put out on the shelves. We stuff sandwiches, cookies, and chips into a knapsack.

"But we had to leave all those behind," Natalie continues as she sets down the scissors. "The military took it. So we grabbed all this stuff and hid it as soon as we got here. There wasn't much left."

Justin reads a label and lets out a chuckle. "Who would make a quiche sandwich?"

It's good to hear him laugh.

"Well, that one's definitely for you," Natalie says, picking up on his mood shift. "I've seen you eat peanut butter and turkey before."

"Because peanut butter and turkey are awesome together." He winks at me, and I grin.

"Soon as this apocalypse is over, I'm having you over for dinner. I'll show you what real food is. My mom's the best cook in the world," Natalie says. Then she sits back on her heels, a faraway look on her face. She blinks fast, like she's fighting tears.

I put my hand on hers.

We're in an abandoned coffee shop, but I can smell her mom's *japchae*, can taste the garlic and soy sauce on the tip of my tongue.

"I'd like that," I say.

"Me too," Justin says.

Natalie gives us both a thin smile, and her voice comes out soft. "It's a date, then."

We're going to get through this somehow. I'm not losing anyone else on my team, and if it means setting up post-apocalyptic dinner dates, then that's what we'll do.

Justin gathers up all the empty bottles he can find and fills them with water from the tap. Fortunately, the shop hasn't reached its daily water quota yet. We put together a stockpile of five bottles each.

We're still stuffing most of our supplies into Justin's knapsack when Billy roars up on a brand new solar-powered Kawasaki.

"We should go get a few more bikes before they're all gone. Good for our new mission, right?" he says. He points at Natalie. "Hop on."

"Can you guys be back here in half an hour?" Justin asks. "I don't know if that cop was telling the truth about curfew, but I don't want to be outside any longer than we have to.

Especially not in the dark."

It's already dark, so we'd see a Xua if it ran past—it'd be lit up like a Christmas tree, edges glowing, silver shimmers everywhere else. But if one of the aliens turned to smoke, we wouldn't see it at all.

Night is even more dangerous than day.

Natalie jumps on the back of the motorcycle. It looks like some of the tension inside her has vanished at the prospect of having something to do. "Don't worry. We'll be back in time. Then we can strategize."

The two of them take off. It's so quiet after they leave, it almost seems like a normal school night. I can't help but wonder if some kids and their parents are home safe, doing their best to be invisible while the invasion sweeps across the city.

That's where I wish I was. At home, listening to my brother's silly jokes and helping him with his homework. Telling him how glad I am that he's my brother and how much I miss him when he's gone—

Anger floods my chest. I'll never have any of that again. Those effing Xua stole my brother, and they need to pay for it.

Even though I'm furious, a tear slides down my cheek, and I quickly brush it away before Justin sees it. I might not be able to control my chaotic emotions, but I vow that I'm going to do whatever it takes to save what's left of the world, if that's even possible.

If I have to kill every single Xua, so be it.

Just before she left, Natalie handed me my knapsack from school. I clutch it in one arm and hold it tight as I sit on the curb.

Justin watches me. Then, without saying anything, he hands me a bottle of Z. My fingers shake as I lift it to my lips and take a sip. He just sits beside me on the curb and slips one arm around my shoulders.

"Has he ever been pulled through those mirror doors before?" he asks, a hint of hope in his voice.

"No."

"Why do you think they took him?"

"I don't know. I've never been able to figure out why they want to kill him, either, and Aerithin wasn't exactly forthcoming about all that stuff," I snap, even though it's not Justin I'm mad at. "Maybe there's some cosmic reason why he's not supposed to be here. All I know is that I want to—"

Someone wails in a building across the street. All my muscles clench, and I jump to my feet. The loud cry goes on and on. It stops, only to echo off the buildings behind us. Then an unearthly quiet hangs over the street, and a chill rushes through me.

"We should get out of sight," Justin says.

I nod. We haven't seen any Xua since we got to this neighborhood, but they could be anywhere, dressed in human skin.

I know we should hide. It's the right thing to do. But I'd really rather fight. My adrenaline is off the charts, and I'd love for one of those monsters to try to take me down.

Justin seems to read my emotions, and I don't think he likes it.

"Let's grab our stuff and move into the alley," he says.

We jog inside the shelter of the store and start gathering up all our backpacks. We're just about to slip out the front door when a man heads out of the building across the street. His shirt is stained with blood, and his left pant leg is ripped, but his movements are smooth as he surveys the street.

My blood runs cold.

Holy crap, it's a Hunter.

The man's head snaps up as if he can hear my heartbeat

speeding up. His eyes narrow on the coffee shop.

Justin grabs me. "Drop the bags," he whispers as he pulls me away from the door.

My knapsack slips from my fingers, and I sink to a crouching position. Together we make our way deeper inside the store, threading around tables and chairs and kiosks until finally we crawl behind the counter, below some espresso machines. A ripped bag of coffee crunches beneath my feet as I scoot farther into the darkness. Justin hunches in front of me, shielding me. I can see out the door, but my line of sight is limited. I lean forward and put one hand on his shoulder.

"We need to kill him," I whisper.

Justin gestures for me to be quiet.

The man levels his gaze on the coffee shop, crosses the street, and heads straight for us. He stops in front of the store, and I'm positive about what he is now. His body is tense, and his eyes are focused as he scans the room. Like he's searching for something.

Hunters don't go into tracking mode until they're looking for their *true* target.

Is it me?

My hands are sweating, and I want to fight, but I want to run away at the same time. I wish I knew where the back door of the coffee shop was. I think it's down the hallway, past the restrooms, but I'm not sure. And even if I could find it, it might be locked. I wish we had checked that out sooner.

The man steps inside the shop, then kicks out part of the plate-glass window with a loud crash. He obviously isn't trying to sneak up on us.

"Sara?" he says in a calm voice. "Are you in here?"

Holy effing crap. Natalie was right. They *are* after me.

WTF is going on?

Justin takes my hand and squeezes it. I realize he's got

the scissors Natalie used earlier in his other hand. I wish he had that bat instead.

I wish *I* had that bat. I'd like to crush some alien skull.

The man takes a step closer, shoes crunching on glass. "Sara?"

Sweat trickles down the back of my neck, and I worry that he can smell it.

"You're in here, aren't you? I heard this is where you like to hang out." He laughs, but it doesn't sound human. It's more of a warble, like a song played on the wrong speed with lots of distortion. "You know you're not going to win. You may as well come out. My friends will be here soon."

I look at Justin. He motions for me to be still.

"Sara left about twenty minutes ago," Justin says.

I can tell he's getting ready to stand up, and I shake my head. He could get hurt.

I can't lose Justin.

"What if he's got a gun?" I whisper.

The man laughs again. "I *knew* you were here, Sara."

Justin gets to his feet and steps out from our hiding place. I peek over the counter. The man isn't alone. Two of his friends have joined him, and they're blocking both exits. One of them is in a woman's body, and the other one is inside a young boy around ten years old.

I'm not about to let Justin fight this battle alone.

I warily come out from behind the counter. Justin begins to swing the scissors, slashing a wide arc, making all of them keep their distance from us.

"Watch out for the boy," I warn Justin as I pull out my switchblade. "He's the Leader."

As I've learned the hard way countless times over, they always put their high command inside an unsuspecting host, the one you'd be least likely to hurt. In this case, they probably think I won't fight a little boy, because I love my brother so much.

They're wrong.

The boy crouches in the shadows, watching me, waiting. He's not trying to hide what he really is anymore. His eyes glow in the dark, and he makes a strange sound, some sort of command in his native tongue, a language I've never been able to learn. I glance away from him, trying to gauge how far away the man and the woman are. She's a hazy silhouette in front of the window, but I can tell she's both older and heavier than me, and she's leaning at an awkward angle. A Jumper. I'm hoping her out-of-shape body and the Jumper's lack of control will make her slow. The man's the complete opposite, however. He's built like a gymnast, short with broad shoulders and a strong body.

Are more of his Xua friends on their way here? If so, we're up a creek.

We have to get out of here.

Justin tries to keep them all at a distance, giving us both enough room to edge our way toward the front door. I've moved behind him, but the boy is still at my back, guarding the rear entrance.

I take another step away from the counter, and I'm temporarily exposed. I'm just about to swing around and put my back to Justin's, when the boy snarls and leaps toward me. He latches onto me like a monkey, then wraps his arms and legs around me. The impact of his leap knocks me down, and we tumble to the floor. My instinct is to cry out, but I manage to keep my lips clamped shut.

I gut-punch the kid with my elbow, three times, hard and fast, knocking the wind out of him. His grip loosens, and I almost shake him off when the woman springs to life, charging toward me on lurching limbs, fast and determined.

Justin slashes her on the leg when she gets closer, slicing her across the femoral artery. She starts losing blood but not quickly enough. She lunges even closer, and it looks like she accidentally tips over a nearby table. But nothing Xua do is accidental. The table falls, and a tray of bottles and mugs crashes to the floor. Glass sprays up, and I cover my eyes with my left hand.

At that same moment, the kid bites me on the arm, sinking his teeth so deep I think he hits bone. This time I can't help it.

I scream.

The Xua inside the woman jumps, splitting her open in an instant, and then the smoky alien sails the short distance between us, and everything happens so fast it feels like I'm in slow motion. The Hunter grabs one of the espresso machines and launches it at Justin. He dodges to the side and, at the same time, the world around us growls, a deep, deafening roar.

The Hunter leaps toward me, jams something between my lips to keep my mouth from closing. The vaporous Jumper flies closer, and I can see its head, like a gargoyle made out of smoke, grinning, sneering.

It pushes inside my mouth, a taste like oil and ashes and death, flowing down my throat. I try to cough, try to shake the kid off my back, try to cry out for help, but I can't. I can't even breathe.

The roaring sound grows even louder, and there's a glistening fountain of glass and noise as two motorbikes sail through the broken front window. One of them crashes into the Hunter and knocks him aside. Justin yells. I think it's Justin, although nothing seems familiar anymore.

Not this world.

Not these people.

The boy on my back speaks to me, *inhale deep and flow deeper*, he says, and for the first time I understand the beautiful Xua language. *Take her body; flow so deep no one can separate you...*

I relax, let the Xua in, open all the doors, let it take over my body.

A dark-haired human boy looms over us. He looks familiar, but I'm not sure. He's smashing his boot into the face of the Hunter—but I don't care about either of them.

Flow deeper, into all the hidden places...

Now the dark-haired human boy pulls the Leader off my back. I want to howl—I don't want to be separated from my Leader, not now, not when I'm in the process of inviting a Xua inside this body. The dark-haired human boy slugs a fist into my Leader's jaw, and my Leader falls slack to the ground. Unconscious.

No! My Leader needs my help.

I stand and swing at a human girl who lunges at me, a glowing weapon in her hand.

"Hold still, Sara," she says.

The tail of my true body is almost inside, another second or two and everything will be as it should be. If I can only keep this human girl away from me for that long, then—

Strong arms pin me in place, and the human girl swings her weapon.

No!

I try to inhale, to suck my beautiful Xua body inside. I lift my chin and expand my chest.

Someone pounds me in the back.

"Get it out. Kill it. Now!" the dark-haired human boy who holds me cries. "Natalie, hurry!"

Another human boy, this one with blond hair, grabs my chin and holds me still.

The human girl swings with deadly precision, slicing through my tail. I growl and moan as pain surges through me, mixing with images of my homeland, memories of the battle that rages in the future, anger at my failure. Every fiber of me catches fire, I'm burning and ripping and all my memories are fading away until only one remains.

Hatred.

And then, I hear the call of death as this planet pulls me onward, toward ashes and fire and a roaring wind that will never stop blowing.

I part my lips, and centuries of death pour out.

An entire civilization is dying in this moment.

28

Fire burns through me, raging in my organs, my chest, my mind. I can't survive this.

I panic.

My face is in a pile of red ash, and it feels like I'm going to choke to death.

I cough, and my throat convulses and my chest heaves.

I'm either going to die or I'm going to live, and I don't know which is worse. Voices are arguing around me, but I don't recognize the faces. I want to run; I need to get away from here.

"What's wrong with her?"

"Didn't you get the Xua out? Maybe it took you too long—maybe it's not really Sara anymore," the blond boy says.

"I killed it! You saw the red ash pour out of her mouth. The Xua is dead!" the dark-haired girl says.

I push myself to a sitting position, then scoot away from them.

A beautiful dark-haired boy keeps watching me, a guilty expression on his face like he's responsible for all this. "I'm sorry," he says, moving closer. "It's my fault, but you're okay now. Tell me you're okay. Sara, please."

I scoot away and hold up one hand. "Don't touch me."

"I'm Natalie," a dark-haired girl tells me. "Say it."

"Natalie. You're Natalie. Let me go!"

She has taken hold of my arm.

"No," she says. "You'll run off, and we can't let you do that. Sorry." Her voice cracks a little. "I can't lose you, Sara. You just need a little time. You'll remember. I think."

She looks at the dark-haired boy, and I think, *He's going to cry and it's going to break my heart.* I have to get out of here.

"Do they remember?" Natalie asks, a thread of panic in her voice. "How long does it take? She never told me. Why didn't she tell me?"

But she still won't let me go, and I'm too weak to fight her.

The girl named Natalie argues with the others. She tells them they need to do whatever's necessary to make me remember.

The beautiful dark-haired boy crouches on the ground a few feet away from me. "I'm Justin," he says, his voice low and soft. It's a deep, soothing rumble in my chest, and it takes away some of the pain. I sigh. He smiles, but I see sadness in his eyes. "I won't give up on you, Sara. No matter what. You wouldn't give up on me. We're going to do whatever we can to help you remember, okay?"

I shake my head.

I don't want to remember.

My muscles tense, my pulse speeds up, my breathing gets short and fast.

"I'll take her home," Natalie says at last, as if she's tired of discussing this. "Maybe that will help." She hangs onto me as she heads toward a motorcycle, and then gestures for me to get on the vehicle behind her.

I shake my head.

"Sara, you have to do this. You need to know who the monsters are. You've always been the one to explain it all to me. Now it's my turn."

Her words are an arrow through my chest. I don't remember her, but she's right.

We all need to know who the monsters are.

I reluctantly climb on the back of her bike, my legs straddling the great machine.

"It's not safe," the boy with the blond hair argues. "What if the aliens are watching us?"

"Then I'll just have to kill them." She shrugs as she kicks her bike into gear. "Like I killed this one."

"We shouldn't split up," Justin says.

She stares at him silently for a long time. I think she might be mad at him for some reason, but there's something about this boy named Justin.

I can't imagine anyone being angry with him for very long.

"Fine, then follow us," she says.

I'm glad she said that. I'm glad Justin will be with us.

And then we're roaring down the street, wind rushing over us, the boys behind us and darkness ahead.

29

The sun has disappeared and, to the left, clouds of smoke and fire rise from the freeway. The motorcycle thrums beneath us as we zip down alleys and back streets. Natalie's trying to keep us hidden from sight, and I can feel the tension flowing from her to me.

She's worried about me.

I still don't remember who she is. She's just a name, a tattoo of letters.

But she *did* cut a Xua out of me. Only a true friend would do that. Most people would run if they got that close to a Jumper.

The ground beneath us loosens as we spin through a patch of gravel. We lean into the spin, barely manage to keep the bike upright, feet touching pavement. She swears, a quick succession of words that I don't understand, and we slow to a stop in front of a large building. Brick against mottled sky. The tang of garbage and rain fills my nostrils. Is it raining?

The ground is wet with it, but the clouds must have passed.

Natalie points toward the nearest tall building, a block

of windows and stone.

"That's where you live," she says. She climbs off the bike, so I do the same. Together we push the bike into a cluster of bushes until it's completely hidden. I rest my hands on my hips, wishing something looked familiar. A moment later, another bike roars up alongside us. Justin and the blond-haired boy climb off.

"One of you needs to stand guard," Natalie says. "You." She points at the blond boy. "You said it wasn't safe. Seems like you should be the one."

"Come on, Natalie. *You* said we shouldn't split up," he says.

"I changed my mind."

The blond boy sighs and crosses his arms. But he stays behind, just like she said.

Natalie leads the way toward the front of the building, where the three of us do our best to keep to the shadows. Up the stairs and in the front door. She stares at me in the blackened hallway, then hands me something. I fumble with it, fingers sliding over a switch until a beam of light shoots from my palm. The troubled expression on her face fades as if she's trying to hide her concern. She gets out another flashlight and shines it on the stairs, gesturing for Justin and me to follow her. We go up several flights, during which time I realize how exhausted I am. I feel like I've been running for hours, my left arm hurts, and my knuckles look like mincemeat. When we finally come to a stop on the fourth floor, I rub the bite on my arm.

Natalie sees me, and her brow knits together again.

"Are you hurt?" she asks.

I don't say anything. I've been injured worse. It's the way of battle. Survive or die.

Together we all stand before a door. She tries running my palm over a scanner, but the power is out. Nothing happens.

She curses, then looks at Justin.

I think he's going to try to break in, maybe slam the door with his shoulder or his foot, but he doesn't. He just curls his right hand in a fist and thumps the door, right where the locks are. They snap, the door flies open, and one of the hinges breaks.

"Show-off," Natalie says to him, but she gives him a smile when she walks through the door.

I stare at Justin, surprised by his strength. He looks like he could be a Genetic. I hadn't noticed before. He's watching me, studying my expression. Like he's worried that I'm afraid of him. But I'm not.

"Impressive," I say.

He gives me a slow smile.

We shine our lights inside the door, sweeping the first room—a kitchen. Natalie drops her backpack on the table and opens the refrigerator, pulls out a couple of bottles, then hands one to me. I press it to my cheek, welcoming the fact that it's still cool. Then I twist off the cap and drink, not caring what's inside, not bothering to taste it. I feel like I haven't had anything to drink for years.

"You have any candles or any—" Natalie stops, probably realizing I won't know the answer to her question. She begins rooting around through cabinets and drawers, says, "Aha," and pulls out a handful of candles, followed by a lighter. A moment later, we have one small candle pooling light on the kitchen table, another in a bedroom that must belong to me. Then we carry a third candle as we walk down the hallway.

I shake my head. I don't want to see what's back there. My heart starts to beat faster, and a wave of panic surges over me.

"No," I whisper.

She opens the door at the far end of the hallway, and I hold my breath. I don't want to go in there; I don't want to see it. But I don't even have to, because a smell wafts out. The scent of spray paint and tennis shoes and leather baseball gloves, and something else that I don't smell but I remember.

A faint smell like urine and a little five-year-old boy who used to wet the bed.

Me, helping him in the middle of the night, stripping his bed and washing the sheets, giving him a bath and washing his hair with lavender shampoo. All so our parents wouldn't find out and so he wouldn't get in trouble.

Me, yesterday, making him wear clothes that smell like piss and having to force him to put them on.

"*Gabe.*"

The word comes out like it's my last, like I'll never say another thing in my entire life, like I might collapse on the ground and never get up. I look at Natalie and Justin. I'm gasping now, each breath deep, mournful, painful, my chest a gaping wound. I can still feel the claws of that Xua inside me, tangling and confusing me. It's like an alien poison runs through my veins.

"My brother's gone, isn't he?" I ask.

"Yes." Natalie kneels beside me, rests a hand on mine. "Do you remember what happened?"

I shake my head. "Only bits and pieces."

"Do you remember me?" she asks.

"We're friends." I pause, remembering the spicy smell of her kitchen.

She sighs. "It's a start. Do you trust me?"

I nod.

"Then you need to believe me when I say we need to leave. Quick. No one else is here, but that could change any second," Natalie says. "Just get whatever you need, and hurry."

We scramble through the darkness, blowing out candles, gathering up supplies, a couple of sleeping bags, a couple of towels. I stop in front of the medicine chest and then instinctively look inside. One of the shelves slides out, and there's a hidden compartment built into the wall.

I pull out a small box and shake it.

There are drugs inside; I know it. I'm not sure what kind of drugs, but I might need things like this to barter with later.

Justin watches me from the doorway. "Do you know what that is?" he asks, nodding at the box in my hand. "Do you remember who it belongs to?"

"Drugs, I think. Is it mine?"

He gives me a gentle smile. "It's yours now."

He's been following behind me, from room to room, carrying everything I say I need. His arms are full.

"You're a Genetic and we're friends, right?" I ask.

He glances away, as if he doesn't want me to see his eyes. I think I hurt him.

"I'm sorry," I say.

He nods. "Where are we going with all this stuff?"

"I think there's an empty apartment down the hall—"

"Apartment 4A."

He's been here before. I stare at him, trying to remember. It hurts. Some part of me aches to know who he is. Another part of me feels like that Xua stole my soul.

I have to fight it. I have to win. I can't let that frigging alien beat me. And I know we can't stay here. It's not safe.

"Apartment 4A, then," Natalie says as she appears in the doorway. "I'll head over there and start working on the door." She opens a kitchen drawer and yanks out a screwdriver. "Maybe this'll help me pick the lock."

I stand in the middle of the kitchen, emptiness in my chest.

This might be the last time I see my home. I might never come back.

Justin has my backpack and most of my stuff in his arms.

We swing the front door closed behind us, then head down the hallway.

I'm following people who are supposed to be my friends toward apartment 4A, my left arm hurting, my heart breaking.

I don't think I've ever felt so lost and alone.

30

A thin beam of light before me, a corridor of black behind, I make my way to our temporary home for the night. Natalie's already opened the door, and I stumble inside, then wrinkle my nose at the stench. A stack of overflowing garbage towers in the kitchen, the floors are filthy, and there's no furniture. I look for the cleanest room and set my stuff on a threadbare rug. Justin lines up our backpacks against the wall, then frowns.

"Uh, I didn't know we were splitting up before," he says. "All our food is in my pack."

Natalie puts her hands on her hips. "And?"

He sighs. "And that means Billy doesn't have any food or water."

She digs through Justin's pack until she finds a sandwich and a bottle of water. "I'll take it down to him," she says, standing up. "Either one of you know if the fire escape on this side of the building is safer than the one that collapsed?"

I frown and shake my head.

"It should be fine," Justin answers. "Just don't come back

up with a hundred people."

"Funny," she says. Then she opens the bedroom window and climbs out onto the fire escape. "Back in a few minutes. And Justin, make sure she doesn't run off, okay?"

"Are we all staying here tonight?" I ask when she's gone. I spread two sleeping bags on the floor and then sit cross-legged on one.

"I think so," Justin says.

I nod and, without meaning to, I run a slow gaze over him. Pictures flash through my mind, almost like a Gov-Net program. They're all pictures of him.

I see him as a young boy in grade school, before anyone could tell he was a Genetic. He smiled and laughed a lot back then.

I see him in middle school, when his genetic alterations came to the surface and other kids started to tease him.

I never teased him, though. I actually got in a fight with two girls my age one day, because they were calling him a Jenny. One of them got a black eye. The other one got a bloody nose.

"I think I beat up two girls once because they made fun of you," I say. "In middle school."

He swallows, then he blinks like his eyes sting, like he's been in the sun too long. "Did you?" he asks. "You never told me about that."

Then I see him when we're older, high school age. He and I are laughing. We're at the beach, playing Frisbee, and every time he gets close to me my heart beats faster and I wish...

I wish he would kiss me.

But he didn't.

We were friends, we were always friends, but there was something beneath the surface, like he might be the boy I could fall in love with.

If only...

Then I started traveling through time.

I sink backward, my eyes widening, my stomach churning, and it all comes back. So many images of what I've lost, all the battles, all the death, the unending heartache.

And the horrible knowledge that it's all my fault.

"Sara, are you okay?" he asks.

It hurts so much to remember.

I touch the center of my chest.

"I can still feel it, here. Like there's too much, too many thoughts and emotions, and it aches and it's hard for me to think about anything else."

A tortured expression flickers through his eyes, and he slowly, carefully, sits beside me.

"I remember you," I say. "I remember...us."

He puts his hand in mine.

"Good. Because I could never forget you," he says. "Ever. You're the best part of all of this. You always have been."

It feels like I've waited a hundred lifetimes to hear him say that.

"I almost lost you. I thought you were dead, back in Snake City."

"I'm not dead. I'm here." He lifts my hand to his lips. "I'm right here and I'm so in love with you."

He turns toward me then, his gaze on my eyes, then my lips. Usually he smiles, but not this time. Instead, he pulls me toward him and he kisses me and it's different than any other kiss. This kiss says more than *I love you*, it says *I need you* and *I can't breathe when you're not around* and *Never do that again, never almost die, ever...*

I melt into his arms, and I hope neither one of us dies in this war, but I just don't know.

This moment might be all we have, and it'll never be enough.

There's a rattling clamor on the fire escape, two people climbing up and probably doing their best to be quiet. But I remember who they are now. These two can't do anything without making noise. Their whispering argument precedes them.

"I didn't say you had to stay down there all night."

"It was implied. I'm not even sure how I was supposed to guard you guys when I can't signal you."

"You could signal us without skin sites."

"Yeah. Honk a car horn. Oh, wait, then everyone in the whole neighborhood would hear it."

Justin and I are sitting with our backs against the wall, sharing a sandwich and watching as they climb in the window. Natalie folds inside the room like a shadow. Billy, on the other hand, thunders in like he's all elbows and knees and bruised ego.

She runs a gaze over us, smiles, and then nods. "Glad you're back."

I give her a smile.

She's the best friend I could ever have. In any lifetime.

Before long, all four of us are stretched out on the sleeping bags. It's like an end-of-the-world slumber party. With aliens outside and an empty place in the room.

It almost feels like Gabe is with us. I keep hearing his voice in the space between our words, like he's trying to make a joke or a smart-ass comment. Or when someone says something funny, I hear his laughter in the chorus. I think I see him in the shadowy doorway, just standing there, hesitating like he can't decide which room to go into.

Twice, I accidentally call Justin by my brother's name and

there's a long, awkward pause. I don't even realize I said it, until they all look at me. Usually Natalie would correct me. Not tonight.

Tonight the mention of Gabe's name brings us all to our knees in silence.

His ghost is here with us. And none of us wants him to leave.

He's the reason I'm planning to take the Xua down.

31

Sunlight slices through bare windows, falling across the room, searing my skin. I startle awake, then sit up with a jolt. I glance around the room, trying to remember how I got here. Natalie was with me, I think. And Justin. Maybe Billy, too. We rode on motorcycles, but I'm not sure.

A vague sense of doom hangs over me.

"Natalie?" I call out.

The sleeping bag next to me is empty.

I stagger out of the room, disoriented. Memories of last night come back. I see Justin then, standing by the living room window, watching the street below. He smiles when I approach.

"Morning," he says.

I give him a shy grin. "Where is everyone?"

"They went up on the roof, trying to see where the Xua are. Or not. Maybe they're just up there arguing about whether the sky is blue."

"He's got a crush on her."

"Well, I know what that's like."

I blush. "I'm going to take a shower."

"My turn next."

I head into the bathroom, glad to discover the water hasn't been turned off. A quick cold shower later, and I almost feel like myself again. Until I look in the mirror.

There are circles under my eyes, my skin is pale, and my hair is going to be a frizzy mess as soon as it dries.

I grimace at myself. Then, I brush my teeth and get dressed.

"Your turn," I call to Justin, then I stop in the bedroom and get a bottle of Z. It's not cold, but the combination of caffeine, chocolate, and raspberry tastes like heaven. I hear Justin shut himself in the bathroom, and the water turns on.

I check to make sure the front door is still locked, then I pause with my hand on the knob.

There's a soft scuffling noise outside the apartment. Somebody's coming down the hallway. At first, I think it's Natalie and Billy, but something doesn't seem right. Maybe because it's too quiet. Those two would be arguing. The power's still out, so the video that monitors the hall isn't working. Instead I peer through the peephole in the center of the door—this building's so old, all the doors still have those old-fashioned, wide-angled lenses built inside.

A man and a woman walk toward me. It's dark, but a little light comes through a window at the end of the hall. The woman is hunched forward, and the man's jaw hangs loose. Both of them look wary, on edge. A heartbeat passes before I realize who they are, and I cup a hand over my mouth, stifling a whimper.

It's my parents.

And they're possessed by Xua.

I pull away from the door, my heart a wild horse racing through open fields, one hand clamped protectively over my gaping mouth. I glance at that gap between the door and the floor. Can a Xua flow through a space that small? I want to look back out the peephole, but I don't dare. They might see my shadow and know that someone's pressed up against the door.

I take another step back, then realize they've stopped walking. They must be standing in front of this apartment.

Oh God, no, oh my God, oh my God, oh my God—

One of them moves closer.

The knob twists.

"Sara?" Mom asks. "Are you in there?"

Can she smell me? Can she hear me breathing?

"Sara? Is that you? Let me in."

The doorknob twists again, then she knocks lightly, three times, like she's trying to wake me up. *Mom's home, sweetheart. Come on now, open the door.*

"They aren't in there," Dad says.

I stagger another step backward, try to muffle the low whine in my throat, my hand still pressed over my mouth.

"This is the wrong apartment," he says. "We live down there."

As crushed as I am, I almost collapse on the floor in relief. They're Jumpers. The fact that they're not Hunters will buy us a little more time.

I cautiously peer through the peephole again as they walk away. Dad's arms are covered with deep, bleeding scratches from his wrists to his elbows, scratches he probably got when he held my mom down and let a Xua get inside her.

I'll never know what happened after I left the rooftop during the launch, but it doesn't matter.

My real mom and dad are gone.

And they're not coming back.

32

The apartment feels like it's shrinking, like the walls might collapse if I don't get out of here fast enough. I've been racing around from room to room for the past several minutes and, so far, I've got our sleeping bags rolled up and tied and our knapsacks filled with drugs, sandwiches, and water bottles.

We can take only as much as we can carry, and we need to get out of here soon, before my parents figure out that I was the one who raided their apartment. Before my mom and dad realize I stole their stash of drugs and MJ, and I really *am* staying in apartment 4A.

We need to run.

I keep remembering what Aerithin told me about the Xua invasion.

You won't be able to trust anyone when it happens. Not your parents or your teachers or the police.

Maybe not even your best friends.

Justin comes out of the bathroom, his hair slicked back, his clothes and shoes on.

"We have to get out of here—now," I say. "My parents were here. They're in my apartment now, but they might come back when they realize I'm not there—"

He frowns. "Your parents are in the building?"

"Yes, but they're *Jumpers*," I say, and the words almost choke in my throat.

His eyes go wide. "Okay, I got this," he says as he grabs all our backpacks and gear. Then we almost run into Natalie when we start to climb out the window.

"Good, you guys are ready. We have to go. *Hurry*," she says. Her backpack is looped over one shoulder, and Billy is a step behind her.

"Seriously, we need to go *right now*," he says.

Alarm ricochets through my body. "Is it my parents? Did they find you?"

Natalie blinks at me, taken back for a heartbeat. "They're *here*? How did they survive—" Then she sees the fear and sadness on my face, and a flicker of sorrow flashes in her eyes. She pushes me down the stairs, one hand on my back. "We'll talk about it later, okay? For now, we need to hurry."

"What's going on?" Justin demands.

"It's a frigging Xua frenzy," Billy says. "I can't tell how fast it's going, but it's headed this way."

"Five minutes," Natalie says as we jog down the fire escape. "Ten minutes, tops. We need to jump on those bikes and—"

Justin grabs her arm and mine and pulls us to a stop. "You weren't watching this street, were you?"

"No," Billy says. "The frenzy's coming from the south."

Justin points down at a truck pulling to a stop below us. "You missed that."

Billy frowns. "So? We missed a truck. We've got bigger problems."

I squint at the truck, and my stomach drops. "Oh, holy

crap," I breathe. I recognize this truck. "This is Blood Lord territory. Those are East Side Dragons."

The East Side Dragons are one of the worst gangs in the L.A. area. They all have retractable metal enhancements—razor-thin blades that run in jagged lines from their forearms to their knuckles—and they're just as deadly as the Xua. If any of them are possessed, this will be a bloodbath.

"Go down slowly and quietly," Justin says.

Natalie pulls away and starts heading down. I follow behind her. I'm not sure how we're supposed to jump the last few feet without being noticed, but we have to try.

Already six of the East Side Dragons have jumped out of the truck. They start running into nearby houses, breaking locks, smashing windows, whatever they have to do to get inside.

They're looting. So they must not be possessed. I'd be relieved if we weren't still in plenty of danger.

Natalie has already jumped down, and I do the same, afraid that they heard me. Billy drops beside us.

Only Justin is still on the fire escape.

A tall man with greasy black hair gets out of the truck and aims a gun at Justin. The razor blades protruding from his arms glint in the sunlight.

"Don't move, Jenny," he says with a dark laugh. "Don't even think about it. You might be strong, but you can't outrun a bullet."

Justin glares down at him. "We all need to get out of here. There's a Xua frenzy headed this way."

"Yeah? What is that?"

"More aliens than you can count, ready to kill you and everyone on this block."

"You high?" the guy asks with a smirk.

Just then, the guy's buddies start to return to the truck, all proudly calling out what they stole. Food, liquor, prescription drugs, jewelry, guns, and ammo. One of them opens a bottle of Johnnie Walker and slugs it down as he walks.

Natalie and Billy crouch down beside me. She holds a gun in her right hand like it's a new piece of jewelry, like she's always carried a firearm. I shake my head. That was how she died in her last life, a gunshot wound.

I've already lost my brother and my parents. I can't bear to lose my best friend, too.

Instead, I stand up and push my way in front of both Natalie and Billy.

"You want to know what a Xua frenzy is?" I call out to the gang leader. "It's every dream and hope you've ever had, destroyed in an instant. It's every person you've ever loved, dead. It's your city burned, your country invaded, your world served up on a platter for alien thugs who will never be satisfied—"

"Sara, don't," Justin calls from the fire escape.

The gang leader turns toward me, a dangerous grin on his face. He flexes his forearms, showing off the line of blades that could easily shred flesh, and aims his gun at me. "I can do that with one bullet. Right between your eyes."

Shadows move across the street, and something glints beside a dumpster. That's all the warning I get before the street comes alive with tatted thugs, sixteen muscular guys strategically positioned up and down the street, all of them carrying guns aimed at me and Justin and all the East Side Dragons.

At first I think they're Blood Lords, but I've never seen any gang do this before. Then I realize some of them are my neighbors, some are Blood Lords, and some are Manny's cousins. L.A. has turned into a war zone in the past twenty-four hours, and it looks like the people in my neighborhood are determined to survive.

It doesn't matter whether the invaders are human or Xua. Nobody's going to get away with hurting the people who live here.

A familiar figure joins the crowd, strolling casually down the center of the street, like he owns this part of town and all the people in it. It *is* his territory, I guess.

"Take your fight somewhere else," Manny says. Three of his boys walk behind him, all of them carrying rifles.

"Manny," I call out. "Don't shoot us."

At first, Manny frowns, while everyone keeps their guns aimed, just like before. Then he flashes me a crooked grin.

"Get down on the ground, Sara," he says, and I breathe a sigh of relief. "You and all your friends. Tell your Jenny to jump and then get on the ground."

We do as he says, even though I can tell Justin isn't really on board with it. I keep my head turned so I can see what's happening. Natalie's lying beside me and Billy beside her. Manny and his boys cluster in front of us, their guns aimed at the invading looters.

"Get back in your truck," Manny says to the guy with black hair, seemingly not intimidated by the amount of metal these guys have in their bodies. Must be the sheer firepower he's got at his back. "And give us back those drugs," he adds. "My grandma lives in that house, and if you took her prescription meds, you're gonna regret it."

The guy eyes him and the rifles currently pointing his way, then shouts, "Ronan, Kristof—give this guy his granny's meds."

"How much time do we have before the frenzy gets here?" I whisper to Natalie.

"A couple of minutes. We'll need to go east to avoid it," she says in a low voice.

A heartbeat passes, and the Santa Ana wind blows down

the street, carrying debris from trees, stirring up the heat. Finally, two guys wearing jean jackets come warily toward Manny, their hands raised. They stop about three feet away, so close I can smell the scotch on their breath. One of them tosses a plastic bag filled with prescription bottles to Manny. He examines the contents of the bag, then nods.

Manny's boys knee the looters in the crotch. The two East Side Dragons crumple over, covering their heads while the Blood Lords kick them again and again with their heavy steel-toed boots.

We have to get out of here; we don't have time to wait for these rivals to come to some sort of agreement. I bite my lip, and my hands curl into fists, nails digging in my palms.

I know it's my imagination, but I feel like I hear the frenzy getting closer, people choking to death, bodies falling to the ground; I think I can smell blood and ash on the wind.

"We have to get out of here," I call out to Manny as I climb hesitantly to my feet. "All of us do. The aliens are coming. Haven't you seen how they take over people? How they turn into smoke and get inside and possess everyone—"

"Yes," he says, his voice coming out like a cold wind. He turns to look at me, and his gaze turns icy, his eyes unfathomable. Shadows from the building fall over his black eyes and the intricate pattern of blue-black symbols on his face. "Yes, I've seen them. One of their demons got inside Gregor, and he came at me with a machete." His voice thickens, and he pauses before speaking again. "I had to shoot him."

I move slowly, cautiously, out of my hiding place behind the bushes. "You have to let us go. Or shoot us, because we're running now. And you should, too."

"Go ahead," Manny says. "This isn't your fight. Here. Take this with you." He extends his arm, rifle in one hand.

"Thanks."

"It's what we do, right? We stick together and fight the enemy who's trying to take over our turf."

His face softens a bit as I take his weapon. Neither one of us wants to admit it, but we have something in common—we both do whatever we can to protect our little corner of the universe.

33

The sky darkens overhead as the sun disappears behind a swift procession of ominous gray clouds. A soft rain starts to fall as we climb onto our motorcycles. We're almost ready to go when Justin glances behind us. He frowns, then shakes his head.

"What is it?" Billy asks.

"I don't know," he says. "I just have a bad feeling about this."

"What?" I ask.

Justin's got an uncanny sixth sense at times. I've often wondered if he can remember things from my past jumps.

"Don't worry about it," he replies. Then to Billy he says, "Follow me. Natalie says we need to go east if we're trying to get away from that frenzy."

A heartbeat later, the motorcycle thunders beneath us, and the street unwinds before us, revealing events from the previous evening. Apparently while we were all sleeping in apartment 4A, a quiet battle raged in Santa Ana. I count five dead bodies between Edinger and Dyer, two car wrecks, an overturned police car in a parking lot on Main, a house being lit on fire, and two more houses being looted as we pass.

We make a sharp right on Bishop and when we do, a Rottweiler charges out of a nearby backyard, the gate left open, a body lying in the driveway. Wearing a thick studded collar and trailing a leash behind it, the dog growls and snaps at my feet, chasing us for three blocks until we turn onto a different road. The dog stands in the intersection for a few heartbeats, barking, before it trots back in the direction it came, probably to protect its dead owner.

Loyalty. It doesn't stop, no matter what happens.

An image of Gabe comes back to me, him turning around one last time to look at me on the freeway, his eyes meeting mine, the realization that I failed him.

Aerithin didn't tell me the truth about the invasion. Maybe there's more to all this than I know.

Maybe there's still a way to save my brother and I just haven't figured it out yet.

I add finding out to plan C.

D rops of rain spatter me on the face and arms and the wind turns cold. A few weeks ago, I would have been glad to see our drought finally ending. Today, all the rain means is that our solar bike could run out of power at any moment, and that we need to be more careful because the roads are now slick and dangerous. Southern California's infamous for long periods of drought followed by sudden flash floods. But instead of being careful, Justin and I lean forward, flying bullet-fast over rain-mirrored streets, beside gutters filling up, water already spilling onto sidewalks and pooling in driveways. We splash through an intersection, rear wheel sliding sideways, my heart thumping when I think I might fly off the bike. A second later, we've got traction again and we're thundering through a world of gray rain, my skin drenched despite my clothes.

The rain is so thick it's impossible to see more than a dozen yards in any direction, but I feel something. It's almost like I'm picking up on that spooky premonition Justin had before we left. I look over my shoulder.

A dark shape flashes just at the edge of my peripheral vision, some sort of vehicle, masked behind a veil of rain. Is someone chasing us?

"Go faster!" I shout in Justin's ear, hoping he can hear me over the storm. His body tenses and the bike whines into a higher gear, a speed I didn't even realize this motorcycle was capable of. We're blinded, the whipping curtain of rain narrowing down our visibility even further.

Then there's a dangerous metallic sound that repeats over and over, echoing dull and threatening. The rain muffles the noise, but it still shoots terror through my veins.

Because I know what it is. I've heard it in too many lifetimes.

Gunshots.

Someone behind us is shooting, maybe at us.

We have to stop. Now.

I grip Justin's waist. "Pull over!"

We almost lose control of the bike. The motorcycle slows, then slides. We almost get thrown off into the water that washes down the side of this humpbacked street. All four of us ditch our bikes and we run, looking for cover, a house or a garage, something that can protect us.

I can still hear that awful metallic sound, and it's even closer now.

Definitely gunshots.

We're somewhat shielded from sight by the rain, but at any

moment one of those bullets could slice through the sky and take us down. Justin and I run side by side; Billy and Natalie morph into gray shadows that hulk beside us, leading us away from the road. We run, crouched low.

I still can't see whoever is shooting.

Who are they?

"Over here," a voice calls from the street.

I don't care who it is—I'm not going back out there. I'd be in the line of fire.

Justin doesn't pause. He wraps one arm around me and pulls me away from the street. Together, the two of us jog across a lawn, still hunched over. Shots smolder in the near distance, some of them ringing so close I can feel them whizzing past, mere inches away. I hold my breath, try to make myself smaller, huddling close to the ground. A cinder-block wall looms up ahead, a dividing line between two properties.

"Not that way!" the voice calls again. It's a girl, but I can't see her.

I run the last few feet, land with my back against the cement wall.

I squint through the rain, looking toward the street, and I think I see a girl with black hair, dressed in camouflage. "Is that Carla?" I ask. "Is she shooting at us?"

"There were two vehicles following us." Justin peers through the rain. "Carla was in one of them, but there's another one out there, too. Whoever's in that second vehicle is shooting at us."

A spray of bullets hits the wall beside us, sending bits of cinder block flying. Justin yanks me under him onto the ground. "Stay down!"

"No! We have to find Natalie!" I wrestle away from him and frantically scan the street, looking for her. Rain strikes the ground with such force it bounds back up, a cascade of water so heavy it erases things in the distance.

I can't see. I can't find her.

Finally I spot a pair of shadows—crouching low as they try to run, as if that can give them protection. I hope it's Natalie and Billy. I want to yell, *Hurry, hurry, run faster!* But then that thought fades away because shots ring out again—a thin, wet sound almost like drumbeats.

Natalie spins away from Billy.

She's been hit!

Her feet lift off the ground, her body turns and flies. She's a dark shadow with wings, airborne, a shadow that falls to the ground with a muddy *thump*.

No! *No!*

Justin tackles me before I even realize I've moved and pins me down. I scream her name into a mound of wet grass, each syllable rocking my body with fear.

"Natalie!"

Somewhere nearby, an engine rumbles and flares to life. There's a flash of headlights, like teeth in the darkness, and a jeep lunges across the grass toward the street. It passes a few yards to my right, and it takes all my courage to hold still. I'm desperate to escape.

"Don't move," Justin breathes in my ear.

It slogs into the rain-filled street. Somehow it misses both Natalie and Billy, but it crunches over both our motorbikes. I catch a glimpse of several strong-jawed soldiers inside the vehicle, all of them carrying rifles.

I clench my fists, still listening as the jeep charges down the street, my eyes searching the curve of lawn and driveway for Natalie and finally finding her. I pull away from Justin, horribly aware of the fact that Natalie isn't moving. Rain washes over her, wave after wave, and she blurs in the gray mist. She's so still. I run across the driveway and stumble to a stop over her body. Billy hunches at her side, one hand on her arm as if that's all it will take to revive her, a puzzled expression on his face.

"Natalie? Are you okay? Natalie!"

Billy and I say the same thing, over and over.

She can't die. She just *can't*.

I kneel at her side, looking for a wound, but the rain runs down my face, getting in my eyes. If there is a bullet wound, shouldn't I be able to see it? It's not until I run my hands over her jacket that my index finger snags on two small holes in the leather, right next to each other, both so small I almost missed them. But once my finger touches one of them, blood oozes out, thin and bright, mixing with the rain, sliding pink over my hand.

Her blood on my hands.

No, no, not again, please no…

"We have to get her to a doctor, right away," a girl says beside me. It's Carla, her arms clutched tight to her chest. "I know where to go. Come with me."

Justin slides his hands beneath Natalie and pulls her to his chest, her arms and legs limp.

That's when I see the pool of blood spreading across the grass. There's so much blood—how will she survive this?

"Get in the car," Carla tells us, taking charge. "I'll drive you guys to a military clinic that's still open."

Justin and I follow Carla to her car, the windows shattered and the doors riddled with bullet holes. Together, the three of us brush aside the glass and get Natalie inside.

"Why are you here, and who was shooting at us?" Billy asks.

"Later," Carla says as she climbs in the driver's seat.

"No," he insists. "No one was following us until you showed up. Were they with you? Tell us now before—"

His last words get cut off as Justin shoves him into the front seat.

"I don't know how they found us," Carla says. "I was only able to track you because of the marker I gave Sara."

Wait. That red poker chip she gave me in Snake City was a tracker?

"Who else has access to the data?" I ask, a sinking feeling in my gut.

"No one," she says firmly. "I destroyed the tracking tech as soon as I found you."

I breathe out a small sigh of relief. If she hadn't and the Xua got their hands on it, we'd never be safe. Still, I'm throwing away that chip.

"I swear the last thing I wanted was for one of you to get hurt," she says as we pull away from the curb. "Everyone else I know is already dead."

She's tough and she's a take-charge girl, but her hands are trembling, and now and then her voice cracks.

I've been there. It sucks.

We race down the street toward the military clinic, Justin and me in the backseat, Natalie sprawled across our laps. I take off my jacket and press it against the bullet holes in the center of her chest, trying to stop the flow of blood. Her eyes flicker open and she stares at me, although I can't tell if she sees me or not. It's like she's focusing on something far away.

"You're gonna be okay, Nat," I say, trying to sound more confident than I feel. She has to make it. I can't do this without her. We haven't even come up with plan C yet. How am I supposed to save the world without Natalie?

Her lips tremble and her face grows pale. That gun tumbles from her pocket, snagging her bracelet on the way to the floor. With a rolling jingle, all those jade and gold beads scatter across the carpet, like her life force is being drained out. But I can't let that happen, so I lean down and scoop up as many beads as I can find and stuff them in my pocket. Then I pick up the gun and hold it between two fingers, far away from my body. I want to toss it out the window.

"Give it to me," Justin says, extending his hand.

I do. Gladly.

34

There's a point in a war where things get so out of control, bodies are left behind like garbage. Nobody has time to cart them away. They just pile up. There's an army of walking wounded left behind, too, all of them trying desperately to survive.

Most of them won't live. They're too broken. There aren't enough people left with the skills to fix them.

That's what the military clinic looks like when we get there.

My gut churns with dread when I see how many cars have crashed into one another outside the entrance; all the people were in such a hurry to get inside they didn't bother parking. The crush of cars flows out into the street, for blocks in every direction. Some people must not have been strong enough to get out—they lean back inside their coffins of glass and metal, unblinking eyes staring into rain-soaked skies.

My hands begin to tremble. "We have to find a way to get Natalie in there and get her treated immediately," I say. "But if we have to wait in line—"

I avoid saying the words no one wants to hear. My best friend might die.

"I have your rifle. Justin has Natalie's gun," Billy says. "People listen to guns."

"I'll take care of it," Carla says. "The people inside have guns, too. There's going to be a military presence here. National Guard or something. We should be careful about letting anyone see our weapons. But just so you know, I have this." She flashes us her gun, then tucks it away in her jacket.

I focus my attention back on what's important. "Natalie, stay awake," I murmur. I smile as her eyelids slide open lazily. She's lost a lot of blood, too much.

"I'll get us in to see a doctor," Carla continues, not taking a breath. "No need to wait in line."

Justin strides toward the entrance, carrying Natalie. She looks like a doll in his arms, fragile and lifeless. My heart skips a beat, and I slog in the rain behind him. It's still coming down in sheets, the sky above us darkening to a deeper shade of gray. I've lost track of time. Is it evening already? It can't be.

We enter the clinic single file, stepping over people lying on the emergency room floor. I think a couple of them may already be dead.

Carla leads the way, Justin a half step behind her. Billy walks in front of me, so we've got our artillery positioned in the front. The boys have their weapons hidden beneath bulky jackets, fingers on the trigger, just in case. I have no idea what might happen here. Right now, my only plan is Natalie getting in to see a doctor and being able to walk out of here.

We pass people slumped in chairs and on the floor. Most of them have physical injuries—broken legs, head wounds, skin burns.

Then I see something I never expected.

Several people my age are scattered around the room, all

of them wearing white T-shirts with orange *V*s painted on the front. They must have watched the videos Natalie and I made. A few of them lift their heads to gaze at us.

I nod and flash them the *V* sign with one hand.

They do the same back to me.

Our single-file line stops at the admissions desk. Carla breaks rank, pushes her way to the front, and pulls something out of her backpack—a card with a military insignia on it. At first the nurse on duty ignores her, but Carla raises her voice, uses phrases like "state of emergency" and "office of the governor" and "national security," followed by "blood loss" and "barely breathing." Then she leans closer to the nurse and lowers her voice.

I don't know what she says, but the nurse snaps to attention.

"Get that girl on a gurney!" the nurse shouts, pointing at Natalie, who's still draped in Justin's arms. "And put a couple of IVs in her. Now! Call a trauma surgeon in here!"

Within seconds, two nurses appear out of nowhere and Natalie's on a gurney, her jacket and blouse cut off. A pair of IV bags hangs above her, tubes snaking down and inserted in her arms. One of the nurses draws blood. A doctor wearing pale-green scrubs, hands already covered in latex gloves, jogs down the corridor toward Natalie, and at first I'm relieved.

Natalie's going to get the medical attention she needs.

But I don't have time to process that thought any further because the doctor slides to a halt beside the gurney and for a second she doesn't move. Time seems to stop and the hair on the back of my neck stands on end.

She's not looking at Natalie.

She's looking at *me*.

The doctor's eyes go wide, then she mouths my name.

I take an instinctive step backward, crashing into Billy.

He braces one hand on my shoulder, while his other hand reaches for the rifle beneath his coat.

Justin's head snaps from the doctor to me to Billy and back again.

She's a Xua, and the three of us know it.

I'm about to jerk out of Billy's grasp, to run over there and push the doctor away from Natalie, but Justin grabs me and pulls me back.

"Let me go!" I snarl.

"No," he whispers.

"But she's Xua," I say. "Why would a Xua want to possess an emergency room doctor?"

"I don't know, but there's something else going on here."

Meanwhile, the doctor turns back to the gurney and quickly examines Natalie. The whole time I keep her in my line of sight, making sure she doesn't jump. But she wouldn't, would she? Xua don't jump into humans who might die; that's not their MO. If they're inside a human when it dies, the Xua dies, too.

"Get her sedated," the doctor says. "She's having trouble breathing, so we need to do a rapid sequence intubation."

A few seconds pass, surely not enough time for Natalie to be fully sedated. Sweat pours down my forehead and my hands are clammy. Is the doctor going to work on her out here, right in the ER admitting room? Everything happens so fast I can barely see what's going on, but then there's a tube in Natalie's trachea.

"Her pressure is too low," the doctor snaps, like it's the attending nurse's fault. "You need to dump more fluids in her with pressure bags. Hurry! We have to get her into the OR and stop the bleeding."

The nurses jog away, one on each side of the cart, rushing off with Natalie.

The doctor turns and looks directly at me. "I'll do everything I can to save her." The expression on her face looks like genuine concern. It's confusing.

"You better," I say.

"Trust me," the doctor says with a slight nod of her head. "You and I have a mutual friend, but I dare not say his name now."

Mutual friend?

Does she mean Aerithin?

Does that mean he's still alive?

35

The doctor hurries away before I can ask any questions, following the gurney through a pair of double doors and down a long hallway.

We pull away from the rest of the people in the room, find a corner with three empty seats, and take it over. Justin makes me sit down. All I can think about is Natalie in that operating room, with that doctor who's obviously got a skin-jumping alien inside her.

The only friend we could possibly have in common is Aerithin. How does she know him? Is this Xua one of his rebels?

Was that cop Justin and I saw earlier a rebel, too? If so, that would explain why he let us live.

I sink back into my chair, but I can't relax and I can't think straight. "She said we have a mutual friend. It has to be Aerithin. Why would she say that if he was dead?"

"She wouldn't," Justin says. "I mean, unless she's lying. But why bother? She could have jumped or attacked us on the spot."

"If he's alive, why didn't he come back? Why would he let Gabe get captured? We need to have a private conversation with that doctor," I say, "as soon as Natalie comes out of surgery."

I'm going to get answers one way or another. Winning this war depends on it.

Another hour passes. I'm on the verge of storming back into the operating room when five people aggressively push their way inside the ER, all of them intent on finding someone and none of them looking injured. All five of them pause, lift their heads in the air, and sniff. One of them, a woman, calls out in a loud, clear voice, "Gabe? Are you in here? Gabe?"

My skin bristles, and my heart thumps so loud and fast I think everyone can hear it.

Xua.

Wait. Why are they looking for my brother? I know these aliens have some sort of advanced tech communication system with one another. Whatever one of them sees or does gets communicated to the rest of them. So, by now, they have to know that a pair of Xua already caught Gabe back on the freeway hours ago. They pulled him through the Corridor of Time.

Then that Xua-possessed woman—a Leader, I'm sure of it seeing how the four Hunters stay a step behind her—turns and runs a gaze over me.

A thought hits me right in my stomach, and it takes my breath away.

Gabe must have escaped.

He must have gotten away from the Xua, and he must be alive. That's why they're looking for him again. Maybe he slipped back out through another door. Or he's in a different time period…

Whatever happened, he's safe. He has to be.

"Gabe, I know you're in here, honey," the Leader calls. She sounds like a frantic mother searching for a lost child. One of the nurses—a tall, slender guy who looks like he's worked three shifts in a row—walks toward her, probably hoping to calm her down.

It backfires.

The Leader slams her fist in his face, harder than you'd think she could, and he falls backward. One of the Hunters kicks the nurse in the gut.

"Hey, what are you doing?" the woman at the admissions desk shouts. She leans forward and yells into an intercom system. "Security, get to the ER now! We have a code red in progress!"

"Sara? Sara, I know you're here," the Leader calls now.

Both Justin and Billy stand in front of me—Justin's got his gun out, but it's still hidden behind his back. It's all I can see, that gun, his finger on the trigger. Carla sits beside me, but I can tell she's ready to fight, too, if she has to.

"We can smell you," the woman says.

If she's trying to scare me, the joke's on her. She just gave me a shred of hope I never dreamed I'd get.

My brother might be alive.

I pull out my switchblade and flick it open.

Three security guards charge into the room.

All five of the Xua at the front door jump at the same time, and spiraling dark clouds spew from their mouths, gargoyle heads grinning.

I have so much adrenaline in my system I think I might be able take them all down myself. I jump to my feet. "Everybody close your mouths and keep your heads down. Now!"

Billy and Justin already have their switchblades open and

powering up, red beams of light flashing.

Three of the smoky Xua shoot toward us. Carla grabs her switchblade, but she's a moment too late. I stand in front of her, then I tempt fate.

I open my mouth in a battle cry, knowing it will lure at least one of them toward me.

Justin and Billy do the same thing.

Fear tingles along the base of my throat as my body remembers what happened the last time I got this close to a jumping Xua. I keep my switchblade hidden behind my back, waiting, heart thundering as a plume of black smoke lunges closer, gruesome head watching me, honing in on me like my mouth is a target.

Then something horrible happens.

Billy accidentally crashes into Justin and knocks his switchblade out of his hand. It falls to the ground and slides across the room.

No.

But Justin's already in fight mode, and there's no way to turn off that switch. And the only weapon he has left is a gun.

You can't kill one of these smoky demons with a gun.

So, I take a step forward, moving in front of Justin, pushing him behind me. I jam him in the gut twice with my elbow—something he doesn't expect—and he crumples slightly.

"Come on!" I scream, mouth open wide, hoping I can get two of them to fight over me. "Let's see if you can take down a teenage girl!"

All around me, people are yelling and running and trying to hide. Even people who looked like they were ready to die. Everybody's got what it takes to get out of the way when a Xua is jumping. By now, nearly everyone in Orange County has seen this scenario before.

Few of them have seen what I'm about to do, however.

Watch and learn if you want to survive.

"Stay back!" I yell at Justin, who's trying to push his way to the front again. "That's an order."

Hopefully he'll do what I said. I don't have the strength to take him down and fight two Xua at the same time. I glance at Billy from the corner of my eye, hoping he's focused by now and ready to fight. His blade remains hidden, just like mine. We can't let these beasts know we're armed.

Not yet.

The black column of smoke shoots across the room, so fast I almost can't tell where it is. It zigzags, maybe some battle tactic the Leaders back home came up with when they realized how many of their kind we'd been killing. No matter. I can still take it down. All it needs to do is get close enough. At that point, its flight trajectory will have to straighten out.

I paste a fake expression of fear on my face.

Then I realize the expression isn't fake.

Gargoyle Head laughs—I didn't know they could make noise while in their smoky state. Warbly, skin-chilling sounds come from its mouth, almost enough to make me turn and run. Everyone in the room—all the humans, that is—have either collapsed on the floor or they've gone running down the hallways.

The smoky Xua screams at me, and I scream back.

"Aaaaaaaaahhhhh!"

The Xua surges forward, giving a burst of speed I didn't expect. I swing my arm up, catching it right where the head joins a snakelike body, its face so close to mine I can smell its strong metallic odor.

My glowing blade slices through the flying Xua in a death stroke. Its thick column of smoke turns bloodred and the expression on its face changes.

I laugh. It's terrified.

Then its smoky body dissolves and pours onto the floor

like a pile of dust.

Beside me, Billy's calling down the wrath of a large gray Xua, and it zips toward him, fast as the wind. It could plunge into his open mouth in an instant—although I know the whole process takes longer than that. I turn, swing my arm down, and catch the beast from the side, slicing it through before it even touches Billy's lips.

Meanwhile, someone flails behind me, strong arms thrashing, legs kicking.

One of the beasts has attacked Justin, and it's already halfway down his throat.

A thin panic surges in my chest as my fears come to life—*don't take Justin, no!*—but I have to push my emotions away if I want to fight.

Carla, Billy, and I all jump into position, but Justin jerks, his left arm crashing against mine, almost knocking the switchblade out of my hand. I stumble, then right myself. Billy lunges closer. He pins back one of Justin's arms, and Carla has the other.

Damn, this guy's strong. It's taking all three of us to hold onto him. But we have to save Justin—we have to.

Fear buckles down my back as I spring toward him. I jump up and latch onto Justin, almost like that kid did to me in the coffee shop yesterday. I wrap one arm around Justin's neck and both legs around his waist. The Xua is right next to my face, gritty smoke pressing against my cheek, tail wagging as it tries to get inside him faster.

Justin lurches forward and almost knocks me off, but all three of us manage to hang on.

My right hand swings down, severing the beast's tail. I only snip off the last three inches, but that's enough. The Xua crumbles into an ashy heap, dust that sifts to the floor.

"Get him on the ground," I say as I jump down.

They lower Justin, but not gently. It's more like everyone just lets go and he falls, face-first on the floor. I wince, then pound him in the back, still working on pure adrenaline. My fist hits square between his shoulder blades and he coughs, puffs of red dust wafting away.

I kneel beside him, hoping that he'll open his eyes and look at me, that he'll remember me. I can bear anything but losing him.

"Justin, are you okay?" I ask.

His eyes flicker open and he turns so he can see me. He smiles as his hand finds mine.

"Hey." His voice sounds rough. "This trumps those two girls you beat up in middle school."

I let out a soft laugh and run my fingers through his hair. I want to stay here with him, glad because he's okay and Gabe might be safe and Aerithin might be alive.

We have hope. We really do.

My team is alive and, for an instant, that's all I care about.

Then someone cries out across the room, there's a crash like a body falling to the floor, and I remember the other two Xua who turned into smoke. Three came after us, but where did the other two go?

I stand up and see that group of security guards. There were originally three of them. Now, one guard sprawls on the ground, his head twisted unnaturally to the side. He must be dead. The other two guards stare at me, muscles tensing, both of them reaching for their weapons. A dangerous chill creeps into the room and I take a step backward.

There's something sinister about them, a cruel expression in their eyes.

They draw their weapons, and then, with a low growl, they both say my name in unison.

"Sara."

36

The emergency room takes on a deadly quiet, so still I can hear every breath I take, and each one sounds dangerously final. My instinct is to run, but I can't leave Justin or Natalie behind. Justin's moving slower than normal—it could be a while before he's ready to fight. Billy has his laser switchblade and Carla reaches for her gun.

This is one of those times when I hate being the leader. I don't know what to do and everyone's counting on me to come up with something brilliant. I wish Natalie were here—I know she'd have an idea. I'm trying my hardest to figure out What Would Natalie Do. My fingers run over those gold beads in my pocket, and those armed thugs grin like they just won the World Cup without breaking a sweat.

A shadow moves in a corridor on the far side of the room, and one of the security guards suddenly falls to the ground like a sack of meat. *Wha-thump*. I don't even have time to blink before I see Natalie's doctor standing behind them, a nurse at her side.

They both have some kind of immunization guns, but I'd

bet my weight in chocolate they're not pumping these guys full of flu shots.

The second Xua-possessed guard already has his gun aimed. But this time, neither the nurse nor the doctor will be quick enough to take him down. That is, unless somebody distracts him.

"Hey, somebody's hurt over here. We need help!" I yell.

I gesture for my team to fall to the ground. We're all in the midst of floor-diving when the possessed guard shoots his gun. Maybe it's hard to hit a moving target. I don't know. I've never fired a gun. All my battles have been fought up close and personal. But there's this nanosecond where he tries to figure out which one of us to take out first.

Both immunization guns fire at the same time. In fact, I think they fire about four or five times.

Then everything's in slow motion, like the world's made out of Jell-O. The security guard's arms are spinning, pinwheels of death, gun firing wildly, bullets *thunk*ing into nearby walls, whining past and shattering windows. People are shouting and the guard is falling, yet his hand is still wrapped around that blasted gun.

Drop the gun, drop the gun, drop the gun.

That's my mantra as I slump to the ground, hands over my head.

People yell, but nobody moves. We all crouch on the floor, wishing we had superhero skin that could deflect bullets.

Blam. Blam. Blam.

How many bullets does that monster have?

Blam, whiz, rip, and *sting.*

Intense pain jolts through my arm, blood sprays the wall, and I spew curse words I've never said before. I clutch my arm, a trickle of blood dripping through my fingers.

I've been shot.

"Sara!" Justin's at my side, apparently recovering from his possession a heck of a lot quicker than I did. He doesn't seem worried about whether that Xua-possessed guard is still shooting or not. He tries to look at my arm, but I won't let him.

"Stay down!" I tell him. "That guy might have more bullets!"

"We need a doctor over here, now!" Carla yells.

The bullets have stopped. I think. Billy springs to his feet, rifle drawn.

"Anybody else think about firing a weapon and you're dead!" he yells, eyes scanning the room.

I expect everyone to be terrified and remain where they are, cowering. A lot of people do just that, especially the adults. But the kids wearing shirts painted with an orange *V* jump to their feet with a loud cheer.

They hold their hands in what our parents used to call the peace symbol. But long before that, Winston Churchill used this same symbol during World War II to represent victory. It gave courage to countries being invaded by Nazis, and as a result, underground movements rose up and people painted *V*s on Nazi tanks. Those who lived in occupied territories refused to give up; they rallied together, rebellious and hopeful.

That's why I picked these symbols. They've helped us win before.

And now, the rebellion against the Xua is growing.

Probably in small groups, like these kids.

"Victory!" they shout.

"You'll never defeat us!"

The shirts, the *V* hand gesture, the cheer and declaration that we will not be defeated—it's all stuff from our vids. Before I know what I'm doing, I scramble to my feet, cheering along with them.

"Victory!" I cry, my fist raised above me.

The adults cautiously climb to their feet. Half of them look at the doctor and nurse who shot down the cops and the guards, and the other half look at me. For a minute, I forget I've been shot.

The doctor stares at all the people, a grin on her face, that immunization gun hanging limp in one hand. I still don't know why she's helping us, but I'm glad she is. Without her, we wouldn't have made it.

I shout again. This time, we all do, even the adults, and our cries echo throughout the hospital and out the broken doors. The sound pours into the parking lot and bounces off buildings, and it circles the earth. It sparks off mountains and cliffs and shoots off into space.

And it aims right at Titan.

One way or another, we're going to win this war.

37

"Where's Natalie?" I ask the doctor as she tends to my bullet wound. "How did her surgery go?"

"She is fine. Needs rest and fluids," she says.

Everything says this doctor is human, from her delicate bone structure to her blue-gray eyes to the fact that her nose is slightly crooked. She even looks a little bit like the woman who used to live next door to me and who used to sneak leftovers to Gabe and me because she worried we were too skinny. But this woman, whose name tag says she's Doctor Hathaway, is anything but human. In my mind, I'm calling her Doctor Xua.

She speaks with a slight, unfamiliar accent when she says, "You have a minor flesh wound. Not serious."

This minor flesh wound makes my arm feel like it's on fire.

"Change the dressing twice a day. Take these." She hands me a vial of antibiotics.

My friends and I are all in a long hallway, sectioned off with makeshift curtains. People still cheer and shout back in the admissions area. I know I should care about those guards who were possessed by Xua—that mob is probably going to kill them—but in reality, they were already dead.

I stare at that vial of pills, shutting everything out except what's right in front of me. "Who are you and why are you helping us?" I ask the doctor.

"I'm a friend of Aerithin's." A half grin slides across her face. She's beautiful in an unusual way. It's not her eyes or her smile or her hair. I can't pin it down. I wonder if the Xua inside her is what makes her seem attractive. "You and I are both rebels, are we not?"

My skin tingles, almost like she gave me an electric shock.

I stare at her for a long moment. "So, you're part of the Xua resistance?"

She nods.

Light fills my chest. "Is Aerithin still alive?"

She frowns. "I do not know. I thought he would be here, somewhere. He doesn't answer my com calls."

"But my brother, Gabe, you must know something about him. He got away, didn't he? He's alive and safe?"

"I do not know."

I frown. "Can you at least tell me why the Xua want my brother?"

She shakes her head. "No. I'm sorry."

Frustrated, I sigh. I have a feeling she knows a lot more than she's telling me. How could she *not* know what her own resistance is fighting for?

"Here." Doctor Xua hands me a card, something preprinted with the clinic's logo on it. I scan it quickly. It has directions for what to do and where to go during an emergency. But the printed address has been crossed out and another address has been handwritten in.

I read the handwritten address twice, mentally imagine that part of town. "There's nothing in this area except abandoned buildings."

Justin peers over my shoulder. All of us act skittish around this woman, as if we're waiting for her to change into a human-killing machine. So far, she's been nicer than my regular physician. Although that's not saying much.

"There are emergency centers set up all over Orange County. Food, medical supplies, beds, water, electricity. I recommend this one. They have a trauma surgeon who will know how to care for your friend." The doctor pauses. "All of these centers have a few of my people stationed there."

Billy nods. "If it's got a doctor who can take care of Natalie, then I say we go there."

Maybe those Xua will give me answers.

"There is one last thing I should do before you all leave," the doctor says as she gestures toward a silver scalpel. "The others will be tracking you, Sara. We should remove your skin sites." She looks to Justin and Billy. "The rest of you who want to stay off the grid should do the same."

I nod, remembering what Natalie said back at the school. The Xua could be listening to all of us. We definitely need to take out our skin sites, as soon as possible.

The doctor gives me a quick local anesthetic for the pain, then the slender knife probes the tissue behind my ear, digging. Blood drips down my neck and I hold my breath, eager to get out of here as soon as possible.

38

The ambulance leaves the military clinic, then drives in silence through war-ravaged streets, where whole city blocks blaze with fire. Bodies are everywhere; cars are overturned, store windows broken. The Xua frenzy that was looking for us must have rolled through here. People shout in the distance, their sporadic cries adding another surreal element to the landscape.

Carla's sitting across from me, staring out the window. Her shirt's ripped, there's a stream of dried blood pooled on her shoulder, her hair's a tangled mess, and she's got a bruise on her cheekbone.

"Why were you looking for me?" I ask her. I've wanted to know ever since Billy and Natalie told me that the military showed up at Century Unified. "And why did you ask if I knew a guy named Noah back when we were in Snake City?"

Carla's lip quivers before she speaks. "It's complicated. I'll explain it later, I promise."

Then I remember what she said earlier. *Everyone else I know is already dead.*

That means her father, the general, must be dead.

It feels like there's a dark cloud hanging over all of us.

I turn and focus on Natalie, laid out in the middle of the ambulance on a stretcher. She's awake. Kind of. Nothing she's said so far has been coherent. Mostly she's been talking about some dog she had when she was a kid—she keeps asking where it is. I just keep holding her hand and telling her the dog is fine.

I'd rather be telling her how much she scared the crap out of me and she better not ever do that again. I've already lost my brother and my parents. I almost lost Justin.

If I lose her, too…

I stare out the window, forcing myself to stop thinking about something that isn't going to happen. Justin senses my mood and draws me closer, his arm around my shoulder.

We've been driving slowly, our lights off, trying not to draw attention to ourselves. Every building we pass is dark. The fires and the chaos are behind us, and this part of Santa Ana feels like a ghost town.

A small building appears up ahead, flaming with light, windows glowing, worship coming from inside. Streams of people line the streets, too many to fit inside, all of them holding hands or with arms around one another, some of them holding candles, others brandishing flashlights. They don't act afraid. Don't they know they're easy targets for the Xua? I want to yell at them out the window.

Then I realize it's a church.

I suddenly remember what my life was like once, a long time ago. How my grandma used to take Gabe and me to Mass every Sunday, how the priest spoke in a combination of Spanish and English. And after church, my grandma, my mom, and I would make lunch together. Later in the afternoon, Dad would take Gabe and me to the park, and we'd all play soccer together.

Everything was different then. We really were a family.

Back before my grandma passed away. Before I started traveling through time.

My throat tightens as I recognize the song they're singing inside that little church. "Amazing Grace." I've heard it so many times I can sing it in almost any language, Spanish, English, Latin. I quietly begin to sing along with the people on the street and, in a moment, everyone in the ambulance is singing, too, even Natalie. More than anything, I want to stop the ambulance, get out, and join that crowd. Part of me craves the faith and hope I know is inside that tiny building.

My heart aches for it. But I know this isn't the time or the place.

Not if I want to make a difference in this war.

This part of town is even darker than the rest. Silence and broken cars and empty streets. It makes the hair on the back of my neck stand up. This is where drug dealers used to lurk, where prostitutes hung out on corners. Nobody with any sense ever came here.

Trash cans overturned, potholed streets, broken windows, graffiti painted on walls. One low abandoned building after another line this long street that spools farther and farther from the world of light. I keep thinking we're going in the wrong direction, the address has to be wrong, we need to turn around and go back.

Then a long building looms up ahead, all the windows painted black. A trickle of light spills out of a pair of doors on the side — an old loading dock. The driver pulls the ambulance to a halt in the parking lot, getting as close as he can to the loading dock. My eyes meet Justin's.

"Does this place look safe?" I ask him.

He does a quick survey of the surroundings. "Yup."

I'm not sure. Nowhere looks safe to me right now. I stand with my hands on my hips. Justin starts to grab one end of Natalie's stretcher.

"It's okay. I can walk," she mumbles.

The driver nods, then speaks in a gruff tone. "Just hold her IV bag above her head and have them hook it up when you get inside."

Ahead of us, the doors widen and more light pours out. It's hard to tell what this building was once, but I think it might have been a factory. Three people jog down the stairs to help us, all of them wearing pale-green scrubs. The closer I get to the loading dock, the more I can see inside.

Hallways lined with supplies, gun-carrying guards—many of them no older than me. Eyes that have gone hollow and fingers that clutch weapons. A handful of adults are serving food and tending to injured people. Meanwhile, a small army of teenagers and young children is eating dinner inside, each of them careful to guard whatever weapon they've found along the journey that led them here.

Baseball bats. Crowbars. Fireplace pokers. Kitchen knives. Hammers.

Half their weapons are already bloodstained.

Billy, Justin, Carla, Natalie, and I weave through the hallways, trying not to trip over anyone in the dim light, catching glimpses of other people who went through hell to get here, many of them wearing bloodstained pajamas because their fight for survival began at home.

Where they should have been safe.

This place reminds me of a village in a war-ravaged country, the kind Gov-Net features whenever they're trying to convince us we're not so bad off. *Look at this—these people are really suffering.*

I shudder and try to stay focused as a trauma surgeon approaches us.

Is he one of Aerithin's people, too?

The surgeon exams Natalie, then says that she should be up and walking in a day, which surprises me. He gives me a grin. "Doctor Hathaway at the clinic is a friend of mine. She used cutting-edge tech, which is why your friend is still alive."

This guy's definitely a Xua. And cutting-edge tech? I wonder if he means Xua tech and if it's safe for humans.

He hurries off before I can ask him about Aerithin and Gabe. I make a mental note to find him later.

Carla stays at my side, while Billy and Justin stop to talk to someone who works here. I hear snippets of their conversation, although none of it reassures me. Apparently there have been more attacks on U.S. cities, so many that dead bodies are piled in the streets. Several kids here—techno geeks like Natalie—charmed the internet into showing suppressed videos, recordings that Gov-Net must have tried to keep us from seeing.

As a result, there's a room set up where people can watch things that are happening around the world. I can hear them describe bombs exploding against night skies, an eruption of billowing bright crimson that devoured an entire city. There were also close-up pictures of Xua, dumpsters filled with aliens that had been slaughtered like cattle. Some people are beginning to fight back against the aliens, but their efforts are too small to make a difference.

I sink to my knees as I listen, not wanting to hear more. Carla places a hand on my shoulder, gentle at first, until her fingertips begin to dig into my flesh. I wince, knowing she means to provide comfort but unfortunately has none to give.

My attention shifts as a familiar face peeks at me through night shadows.

Ella.

Relief washes over me. She's alive. Safe.

Like a skittish woodland animal, she creeps closer, glancing around, red hair spilling in matted tangles over her shoulders, a four-inch gash carved across one cheekbone. She looks first at me, large eyes full of surprise, then with her mouth open, she scans the others around me. Her gaze darts from me to Carla, then it sweeps over Billy and Justin.

I nod at her, hoping she'll come closer. She does, one timid step at a time. I know what she's going to say before she reaches us, even though this particular scenario has never played out before.

"Where—where's Gabe? Is he with you?" Her voice comes out raspy and thin, like someone who hasn't had anything to drink for a long time.

Like a knife, her question forces its way between my ribs, searching for my heart and finding it. It takes me longer than I expect to answer and, during that time, Carla is watching me, too. She probably doesn't know what happened to Gabe, either.

I shake my head, words too painful.

"But he's okay, isn't he?" Ella's close enough to touch, her knees bent and her hands trembling. "I know he can't be—he just can't be *dead*." Her last words soften, as if she's trying to convince herself.

"He's alive, I think," I tell her. The Xua wouldn't be looking for him again if he'd been killed. "The aliens took him, but I think he got away. So we have hope." I give her a smile.

Tears glisten in the corners of her eyes. I put my right arm around her shoulders and pull her close. I have a feeling she might be alone here.

"Stay with us," I say. She doesn't balk or pull away. Instead she leans into me, her head on my shoulder, not speaking.

That's all it takes.

Ella is one of us. Again.

I'm glad. Gabe would want her to be safe.

There are six of us now. That's how many there were before we lost Gabe.

Ella joins us as we spend the next hour figuring out which room we're going to make our base, during which time I ask about all the wild stuff I overheard. Eventually, we find an unused office. Soft voices drift in from the corridor while Carla, Ella, and I carefully arrange Natalie's bedding; the boys just toss their stuff on the floor. I spread out my sleeping bag between a cot set up for Natalie's IV and a mat Ella's been carrying around. Even though everyone says our stuff will be safe, I hang on to my backpack. No way do I want a little kid or an addict stumbling onto the pharmacy I've been carrying around.

"Did you guys hear about the Xua that were killed somewhere in South America?" I ask. A girl just brought us each a bowl of hot soup and I take a sip. It's a thin broth with lumps of potato and carrots, and it tastes like ambrosia.

"Yeah," Billy answers. "A team of Xua attacked a coffee plantation in Columbia."

"Why would they attack a plantation? Up until now, they've been going for cities."

Billy shrugs. "Must have been a mistake. Anyway, the guys working in the fields charged the aliens and killed 'em all with machetes."

"Brutal. Wish we had them on our team."

Billy and Justin grin. Carla retreats to a nearby corner, and apparently her head's full of dark thoughts, because she sits with her gaze focused on the floor. Natalie lies down on her cot and quickly falls into a deep sleep. I pull a blanket over her and check to make sure she ate her soup. She did.

I motion for the rest of us to go in the hallway. There we sit, side by side, none of us ready to mingle with the other people here yet. They walk past us, most with heads down, one hand always carrying a weapon. Even the smallest ones have something.

My heart twists when I see a little boy—he can't be more than five—trudging past all alone, a ragged blanket draped over a shoulder, thumb in his mouth, one hand dragging a T-ball bat behind him.

"Hey, where ya going?" I ask him.

He stops and gives me a blank stare, his cheeks pink, his sandy brown hair mussed. His thumb slides from his mouth, and he tries to speak several times, but no words come out. I settle down beside Justin and pat the floor in front of us.

"Come and sit with us," I say.

He hesitates. I stretch out my arms, remembering how many times I used to hold Gabe. When he had nightmares, when the kids at preschool teased him. When I just wanted to give him a hug.

"What's your name, buddy?" Justin asks with a grin.

"Bran," the boy whispers, although it's barely audible.

I see marks on the side of his face as he shuffles closer. They could be burns; I'm not sure. It looks like the medical staff has already treated him, so he's got to be on some pain meds or antibiotics. He sits beside us, and I lightly put my arm around his shoulders, that knife in my chest twisting even harder when he leans into me.

"Are you taking medicine?" I ask.

He nods and pulls a small vial from his pocket. I read the label and try to figure out when his next dose is. Looks like it's in about an hour, at bedtime.

There are a lot of questions I want answers for. Things like, where is my brother; if Aerithin is alive, then why didn't he come back for me; and what am I supposed to do next? I'm supposed to be saving the world, but so far all we've done is struggle to survive.

But I can't talk about stuff like that in front of the kid. My gaze slides toward Carla. She's crying so softly you can't hear it, her shoulders shaking, her lips curled in.

What brought you here, Carla? I want to ask. She had a gang of her own, even bigger than mine, and her dad still had connections with the military. So how did they all die, and why was she looking for *me*?

But I don't say anything. I just pull Bran onto my lap, careful not to touch the burns on his face.

Bran takes his thumb out of his mouth. Long dark eyelashes blink up at me. He looks like a tiny angel, wounded and broken, but still carrying a piece of heaven in his eyes.

"My mommy's sleeping," he says.

For the first time, I notice the blood stains on his clothes. There's a clean spot across his chest and waist, as if he was in the backseat of a car, strapped into a booster seat.

I wrap my arms around him, hiding my face. I can't hold the tears back any longer. They slide down my cheeks. I try to wipe them away but they won't stop, so I close my eyes and I pretend that it's ten years ago and this is my little brother in my lap.

39

About an hour passes, then everyone around us starts heading toward the far side of the building. I wonder if it's some sort of evacuation. Have the Xua found us, and are we all responding to a silent signal the people at the front door forgot to mention?

Natalie's still asleep, and I don't want to leave her. Then I realize Billy has pulled a chair beside her cot, a blanket draped over his shoulders.

"You going to stay here?" I ask him.

He nods, then answers in a soft voice. "I'm not leaving until she wakes up."

Maybe there are some good things going on during this apocalypse after all, besides Justin and me. Billy's got it, right through the heart and then some. Any doubts I had before about his feelings for Natalie have vanished. He's waist-deep in the ocean, waiting for the next wave to pull him out to sea.

Love. Makes you do funny things.

"We'll come back for you if anything important happens," Justin says, pulling me to my feet.

Billy nods.

At least he's got that rifle Manny gave us. He can protect Natalie.

Meanwhile, all the other kids continue to head in the same direction. Both Carla and Ella watch me, waiting to see if I'll join the crowd. Bran holds out his hand, T-ball bat in the other, and I take his tiny fist in mine, letting him lead the way. The rest of our small group follows behind.

Justin walks at my side, holding my hand. Then he reaches down, picks Bran up in his other arm, and carries him. I listen to how he talks to the kid, tries to get him to laugh by telling stupid jokes, and finally, believe it or not, he gets the kid to smile.

I'm so in love with this guy it makes my insides hurt. Just watching him gives me hope. Just having him at my side makes me think we can win.

Together.

Then he glances at me and notices the expression on my face. "You all right?"

I swallow, my throat dry. "Later, okay?"

"Sure." He leans closer, kisses the top of my head, and then gives me one of those grins that makes me melt.

Up ahead of us, the doors to a large conference room hang open. Several members of the adult staff guard the doors, rifles strung over their shoulders, weary grins on their faces. Right now, they're handing out watery hot chocolate to everyone who goes inside. I take mine, slip my fingers around the paper cup, let the warmth sink into my bones.

I'm just about to walk through the door when a hand touches my elbow and pulls me to a stop. I nod for Justin, Bran, and Ella to go inside, but I stay in the hall.

Carla has one hand on my arm, and apparently now is a good time to talk.

I'm expecting her to open up, but we just lean against the wall, drinking hot chocolate. The first sip burns my tongue and, after that, I can't taste anything. We both stare across the hallway, waiting until all the kids and the adults have gone inside the conference room and the door closes. I'm hoping there's no wacky Kool-Aid ceremony going on in there. But then, I always worry about the stuff I can't control.

After the last person has gone inside, I realize the other side of the hall is covered with poster-size stills from those videos Natalie and I made. You can't tell it's me in those photos, but that was never the point. Beneath the posters, someone used orange spray paint to write "Death To The Zow" in big dripping letters.

I can't help but smile at the misspelling.

And then farther down the corridor, in all caps, the word "VICTORY!"

My left hand slides into my pocket, fingers running over Natalie's beads. None of this feels right without her at my side.

Carla nudges me. "Here." She opens her palm and reveals a small plastic wand drive.

"What's this?" I ask as I take it.

"My dad wanted you to have it." She tries to smile but fails.

I turn the drive over in my hand. "Is there something about Noah on here?" That's the only thing I can think of.

"I don't know. It's top-secret. My dad wasn't working on that project, so he only heard bits and pieces about it now and then. But he always said there would be a war in my lifetime that would end everything, unless some guy named Noah could help us."

"Do you want to tell me what happened after you left

Snake City?" *Or maybe why men with guns were chasing you and that's why Natalie got shot?*

Eyes focused on her shoes, she starts to talk, her voice an eerie monotone. It's almost like she saw a ghost or a horror movie, and she's trying to keep her emotions in check.

"I stayed and fought with Justin almost all night. My team was there, too. But then I got a call from my dad—the Xua were attacking Camp Pendleton and other military bases nearby. He wanted me to meet him."

Her voice cracks, and she pauses, closing her eyes before continuing.

"You know I'm a Genetic, like Justin. Except my parents didn't go through the GEIVE lottery to get me. My dad pulled a lot of strings because…" She pauses, her eyes tearing up. "Because he wanted a child who would be able to survive *this*." She gestures with her arms. "My dad trained me himself. Morning and night, every single day. That's why I know how to fight and shoot and survive, but what good did it do me? Or him? He's *gone*! *He's one of the Xua that shot at us!*"

Her dad must be a Hunter now.

I blink, fighting tears. When I speak, my words come out as a whisper.

"I'm sorry, Carla. I didn't know."

She shrugs. "It is what it is, right? You lost your brother. We all lose someone."

I take a shallow breath. Whenever anyone mentions Gabe, it feels like I got punched in the chest.

"Last night, I left Snake City, found my dad, and together we fought the Xua," Carla continues in a broken voice. "A group of us managed to escape, and that was when I told Dad about you. He said he had to talk to you. At first I thought you were at your school, but you were already gone."

I think about that chip she gave me and how I left it in

my backpack at school. Natalie didn't give it back to me until the coffee shop.

"It has a GPS tracker in it," she explains. "That's how we keep track of people down in the river."

I nod.

"We were attacked again after we left the school and were driving along the coast. The world filled with mirrors. None of us could see where we were going—not even the guy driving—and I thought our jeep was going to crash. We spun in a circle, and the car next to us flipped over and rolled toward the ocean."

I bite my lip. I've seen those mirrors too many times. A shiver turns my arms to gooseflesh.

"Then aliens came out of nowhere, more than I could count. Most of them were behind us, attacking other cars on the freeway—but some of them came after us. The Xua turned into smoke, and they got inside our jeep. It was awful. They were swirling around our heads, and we couldn't see. Then another car crashed into us, and we got pushed off the freeway, even closer toward the ocean. Those smoky Xua were still curling around us. I knew I had to keep my mouth closed, so I did. Without saying anything, my dad yanked the door open and pulled me out. Together we ran toward the beach. Once we were there, on the sand, I thought we were going to get away—"

She shudders and stops talking.

"But you *did* get away. You're okay now," I say.

"Not really."

The conference room door thumps open, and Justin steps out. He pauses on the other side of the hall and leans against the wall, watching us. He just waits, like we might need him soon. His eyes meet mine.

"My dad put this in my backpack and told me to find you,"

she says, gesturing to the plastic wand drive.

"Why me?"

"I don't know. He just pushed me into the ocean. He told me to swim and not to look back, no matter what. I almost drowned with that stupid pack on my back. I probably would have, except I've been training since I was four…"

"Whatever happened, it's okay," I tell her. "You're safe now."

She catches a long breath, then closes her eyes again. When she starts to speak, it sounds like she's a million miles away. "I did what my dad said. I started swimming, but I didn't get very far before the aliens showed up. I didn't look back; I couldn't. But I know they came down on the beach, because my dad started yelling."

Another long pause and I'm trying hard not to see that beach in my mind, but I can. I can see it all—her dad surrounded, them holding him down. I've seen how the Xua torture humans. It's awful.

"They didn't possess him. Not yet, anyway," she continues. "It would have been quiet if they did. So they probably tried to make him call me back. But he wouldn't. He just kept cursing at them, telling them to go to hell. I wanted to help him—"

"There were too many of them, Carla," Justin reminds her.

"What good is being a Genetic if you can't save the people you love?" she asks, tears spilling down her cheeks. "I bet I could have killed at least five of those monsters, maybe ten. I could have saved my dad."

Again I'm running the tiny flash drive through my fingers. It has a waterproof casing and a loop on one end, like it was meant to wear on a cord around your neck.

"I kept swimming," Carla says, her words a dark confession. "Even though my dad was yelling, I just kept swimming away from him. I thought the Xua were going to follow me, but they didn't. I swam up the coast, until I came to San Onofre Beach. There I crept onto the shore and hid for a while. After that, I made my way to Pacific Coast Highway and, from there, I stole a car and drove back to Santa Ana, looking for you and following that marker."

"I'm sorry, Carla, really," I say.

But her words keep playing over and over in my head. Something that Carla just said is *really* important—I can feel it. It's like my brain is on fire. I force myself to go back over every detail, looking for a clue.

"You were in the ocean," I say, thinking.

Carla nods.

"And the Xua didn't come after you?"

She shakes her head.

Okay. So they don't like the ocean. But why? Is it that they can't swim, are they afraid of sharks, are they allergic to water? There must be *something* they were trying to avoid...

I gasp. "Oh my God!"

Both Carla and Justin just stare at me.

"Don't you see it? The *rain* today didn't bother them. There was still a Xua frenzy, plowing through Santa Ana. So it wasn't water that stopped them from following Carla. There's something about the *ocean*," I say. "Something they really don't like."

Lightness, like a houseful of sunshine, fills my head. I think I just figured out one of the Xua's weaknesses.

The ocean, a large body of water, stopped them.

A large body of *salt* water.

40

Once I've convinced Justin and Carla that I'm right, we slip into the conference room where the kids have been telling stories about what's happened since the invasion. I'm practically vibrating with the need to either demand one of the Xua stationed at this abandoned building talk to me or wake up Natalie and figure out what to do with our salt theory. Justin wants me to wait until morning, and Natalie needs rest. Honestly, we all do.

After half an hour, the kids begin to fall asleep. Some of them curl up together in the middle of the floor, a mass of little arms and legs, sharing blankets. Others hide in the darkened corners of the room, their weapons still clutched to their chests.

At that point, Justin, Carla, and I tiptoe out of the room, Bran in my arms. Ella follows us. The door swings open, and a flow of fresh air calms me just a bit. Tomorrow morning, Natalie will be feeling better, and we'll come up with the plan that'll win this war.

We're passing the makeshift cafeteria before we realize

we're being followed.

Two little girls about eight years old are just a few feet behind us. I know the instant I see them—the lost expression in their eyes—that they have no one here, no older sisters or brothers.

We stop and wait for them. Justin reaches down and scoops one of the girls up into his arms. She leans her head against his chest, her brown-gold hair tumbling over her face. Carla takes the other girl's hand and then, together, we head back to the office we claimed, taking a small army of children with us.

There are eight of us now, eight children who have no one but ourselves.

Our room fills with shadows, a puzzle of sleeping bodies on the floor. We've been given blankets and sleeping bags, but there aren't enough to go around, so I open my blanket and lay it out flat so it's twice the size. Then I give it to Bran, Ella, and the two new little girls.

"Hey," Justin says in a low voice. He motions for me to join him. "It's not much, but I scored a couple of pillows and a blanket. If you want to share."

"Sure." I set my backpack on the floor, then my heart skips a beat or two as Justin and I lie down next to each other. I have no idea how I'm supposed to fall asleep, especially when he wraps one arm around me and kisses me.

"We're going to survive," he says. "I know we will."

"I hope so," I whisper.

He runs his fingers through my hair. "And we have something to look forward to, don't we? That Gabe is still alive and we'll find him?"

I nod and then nestle closer to him, my head tucked under his chin, my hand on his chest, his heartbeat strong beneath my fingertips. It feels so good to be with him again, so safe. Like nothing can ever hurt me.

Some older boys whisper in the hallway outside our room. I keep hearing words like "run" and "knife" and "blood," so I quit trying to listen. From what I've overheard so far, one group of kids formed a gang last night. They rounded up eighteen kids from their condo complex—most of them went to Thorpe Fundamental, the nearby elementary school—and every one of them had lost either one or both of their parents. Together, these kids managed to fight off a small band of Xua. After that, they wandered in here the next morning, hoping they could find something to eat.

Apparently, most of the kids who have survived are the ones who watched my videos. Except for Justin and Billy, nobody knows that Natalie and I made those. I wish we'd made more. There were a lot of other things I wish I had told them.

My mind is like a race car, going around and around the same track.

I try to sleep, but I can't.

Justin has rolled over on his back and he's already in REM sleep, his eyes flitting beneath his lids. I hope he's having good dreams, but I doubt it, the way his muscles keep flinching. It's more like he's practicing a battle.

My fingers slide over that flash drive Carla gave me. Earlier, I rummaged through one of the desks and found two pieces of cord. One, I used to restring Natalie's jade and gold beads. The other I made into a short necklace and attached that flash drive, so it now hangs beneath my shirt.

Why did Carla's dad tell her to give this to me?

I sit up, careful I don't wake Justin. The other boys in

the hallway are finally quiet. Hopefully, they left. Everyone else in the room is asleep. I grab my backpack and creep out into the hallway. Light falls in through an open window. A full moon hovers outside, the same moon as yesterday, the same as tomorrow.

The earth, the moon, the stars, they all stay the same.

But we don't. We change.

I find a quiet spot down by the drinking fountain, lean against the wall, and pull the tablet from my pack. I hold my breath as I flick it on, and it powers up with a soft *bleep*. Plenty of power left. I run a finger along the edge, locate a port, and slide the flash drive in, waiting for the drive to show up on the screen.

Nothing happens.

I turn the power off and on a few times, pull the flash drive out and reinsert it, but all I see is my home screen image, a photo of Dad, Gabe, and me at a Dodgers game, one of the rare times my father took a day off work and spent it with us.

The flash drive clicks and spins, but it never registers. Instead, my tablet inadvertently hooks up to the internet. After what everyone has been talking about—all the dead bodies and the cities that have been destroyed—I'm not sure I want to go online. I consider flicking that connection off.

But I don't.

The first image has already popped up. It's today's top news flash, a list of U.S. cities that have been attacked by the Xua. Buildings have been destroyed, whole city blocks are on fire, and blackened ash floats down from the sky. Detroit, Seattle, Atlanta, Houston, New York, Chicago, Boston—

Washington, D.C., is still dark. No news has come in yet about what happened during the attack on the White House. Did the Xua get in?

I set my tablet on the floor, then start pacing the hallway.

My adrenaline's kicking in at the wrong time. I should be asleep. I shouldn't be worried about aliens or wars or secret messages from the government. I'm just a kid and I'm tired of fighting and never winning.

This abandoned building looks eerie at night. There's a ghostly quiet. With this much open space, everything is cast in shadow. Too many doors lead into black rooms and hallways disappear into shadow. I wonder if the Xua know I'm here. If they do, they could come at any time, and we wouldn't have anything to stop them.

Except maybe we do.

I don't stop to think. I stuff my tablet in its case, hang the flash drive around my neck, sling my backpack over my shoulder, and make my way to the cafeteria, hoping the door's unlocked. Thankfully, it is. I swing it open, then run a gaze across the room. This side of the building doesn't have black paint on the windows, and moonlight pours in, outlining lunch tables and chairs.

Compared to the rest of the world, this space looks surprisingly organized. I start hunting, and the first thing I grab is an empty bowl. After a few minutes, I find a tray filled with saltshakers. One by one, I screw the lids off the shakers, then pour their contents into my bowl. A few minutes later, I have a cereal-size bowl brimming with salt.

I sneak out of the room, much quieter than when I came in.

The next step in my plan requires stealth. And a mean streak, which I already know I have.

That Xua doctor back at the hospital told us there would be more Xua here at the school, so I've been watching all the adults, looking for signs. So far, I have three people figured out. The trauma surgeon who's taking care of Natalie, one of the paramedics, and Mr. Malone, a counselor who ran that "therapy" session for the kids earlier.

I saw Mr. Malone walking toward the main office when we all left the conference room. So I head over there, careful not to spill any salt on the way. I'm going to need every grain. The entire wall leading into the office is made of windows. I hope he doesn't see me coming. Otherwise —

Otherwise, I could be in trouble. Even a "nice" Xua might not be so friendly if he catches me trying to poison him.

I open the office door, hoping it doesn't squeak, wishing I had brought Justin or Billy with me. Even one of those fourteen-year-old boys who fought off a band of Xua would be a welcome companion right now. I don't know where Mr. Malone is, but I'm guessing he's asleep on a cot in here somewhere. The smell of old carpet greets me as I sneak down an inner corridor. I can barely see, it's so dark. My left hand runs along the wall, trailing the edge of a bookcase, bumping over a row of hanging photos, dipping into a recess in the wall.

It's an open doorway.

I stop and listen for breathing.

Silence.

He can't be in there. Unless Xua don't breathe at night.

My fingers continue to slide along the wall and then finally I find another doorway. I stop and hold my breath. I command everything in the universe to be quiet, but it refuses. Instead, a nearby clock ticks and water rushes through pipes and somewhere, out in the hallway, someone coughs.

I freeze, hoping the cough doesn't wake Mr. Malone.

There's an unpainted window at the end of his room. It's curtained, but pale light still shines in, exposing a long, narrow room with a desk at the far end.

And on the right, a cot.

He's there, asleep.

His chest rises slowly, methodically, peacefully, his head

hidden behind a bank of filing cabinets, his torso and feet stretched out on the bed, a blanket drawn over him.

I quietly and hastily pour my bowl of salt across the doorway, creating a thin white line, almost invisible. Most people wouldn't even know it was there.

I swallow nervously, then take a step backward, hoping I'm far enough away from the door that he won't be able to reach me. Then I call his name.

"Mr. Malone! Mr. Malone, help!"

My heart thunders; I can't believe I'm doing this. It feels like dangerous magic, like I might be stirring the powers of darkness. I'm pressed against the wall as he stumbles out of his bed.

"What is it?" he calls into the night. "What's wrong?"

I move a few more steps away and call again in a softer voice this time.

"Stop, stop, don't! Mr. Malone, help!!"

He flicks on the light and scurries toward the door, turns into a silhouette outlined with yellow light. Then, when he reaches the doorway, he slams to a halt. He glares at me, hissing, an almost supernatural sound that makes my skin crawl. He speaks in Xua, in that dreaded secret language, a succession of words that sounds like curses. Sharp, brutal words, his eyes narrowed, his back hunched.

Holy. Effing. Crap.

I almost can't believe this.

Mr. Malone stands frozen at the edge of the room, unable to cross the barrier of salt.

I move a step closer, terrified, but curious at the same time.

"Why did you do this?" he asks.

"Why can't you come out?" I ask.

His eyes glisten with dark light, and I know I've made an enemy. He's not speaking English. I've triggered something primal inside him—the need to survive. His head swivels, and he stares back at that window on the far side of the nurse's office. Too late I realize I should have spread salt there, too. But I wasn't trying to trap him, was I? I mean, I knew he was a Xua. I only wanted to test my theory.

He's still hissing and spitting, but never once does he cross that line of salt or even extend his hand across it.

"Why can't you touch the salt?" I demand, my voice bolder now.

"We should have killed you the moment you came in the front door," he growls, his words barely intelligible. "I don't care what the rest of the Rebellion says. You can't be trusted."

Then he lunges across the room like a fierce beast. In a single fluid movement, he grabs the desk chair and swings it against the window, again and again. I don't realize I'm screaming, but I am. I'm terrified, and I don't want him to escape. Not if I accidentally made him mad enough to join the other Xua that want to kill us. The chair continues to strike the window until glass sprays across the room, followed by the smell of night air. He bounds through the open window, not seeming to care that the edges are like glass daggers or that he'll get cut.

One moment, he's there in front of me, mad as a caged beast.

The next, he's leaping through the window, down to the ground. I run inside the room, see blood on the window frame and him on the ground, hobbling to his feet.

And then, after a final hiss back at me over his shoulder, he dashes away, disappearing into midnight shadows.

41

"What were you thinking?"

"Are you *nuts*?"

"There were a million ways you could have tested your theory, Sara." Justin's hands are on his hips, and he towers over me. "This was probably the worst way imaginable."

"Okay, okay," I say. "I get it. I should have waited or discussed it with you guys or done something else, anything but what I did. I just couldn't sit around and do nothing anymore. We need to act, and now we know how!"

The office is filled with too many people, and I can't breathe. I want to get out into the hallway or, better yet, outside. That trail of salt got brushed away when I first ran into the room, trying to see if I could stop Mr. Malone from jumping. Now it's my word against anyone else's whether I put salt there in the first place. Carla leans out the window, staring down at the parking lot. She accidentally brushes a shard of glass, knocks it out, and it tinkles to the ground. Natalie moves slowly around the room, like a private detective trying to figure out what really happened. I wish she was back in bed, but apparently the trauma surgeon was right.

The "cutting-edge tech" that Xua doctor used back in the clinic is working faster than our own medical techniques would have.

Billy's the only one who's excited about what I did.

"Salt? No kidding, *salt*?" He keeps saying the same thing over and over, a goofy grin on his face. "Holy wow, that's cool."

"What's cool about it?" Justin asks. "Sara could have gotten hurt."

"But she didn't," Billy answers. I'm proud of him for not letting Justin bully him. "Don't you see?"

We all stare at him. Apparently, we don't.

"All we need to do is get a lot of salt and pour it around the building. Then we'll have a fortress, just like in *Battle Mania III*."

"Video games? Really?" Carla asks.

I never even realized Billy was into video games.

Natalie frowns, but not for the reason I expect. She's nodding. "I think it could work."

"I agree," I say. Also, this will buy us enough time to gather more information. Maybe we can find more Xua rebels who will help us find Aerithin. And Gabe.

"Where will you find that much salt?" Justin asks.

"It shouldn't be that hard to find," I reason. "And if we're going to get it, the middle of the night seems like the best time. So where can we find salt?"

Billy grins. "Target and Walmart sell forty pound bags for pool supplies. I used to clean my uncle's pool in the summer."

"Natalie, you get the addresses and directions to the nearest Target and Walmart," I say. "Justin, you find a truck or a car we can use. And Billy, you find some gear for breaking into the stores, in case the windows and doors aren't already broken."

I don't know where Justin found an old truck or how he got it started. All I know is, half an hour later we're all crammed inside and heading toward the nearest Walmart. It's about four in the morning, so I'm seriously hoping no one else will be there.

Billy's the only one who knows how to drive this ancient beast with a stick shift and no automatic GPS controls. We pull into the parking lot, then slide sideways into a spot by the door.

The lot looks like the clinic, cars jammed into one another. A few still have dead bodies inside, people who are never going to leave that spot behind the steering wheel. I'm getting tired of this whole *Night of the Living Dead* theme.

Justin and Carla jump out of the trunk bed and head to the front of the store. Billy follows a step behind them. It doesn't look like they'll have any problem getting inside, since all the windows are broken. I couldn't convince Natalie to stay back at the school, but I'm not about to let her wander around the store. She stays in the truck with me.

Just before they all disappear, I call out to Justin. "Hey, give us Natalie's gun."

He jogs back to the car and hands it over. Billy has that rifle and Carla has a gun, so this way both our groups will be armed.

"Make sure you all stay together, okay?" I say.

He leans in the window and kisses me. Then he grins. "I figured that might be the only way to make you stop giving orders," he says. Then he kisses me again, long and slow enough to get my heart thumping.

"Funny," I say, but as soon as he disappears, I'm rubbing

my thumb across my lips, remembering his kiss, replaying it over and over.

For the next several minutes, Natalie and I both stare at the darkened store in silence. Waiting. My stomach feels like there's a nest of snakes inside, squirming around and biting. I change position, hoping that gnawing sensation will go away. It doesn't.

"Did you ever get a chance to catch up on the news?" she asks.

I nod. "Part of it."

A car races down the street. Natalie and I sink lower in our seats, trying to not be noticed. Now I'm glad Billy parked so crooked. We blend in with the rest of the cars in the lot. My left hand tucks inside my pocket, and I remember Natalie's broken bracelet. I pull it out, thinking the way I strung it back together looks like an art project done by a fifth grader, the beads out of order, the cord so long it's more like a necklace than a bracelet. I wish I could tell her how worried I've been about her, but all I manage to do is open my fist and say, "Here."

She stares at my hand for a long time, so long I wonder if she even recognizes her bracelet. Then her eyes glisten with tears as she reaches out to take it.

"I thought I lost this," she whispers.

"Maybe later we can figure out how to put it back together right. It's pretty messed up—"

She slides it over her head. "No, it's perfect. Thank you."

Silence lingers between us for another moment before I get the courage to say what's been in my heart. "You know, your dad is really smart, and he knows how to take care of himself," I say quickly, hoping she doesn't try to stop me. "He's probably safe somewhere, just like us. He's probably being careful because he wants to see you again."

She nods. "I hope so."

I've known all along that this is why she's always been willing to help me save my brother. She knows what it's like to be separated from someone she loves.

Then I pull the flash drive out and show it to her. "Carla gave me something," I confess, my voice hushed.

"What's on it?"

"I have no idea. Her dad told her to give it to me, but my tablet can't open it. I think it's encrypted or locked. The contents are supposed to be top secret." I try to hide the fact that I'm terrified. I have no idea what information this thing holds. Best-case scenario, it'll have the rest of the Xua's weaknesses, and one of them will be something I can work with. Worst case, we find out the world really is screwed.

Natalie frowns. "It's top secret and some guy in the military wanted *you* to have it? Why?"

I shrug.

"We should take a look. Give it to me." She pulls out her tablet—she never goes anywhere without it. With a flick of her wrist, she's got the flash drive hooked up, and it only takes a minute or two for her to access the files. It downloads onto her internal drive. Images and charts and word documents fly up, one after another.

"Hey, what's that? Is that a picture from Titan?" I ask.

She tries to find it, then opens it, and we both stare. It's a shot of a mining camp on another planet, but it looks old, like the camp has been there for years, which is wrong, since the *Valiant* hasn't even landed yet. The image is slightly out of focus, but I can definitely see a group of people approaching in the distance, dust blowing around them.

They glow in the dark. They've got to be Xua.

"That's from the future," I say, confused.

She nods.

"Open that video." I point.

She clicks on it and, a moment later, we're watching a general as he talks to a group of soldiers. The really weird thing is, the video's got an embedded time stamp from forty years in the future.

"The real battle can only be won in the future—in the twenty-second century. No matter how many times we try to beat them in the twenty-first century, we always lose," he says. He stares at the camera, his gaze piercing.

The Xua have been fighting battles with us in different time periods? Aerithin never told me that.

A shiver flows through me as the video continues.

"So far, we've only found a few weaknesses." The general holds up his hand and starts flicking off his fingers, one by one. "First, if you kill one of their Leaders, you immediately weaken the rest of that cell. Second, every time they travel through time, their genetic material breaks down a little bit more—"

I nod. I already knew this.

The general continues with his list of Xua weaknesses.

"And, as a result, the decisions made by the Xua keep getting more erratic, more unpredictable."

Again, he's staring at the camera, and I almost feel like he's talking directly to me. I knew this message was going to be horrible. I wish he would stop, but he doesn't.

"And finally, for some reason they always go after the adults first. I think they've made a huge mistake by ignoring the children. I sincerely believe that, even if we fail, our children will be able to carry on the battle for us."

Natalie pauses the video and stares at me.

Neither one of us can speak.

My heart races and my stomach churns.

"They haven't been ignoring the children," Natalie says. "They've just been going after one particular kid, over and over. Gabe."

"But he's gone."

"And then they started going after you, Sara. There was that group of Xua that attacked you in the coffee shop, that frenzy that was heading right for your house…"

"And that Leader in the clinic. But why me?"

"Maybe Aerithin triggered something by trying to save you and Gabe. Maybe he broke the rules."

"So this is vengeance for that?"

"I don't think so," Natalie says. "But maybe we've been looking at this all wrong. Maybe this isn't *your* last chance to save the world. Maybe it's *their* last chance to destroy it. If Gabe is still alive—and I really, really want to believe that— then maybe he's stuck in the future and he's trying to find his way back through the mirror doors somehow."

"I like that idea."

"Me too. Except it's possible that whatever is happening in the future is what's making the Xua fight so hard this time. In the past twenty-four hours, they've almost killed you multiple times. Remember, if you die, we all die."

I nod. "Then we better get that effing salt and get out of here. Fast."

42

We work all night long, but the sun still comes up sooner than we expect. Blue shadows stretch behind the building while yellow light reflects off the few unpainted windows. The air's cool and brisk and welcome as it blows across my neck. My hair's damp with sweat when I finally stand up and glance around, noting that we've got all our bags of salt positioned around the building. Next step: start pouring. I'm going to leave that part to the others. I've got something to do inside.

First, I check on Natalie. She's back in our room, finally asleep again. I check the younger kids, cover those who have kicked off their blankets, then glance at Billy. He traded places with Ella when we got back from Walmart so he could guard everyone in our room. He was quite insistent on it, in fact. I watch him now, his head nodding on his chest, rifle draped over the back of his chair.

Even though he's almost asleep, he's still holding Natalie's hand.

She hasn't said anything about this yet, but she doesn't

have to. If she didn't want his attention, she'd tell him to back off. If there's one thing I know about that girl, it's that she's not shy.

I'm smiling when I leave the room.

The rest of the building is silent, even more so than it was in the middle of the night. No one wants to wake up and face this new world. Better to stay asleep as long as possible, dreaming about things we've lost.

I wish I had time for dreams.

But even if I wanted to sleep, I can't.

Something's coming. I can feel it, like a steady tremor beneath the balls of my feet.

I just hope we're ready in time.

Once I get out of our hallway, I hear vague movement and soft voices. Someone is already working in the cafeteria. Smells like they're making oatmeal with brown sugar. My mouth waters as I pause before the open door and spot a woman inside, slicing apples. I wonder how much time we have before we run out of food. That's got to be our next priority—send out a search party and bring back as much food as we can. After that, we need to find a way to go on the offensive, maybe form teams and attack the Xua with salt.

We should have gotten some high-pressure water guns at Walmart. I could have made a saltwater slurry to put inside and handed them out to all the kids here.

Note to self: *Head back to Walmart ASAP.*

People are waking up now. Shadowy figures appear in doorways, rubbing sleep from their eyes, mouths opening in wide yawns. Two girls wave as I pass—I think they were in my algebra class last year, back at Century Unified. I don't remember their names, but I notice they've both drawn large black *V*s on their hands with marker.

I should start getting these people ready for what's ahead.

Maybe I'll hold a training session in the conference room later today. Make sure they all know how to use those weapons they've been carrying around. They need to get ready for the next step.

But first, I need to make a change in everyone's diet.

The woman making breakfast isn't happy to hear my request. I do my best to explain it to her, and she keeps shaking her head, refusing. In the end I do it myself when her back is turned. Then I head back through the building, passing a group of four sleepy ten-year-olds, all heading toward the showers. I overhear one of the boys boasting about his last round of *Virtual Street Racing*, how he managed to beat everyone online that day.

In my mind I see Gabe, fingers curved around his game controller.

He's a welcome ghost, haunting me, following me, waiting for me to figure out where he is.

Sunlight sears the hallway up ahead, bolder and brighter now, through the open doors on the loading dock. I'm heading toward our makeshift infirmary, set up in the first room past this entrance. I'm trying to figure out if there might be other people on staff who are Xua. I think there's a nurse, too, or maybe she's a nurse's aide. She mainly does whatever the other two staff members tell her to do. As far as I can tell, the surgeon must be in charge. A burly man with a rattling smoker's cough and fingers like sausages, he doesn't look capable at all. But somehow he manages to spin magic with those broad meaty hands. I saw him lace up a boy's bleeding arm with nearly invisible stitches, and I watched how he tended to Natalie's bullet wounds.

I'm dreading this conversation.

The door hangs open, and the first thing I see is an empty cot. All the computers have been moved to a counter along the far wall, and medical supplies cover the desks. The doctor is half asleep, leaning back in an office chair, feet propped up on a desk. His eyes flicker open when I walk in, and I worry that he already knows why I'm here.

I have to tell him what happened last night, and I have to be honest with him, because my next step is to ask what he knows about Aerithin and my brother.

I do my best to be diplomatic as I tell him about Mr. Malone. About how I trapped him in another office with a layer of salt, how he panicked and jumped out the window. I mention that I didn't mean for that to happen and that I wasn't trying to hurt him. The doctor's first response is to glance out the window, as if Malone might still be out there, waiting for him. Then he rises to his feet and, now that there are just the two of us in the room, I realize he's a massive brute. Broad shoulders, muscular arms.

I hope he doesn't wig out like Mr. Malone.

"You did *what*?" he demands, leaning over me. I hear that slight accent creeping into his words, and he sounds almost like Doctor Hathaway last night. "Why would you do that? We came here to help you."

"I—I—" I can barely get a complete sentence out. Meanwhile, I slip one hand inside my pocket and wrap my fingers around my switchblade. Just pressing it into my palm restores my courage. "If there was a way to stop the Xua—the bad Xua—I needed to know. I had to test it. I'm sorry, I didn't mean for him to run away. I just wasn't thinking that—"

"Blast it, girl! We're shorthanded now," he says, glancing around him as if he's trying to count his allies. "If the others attack the building, we won't be much use to you without

Malone."

"But we're making a barrier right now." I point toward the window. "It should keep the other Xua away. We should all be safe."

He studies me suspiciously, then goes to the window and stares outside. I join him, both of us watching as Justin slices open another bag of salt and starts pouring. He's making a thin line that traces the shape of the building. I know Carla and Ella are doing the same thing, each of them positioned in different sections around the perimeter.

The doctor curses, loud and long, then he swings toward me. I back up and pull out my switchblade, afraid he's going to strike.

"You're making a barrier out of *salt*?"

I nod. Either he doesn't notice my weapon or it doesn't impress him.

"They told me about you." His eyes narrow, and I feel like I'm getting a repeat performance of last night. "But I didn't believe you'd be this much trouble. 'How can one girl possibly harm us?' I said. But you're trapping us in here and giving us a death sentence. The other Xua already consider us traitors. If they find us, they'll kill us first. If you think what Xua do to humans is bad, you have no idea what they do to their own kind."

I swing my blade, just to make sure he sees it, just in case he's thinking about doing anything. Like jumping.

Instead, he opens his mouth wide and screams. It's a long, high-pitched shriek that warbles between octaves and shreds every nerve in my body. I can't stand it. I fall to my knees and cover my ears, cringing in pain. Down the hall, I hear a resounding cry, in a different pitch but equally horrid. A moment later another one screams, from the far side of the building, I think.

The alien cries seem to go on forever, and I swear they can be heard on the moon.

Then the doctor shoves me aside with a brawny hand. I tumble to the floor and hit one of the long tables on the way. Bandages and vials of medicine bounce down, some of them striking me on the head. I'm still shaking from the screams. I think they may have stopped my heart for a second. I'm gasping and trembling, one hand still clinging to my switchblade.

And then the screams echo through the building one more time as the three of them head toward the exit.

43

They leave, all three of them. One more Xua than I knew about. They cover their mouths, probably trying to keep salt from getting in, and they race out the front door side by side, as if we might try to stop them. Most of us, me included, are cowering, hoping we never hear another trio of screams like that again. None of us speaks for several minutes. We walk around, numb, trying to regain our composure.

My friends must know what I just did. Natalie will forgive me, I'm sure, even though this will affect her the most. Losing her doctor was the last thing I wanted.

The barrier's almost finished, and volunteers are passing out breakfast. Sliced apples and steaming bowls of oatmeal laced with brown sugar.

And lots of salt.

I wince as I watch everyone bite into their food, then spit it out. Time to man up. Not that I want to. I stand in the middle of the hall and speak as loudly as I can, which isn't really that loud. "Okay, I know it doesn't taste very good, but you *have* to eat it!" I yell. "We can't waste food. Not now."

A couple of people try another bite, then swallow with great reluctance.

"And from now on, at least one of our meals every day will contain a large quantity of salt!" I'm still yelling. They stare at me with furrowed brows. "I don't have time for explanations. You need to trust me. The Xua can't stand to be around salt, so this is necessary for our survival."

That gets everyone's attention.

I have to keep this place Xua-free. No more Jumpers. And apparently, no more hidden "we're the good guys" Xua, either.

Justin and Carla walk in the front door while I'm explaining the food situation, both of them looking exhausted. Someone hands them each a dish of oatmeal. Carla tastes hers and wrinkles her nose but manages to eat it anyway. Justin pushes his away.

"I raided our food supply last night, right before we headed out to get the salt," he says. "I'll take my dose later."

Meanwhile, Billy jogs down the hallway toward us. I can tell by his expression that he's upset. His cheeks are red and his fists clenched.

"The doctor's missing. Do you know where he is?" he asks.

"Yeah. He left with the other Xua," I answer. "I told him what happened last night with Mr. Malone."

"Why?" He stares at me with an incredulous look.

"Because I wanted him to trust me," I say. "I was hoping he'd tell me where my brother is."

Justin stands beside me, his arms crossed.

"But now we don't have a surgeon," Billy says. "What if something happens to one of us?" Then he says what we're all really thinking. "What if something happens to *Natalie*?"

"I'm fine," Natalie says, her voice quieter than usual. She's pushing her way through the crowd toward us. "Look, Sara's right. She gave them the choice to stay or leave. Once that circle of salt was finished, they wouldn't have been able to get out. Not even if they jumped into smoke. Would you want to be trapped in here?"

"I *am* trapped," he says.

"Nobody's *making* you stay." Her hands are on her hips. I'm not sure if anyone else notices it, but there are two small bloodstains on her T-shirt. Right where those bullets slammed through her yesterday.

"Okay, guys, enough," I say. "Natalie, you need to get back to bed. Carla, find that nurse—I know she's still here somewhere—and get her to take a look at Natalie's bullet wounds. And we can't wait till the last minute. We need to send out a team for food and supplies. Any volunteers?"

I scan the raised hands, note that almost all of them are kids below the age of twelve. I shake my head. "You gotta be at least fourteen to go off-site. Now let me see who wants to go."

Nobody lowers their hands.

I sigh.

I guess having too many people willing to risk their lives is slightly better than none.

Billy's helping Natalie back to our room. Justin and I are trying to figure out who's really old enough to go out looking for food when Ella comes in the front door. She wipes a hand across her forehead, brushing damp red curls aside as she grins and announces that our salt barrier is finally done. Right then, when I think maybe we've accomplished something that might help protect us, we all get some news.

Some very bad news.

44

The Gov-Net announcement comes when we all stand in the hallway. Ella's mouth hangs open as everyone around us freezes in place. Those who have working skin-site connections stare off at the holographic transmission. I'm just about to ask someone nearby what's going on when the building loudspeakers unexpectedly kick in. They're part of an old emergency broadcast system, wired about fifty years ago, long before skin sites were invented. The original owner of this building must have decided to leave the old systems in place, just in case.

This is one of those emergencies they were hoping would never happen.

The president is speaking. I don't need to see his face to recognize his voice, that rich baritone that carries a hint of a smile in its tone. Up until now, Washington has been dark, and as a result, we've all been too scared to talk about what happened. I'm silently praying he gives us a message of hope, something to encourage us and keep us going.

And that he isn't a Hunter. Because if he is, our country

is toast.

"I know all of you saw the attack on Washington two days ago," the president begins. "But you may not know that we weren't the only city invaded—Los Angeles, New York, Chicago, Detroit, Atlanta, Boston, Seattle, and Houston were assaulted as well, and the effects have spread throughout the country. We're hoping to get our communication systems back up soon. But in the meantime, I need to ask all of you to stay strong and carry on. If at all possible, get back to work— especially if you're a doctor, nurse, paramedic, or volunteer firefighter. The police force, the firefighters, and the armed forces are doing the best they can under the circumstances, but we all need to pull together if we want to win this battle—"

I agree with what he's saying. We do have to pull together if we want to win. It's our only chance for survival. Then I notice a couple of preschoolers huddled together in a corner, crying. I go over and kneel beside them. They throw their arms around my neck.

"Is it the end of the world?" one little girl asks.

I shake my head and hold my finger to my lips.

"The White House was attacked," the president continues, his tone sounding upbeat and confident despite the situation. "But we managed to fight off our enemies—*most* of our enemies."

He pauses, and several kids around me stare at one another, eyes wide.

He's not telling us the whole story. Apprehension swells inside me.

This is exactly how a Hunter would talk.

"We know who's behind all these invasions. And we plan to retaliate soon. But first, I must ask you not to give in to fear. We may need to go through a few more dark days before we begin to see the light again—"

Natalie has come back down the hallway, and she's

looking at me. That bloodstain on her shirt has widened. It seems to be spreading with every heartbeat.

"It looks like we're in the midst of another kind of war," the president says, and a collective gasp sweeps down the hallway. "Already Iran, Iraq, England, Japan, India, Russia, and Australia have experienced this. As I mentioned, several American cities have been attacked. What I didn't say is that this new enemy, this race of aliens from another planet, has gotten control of our white bombs."

No.

In an instant, all my strength is gone.

This is the nightmare we've all had since we were children, that someday one of our enemies would send the white bombs to kill us.

Except the nightmare just got one hundred times worse.

The Xua have white bombs.

Some military leaders claim this is humane, the death is quick, and, hey, it doesn't destroy any buildings. But we all know that's just propaganda. When a white bomb explodes, Agent-X rains down like acid, so strong it can penetrate through steel-plated buildings. When it gets within twenty-five feet of you, your skin begins to melt. At ten feet, your brain starts to boil, right inside your skull. At five feet, your bones begin to dissolve. Once Agent-X hits ground zero, all the people and animals within a twenty-mile radius are vaporized.

Almost nothing left behind to prove you ever existed. Not a shadow, not a whisper. You're gone.

No one around me moves; no one breathes. It's like we're all trying to be quiet so the white bombs won't find us. The only sound I hear is the wind blowing through the trees outside. It's an eerie, constant rushing almost like the sound of the ocean. Relentless. Merciless.

No matter what I do, no matter how often I travel through

time, I can't stop the inevitable.

I can't stop people from dying.

"Did he say white bombs?" Billy asks, a tremor in his voice.

"Are the Xua going to bomb us?" Ella asks. She shelters the little kids in our group by draping one arm around their shoulders. Bran leans against her, his thumb in his mouth.

I stand, listening to the whisper of the wind as it continues to moan through the trees. It almost sounds like a thousand voices, all of them reminding me of my mistakes. Why is everything else suddenly so quiet? Then the lights in the hallway flicker. Light spatters on, off, on, and finally off with a crackly hiss that wicks its way throughout the building. I keep waiting for the president's speech to continue, but it doesn't. I notice the people around me are more alert than before. Gov-Net must have switched off, too.

Maybe the president, wherever he is, was the first target hit by the white bombs.

I glance at Natalie. She's just staring off into space.

All I can think about is the Xua having control of our greatest weapon. Meanwhile, the bloodstains on Natalie's shirt continue to widen. Where the heck is Carla and that nurse?

"The Xua have gotten the advantage," Natalie says, her words hollow.

Finally someone moves. Footsteps race down a distant hall, doors swing open, and a girl calls to us.

"Look! Look!" she cries.

It's Carla, and she swings into my line of vision then, eyes wide like she's just seen an army of ghosts. She slides to a stop next to Justin. It takes a heartbeat for her to catch her breath.

She points toward the front door, wordlessly.

We all turn and look. Nothing's there.

"Outside," she says, her words little more than a gasp. "They're here."

45

The front doors are still closed, but the whispering wind has grown louder. It murmurs now, an eerie sound that both unnerves and compels. I want to tell everyone to stay where they are, but we're all straining to listen. Carla stands frozen in the middle of the hallway, still too frightened to speak.

But Natalie's not afraid. She pushes through the crowds, heading toward the exit. I follow her, realizing that a cluster of kids and young children has already gathered there. A few adults are trying to peer through the nearby broken windows. Every single person with a view to outside wears an expression of horror on their face. Before, we had a constant backdrop of chatter, people talking to one another, even while they were listening to the transmission from the president. Now an unnatural silence fills the building, and we all hold still, trying to understand what we hear outside.

Natalie glances back at me.

"What's going on?" I ask.

But before she can answer, the other kids begin to flow past us in a brisk stream, all of them converging on the exit.

Up ahead of me, the door swings open, light pours in, and kids flow out. I'm swept up in the crowd, trying to catch up with Natalie. I know the others in my crew are nearby; I see them from time to time—Justin's broad shoulders, Billy's blond-streaked hair, Carla's frightened expression, Ella's wild red hair—but the crowd separates us. I push my way through a sea of shoulders and elbows until I find Natalie. I pull her to a stop before she reaches the door that leads outside. "What are you doing?"

She strains against me, her face a mask, like she's in the midst of a nightmare and can't wake up. "Don't you hear them?" she says, her voice choking at the last word.

"Hear what?"

But the door is open now, and I realize I do hear something, like murmuring, indistinct words being spoken, over and over. I tilt my head, listening, my heart skittering. I freeze, unable to believe what I hear. In the midst of the clamor, two familiar voices are calling my name.

"Sara—Sara, sweetheart—"

My parents.

Oh, dear God, no. Please, no.

Natalie nods. "They're all out there. Calling us."

The door hangs open, and a crowd of people pools outside, all of us stunned, unable to think clearly. Voices are calling out to us in every language: Chinese, English, German, Russian, Korean, Farsi, Czech, Spanish, Hindi, and more.

"Don't go out there!" I yell. But how can I compete with this?

The building is surrounded on all sides by the worst effing body-snatching army in the history of horror. It's made up of our parents, sisters, brothers, cousins, and best friends. Every one of them calling our names, arms outstretched.

"Sara—Natalie—Ella—Justin—Carla—"

The list goes on and on, until every one of us has been shot through the heart and we're dead; we can't fight. Natalie's sister and mom stand in the front row, bruised and beaten. Her mom's clothes are scorched, and her sister has bloody scratches all over her face, like someone forced her jaw open to let a Xua get inside. Both of them call to her, feigning heartfelt love.

"Join us, Natalie. Come here, my precious daughter—"

Natalie's crying, tears running down her face. She brushes a palm across her cheek, then shoves her way haltingly through the crowd until, at last, she stands on the pavement outside.

I follow her, terrified she's going to run out and join them.

I grab her by the arm and stop her from going any farther.

"That's not your mother or sister," I tell her.

"I know—it's just all that's left of them." She turns toward me, her lashes thick with tears. "I was hoping they were safe."

Then I realize most of the other kids are rushing past us; they're racing toward the parking lot. Toward the Xua horde that surrounds the building.

These kids need to be stopped. We can't afford to lose even one of them.

"Stop!" I yell, but they aren't listening to me. "You all need to get back inside! These aren't your parents or friends! They're here to *kill* you!"

I see Justin behind me, head and shoulders taller than the rest of the crowd. He has that same look of torment in his eyes as Natalie. I want him to be the sensible one, to help me, but I can tell he's fighting the same emotions as all the others. I twist around and follow his gaze, then locate his mom and dad in the tangle of broken bodies standing at the edge of the salt perimeter. He thought they were safe, too. He thought they got away, that they made it to his sister's house and somehow the alien curse had passed them by. Most of us don't know what happened to our families—they just went missing, like a runaway dog with the backyard gate left open. And now, here they are, calling us to come home.

Home. It's what we all want. Mothers and fathers who love us enough to turn down the volume on the endless stream of Gov-Net news and music and pay attention to us.

I turn toward Natalie. She's lost interest in me for a moment. She's staring at her mother again.

Holy crap, I've got to do something fast.

I lunge forward, reach into Natalie's pocket, find that gun she's been lugging around since last night, and I pull it out. It's heavier than I expect, and it yanks my hand toward the ground. My fingers latch onto the barrel just in time, before it slips away. I find the trigger, and it becomes my new best friend. Then I dash through the crowd, elbowing everyone out of my way. I race, gun hidden at my side, until I'm standing in between the kids and their Xua-possessed loved ones.

Feet braced, chest surging, shoulders back, and head high, I face them all.

"Nobody's leaving!" I shout, louder than I've ever done before. It's a shout so loud it burns my throat and empties my lungs. I draw another savage breath and yell again, "Do you hear me?"

But they all just keep trying to push past me.

In horror, I see a little silhouette darting between everyone's legs. Behind me, Ella is yelling. A child is running toward the Xua, weaving between people. He's too far away for me to reach him in time and he's crying.

"Mommy!"

No. It's Bran.

Panic shoots through me. "Somebody stop him!"

Meanwhile, the crowd surges forward and a few people have already stumbled over that line of salt.

"Come back, Bran, come back!" Carla and Natalie and I

are all yelling. Ella is chasing him and her fingers latch onto his shirt, but he wriggles out of her grasp.

My heart freezes when an older boy picks Bran up in his arms and carries him across the line of salt. Someone who must be Bran's mother reaches for the little boy, a broad smile on her face. He drops his T-ball bat, takes his thumb out of his mouth, and tries to wrap both arms around her.

"Put him down!" I cry.

It's too late.

The woman has already snapped his tiny neck.

She leers at me, then drops his lifeless body on the ground.

I don't even stop to think. I aim my gun at her chest and fire.

She collapses next to him. Her body twitches, like there's a live snake trapped inside, and everything I've ever heard about Xua anatomy proves true. If they're trapped inside a human host when they die, they die, too.

I feel like someone just ripped my heart out of my chest, but I can't stop. I just can't. Bran isn't the only one to die. Every single person who crosses that line of salt is murdered while we watch.

One by one.

And now, I've got an out-of-control crowd on my hands. They're all being called to their deaths. Most of them are trying to stop, but some of the people behind me don't know what is happening and, in their panic, they keep shoving me forward. That line of salt is growing closer and closer. If I can't stop this madness soon, I'll be pushed into the arms of this nightmarish horde, too.

"Get back inside the building—now!" I yell. "All of you!"

Then I raise the gun over my head, and I fire it toward the heavens.

Ba-boom!

Everyone in Santa Ana knows the sound of gunfire. We've

been raised on it. It thunders through our sleepless nights; it echoes down our dark alleys. It ends every fight and it begins every gang war. It sends our loved ones to the morgue and invites us to too many funerals. Our streets are always lined with memorials—flowers and candles and tear-stained letters of goodbye.

Not this street. And not today.

"If anybody moves closer to that crowd, I'm going to start shooting. Right at them!" I face the people still poised in front of me, but my right arm is aimed back toward that crowd of alien body snatchers. "Do you hear me? I'll kill them if you don't get back inside!"

The children closest to me start crying, deep soul-stealing sobs, their chests shaking. They're pleading with me, all of them.

"Don't kill my mom, please—"

"Not my sister, don't shoot her—"

"Please don't, please—"

I'm the monster now, and I can't believe I'm doing this. Behind me, my dad's voice rises above that unending chant of names.

"Sara, Sara, don't, little girl. Put the gun down, baby—"

Oh, sweet Jesus, he's never sounded like he loved me so much. Not even when I *was* a little girl.

"Sara, sweetheart, we just want you to come home—"

I fire my weapon toward the sky again, and this time the crowd responds. They look around, wide-eyed, and then slowly begin to move back toward the doors.

They don't know I'm fighting my own personal demon.

I'm the girl who can never save her own brother, so how can I possibly save anyone else?

My gaze flickers over the remaining crowd. I can't bear to look behind me—I can't look at my dad, I just can't—then

I see Justin, still staring at his mom, sorrow and panic in his eyes. The two of them have always been close. It's one of the things I like about him.

"Get back inside the building!" I say, and I hate myself because my words quiver at the end.

The last few people disappear back into the building, but Justin doesn't move. Billy now stands beside him.

I can't stop the helplessness that floods through me, a river of bad water, a riptide pulling me out to sea. I turn and glance behind me. My father has moved. The entire Xua-possessed throng has. They've come several steps closer, almost close enough to lunge at me and grab the gun.

But it's the look in my father's eyes that reaches inside my chest and stops my heart.

His expression has changed; the light has darkened, and now a sinister grin reshapes his face. It's hatred, as dangerous as a lightning storm, bolts of jagged light striking down, killing everyone. The gruesome expression on his face sickens and terrifies me. I can't move.

And at that moment, when I'm the most vulnerable, someone grabs the gun from my hand—Natalie. Her chin held high, her tears dried. She stands at my side, aiming the weapon at my father, something I was too weak to do.

"You'll be the first to go," Natalie says. "You frigging monster."

She shoots him in the leg, and he stumbles to the ground, still alive, but at least he's not looking at me anymore. He continues to call my name, his face buried in the grass, his words muffled. My mother stands at his side, oblivious to what just happened. No compassion for him, no notice that his blood is pouring on the ground, painting the brown grass a brilliant red.

And then, just when I think it can't get worse, it does.

46

My team has all drawn their weapons, even though we know we won't be able to hold this horde of Xua back for long. Not if they find a way to cross that narrow bridge of salt. Even the wind could brush away a patch and give them an opening.

That's when it happens.

The sky overhead rumbles. Like distant thunder.

Rain would wash the salt away.

My heart races as I look up. Nothing but blue sky overhead. No storm. No clouds. Still, the thunder grows and the ground beneath me trembles like the earth itself is afraid.

My father has crawled to his knees. As much as it hurt me, Natalie was right to shoot him.

That horrid grin on his face grows.

"You had to know we had a backup plan," he says to me, his voice loud and clear, carrying throughout the crowd and beyond.

The Xua-possessed army begins to laugh, heads lifted. Some of them even dance, though the only music is the sound of engines, whining and raking the sky like monster hands ripping the heavens.

Airplanes. I can't see them yet, but I know that's what they are now.

My heart sinks until my chest feels like a black hole.

The words of our president echo in my mind: *"We may need to go through a few more dark days before we begin to see the light again—"*

He was telling us the end was near. That a lot of people would die before there was any hope of winning this war.

The trembling in the ground intensifies just as a formation of planes appears in the distance. I lose my balance, tumble, and hit my knee on pavement. The universe has shifted, mirrors surround us, higher than mountains, wider than oceans, what is and what will be, hope and destruction and every beginning and ending opens up in front of us. I see the beginning of the earth, the first man and woman, babies without number dissolving into unmarked graves, we live, we die, we are dust. I turn, and behind me the Xua have already left their hosts; a cloud of black dust is transforming into a crowd of slender silver bodies, every one of them braced and ready to run as soon as the doors to the future open.

They leave a pile of human carcasses behind, and I can't bear to look at the bodies.

But the mirror doors haven't opened yet.

It's hunting season.

We start shooting the aliens, weapons firing and striking silver flesh, glowing blood pouring out, Xua bodies slumping to the ground. We have only so many bullets, and they're gone too soon. Before long, both Carla and Natalie are pulling triggers that echo with a hollow *click*.

Across from me, just a few feet away, the dead bodies of our parents, sisters, brothers, and friends litter the ground—

And overhead the planes fly, close enough to see.

A big black *X* is painted on the side of each and every one. The mark of a plane carrying white bombs.

Billy bolts toward his father's body. He uses the butt of his rifle to sweep an opening in the path of salt and then runs across bare earth. Likewise, Justin rushes to his mother's side, and I can totally understand why he's doing this. We might all be dying in a few minutes, and he wants to see her one last time. He lifts her into his arms, shakes her gently, as if trying to wake her up, as if he can't believe she's really dead. Some of the bodies do look as if they're merely sleeping. Maybe the Xua have another way to leave without ripping us apart. Maybe they only do that when they're in a panic.

Justin's mother opens her lips, and I gasp.

Maybe she wasn't possessed; maybe she's still alive!

But then a black-headed Xua pours out of her mouth.

I stumble forward.

No.

No!

"Justin!" I scream as it pushes its way inside Justin's mouth, and I take off at a dead run. "Billy! Kill it!"

It's no use. Justin falls to his back, and the last of the Xua slips inside.

I skid to a stop just inside the salt line and choke back a wail. I've never seen a possession happen so fast. There's no way I could've gotten there in time, and Billy froze in place, but it doesn't matter. He wouldn't have been fast enough to stop it even if he'd been standing right beside Justin with his switchblade open.

But one of the things I've learned from my time travels is this: Just when you think things can't get any worse, they usually do. They get a *lot* worse.

Billy whirls around and aims his rifle at me.

"What are you doing?" I ask.

"You never understood how dangerous your brother is," he answers.

A chill floods through me. *"What?"*

But I already know, don't I?

He swept the salt away with the rifle.

He didn't try to save Justin.

He's a frigging Xua.

Now I know why they've been a step ahead of us the whole time.

Planes of death are heading our way, Justin is still flailing and choking as the Xua takes full possession of him, and Billy is a traitor.

All I can do is whisper, "Justin."

Worse. And then even worse.

The mirror doors open. The Xua who are still alive race toward them.

Billy tosses us a cavalier grin, then he pulls Justin to his feet.

I know Justin has a Xua inside him and that makes him my enemy now, but all I can see is the boy who was always there for me, more than anyone else.

Justin turns and looks at me, his eyes dark, a troubled expression on his face.

I've never seen him look so lost.

Then he runs through a mirror door, disappearing from sight, Billy a step behind him.

"When I find your little brother, I'll tell him you said hi," Billy says to me, the mirrors embracing him, distorting his features. "Right before I kill him."

"Bastard!" I scream.

But both of them are already gone, and my curse just circles the parking lot and the street without purpose.

The mirrors disappear and, at that same moment, the heavens overhead darken. The formation of planes is right above us, all of them white against indigo sky, flying so close together they're like an interlocking puzzle of positive and negative shapes.

The building windows rattle from the noise of the engines. Can the pilots see the expressions on our faces? Do they know they're killing a bunch of helpless kids?

My mouth is filled with dust, and I can't speak, I can't move.

Beside me, Natalie is speechless, something that doesn't happen very often. She just slips her hand in mine. Ella takes my other hand and presses her trembling lips into a thin line. Carla slides one arm around my waist. Still as stone, we watch the pattern of white and blue that moves and shifts and drones, the hatches that swing open, and the glistening white cylinders that slide into view.

We gasp.

I want to close my eyes, but I can't.

The cylinders, the bombs, all release at the same precise moment, and they plummet faster than I expect, growing larger and larger as we watch, the air filling with a whine that changes pitch.

Natalie leans her head on my shoulder, and I wonder what would have happened if we'd never been best friends. Maybe she'd be free somewhere right now, or maybe she'd be in some part of the city where the bombs aren't falling, or maybe she could have gone to Seoul one more time to see her father.

If I hadn't fallen in love with Justin, maybe the Xua wouldn't have chased him for countless lives; they wouldn't have possessed him and pulled him into the future. He and Billy wouldn't be hunting for my little brother right now, hoping to kill him.

If I had never cared about anyone, maybe they would have found a way to be free. There has to be a place in the universe where it's still safe, where children can be just children, where they don't have to learn to fire weapons or swing hammers at their parents to survive.

Up above, the bombs explode and Agent-X begins to spray out, a mist that glistens and catches the sunlight in a glittering rainbow. Horrible and beautiful.

At this moment, I am anything but valiant.

I am weak and pitiful and ashamed and broken and defeated.

I wrap my arms around Ella and Natalie and Carla, trying my best to offer a few inches of protection for them, my head lowered.

The whine overhead has turned into a hiss, like the sound of sprinklers on a lawn. Agent-X is drifting down, filling the world with silence, wrapping us in a bubble that both traps us and blocks out everything else. The sunlight dims, and everything around me is white.

I'm blinded.

Even if I wanted to run, I wouldn't know which way to go.

I think I hear something, almost like music, like metallic chimes, hollow tubes sliding against one another in the wind, the rhythm erratic, the sound growing louder, then softer, a clanging and banging of metal against glass—

The light around me grows brighter, then dims. Almost like sunlight when it reflects off a mirror, casting beams of light that move closer.

Heat so strong I can barely breathe wafts over me, and I whimper, waiting for the end to come, for my skin to start melting like wax.

"Sara—"

"Sara, hurry! This way!"

Voices, soft and indistinct—I can barely hear them over the chimes, over the silence, over the movement of mirrored doors.

A thousand mirrored doors are sliding open, only this time it's not for a Xua army. It's for us.

Hands are latching onto us, pulling us up.

"Climb up, all of you, take hold of his fur. Hurry!"

Arms are reaching down and grabbing onto us. I realize that I recognize one of the voices—

It's Gabe! My brother is here.

He's riding a fire-beast.

Another person is with my brother, but I don't know him. He smells like a forest, earth, moss, leaves.

"Noah, hurry!" my brother yells at him.

It's the boy Aerithin told me I would meet one day. The unavoidable cascading event in my future was him saving my life.

Noah.

He grabs hold of Natalie and yanks her up onto the fire-beast, then reaches back down for Carla and Ella. The beast radiates heat and, as soon as I touch it, a vibrating purr runs through me.

My brother wraps one arm around me, pulls me up onto the beast in front of him, and holds me safe. His other hand latches onto a fistful of burning fur. The sound of Agent-X is like rain now, the planes above, one last echo of thunder and the descending mist, a hissing wet curtain.

"Now, fly!" Gabe yells from behind me. He must be directing the fire-beast, just like Aerithin used to do. "Faster than you ever have before! Take us back, now!"

Agent-X is so close I can feel the skin on my shoulders sting, and we're all howling in pain as my brother leads us in a charge, back through the mirrored doors, all of us temporarily blinded by the falling white bombs.

47

2137 A.D.

Within moments, we've gone from a field of blinding white through the Corridor of Time to the edge of a forest. The gray sky overhead is even darker here, and birds sing in the nearby trees, warning one another of our presence.

A city that I think is Los Angeles looms in the distance, but everything looks so different that I'm not sure. I can see the remnants of a freeway to the right, but it looks more like a green river with vegetation growing up the sides. Trees sprout up on overpasses and rusted metal pokes through. A shopping center stands on the far side of the freeway, but it only vaguely resembles a building. Trees cover the roof and vines creep up the walls.

Is this where my brother has been all along?

Another boy, a bit older than me, stands at the edge of a forest, watching me. His pants are torn and dirty, and his long blond hair is braided and woven with feathers.

Noah.

He hasn't spoken to me since we got here.

Except for Natalie, Ella, Carla, and me, there are no other girls here. I haven't been able to count exactly how many boys there are. They keep darting in and out of the woods, stopping to talk to Noah, who nods from time to time. He must be in charge.

Just like me.

Aerithin's fire-beast sits away from us and, even at this distance, the creature's light and fire warms us. Its long liquid strands of fur shift with each breath of wind, and occasionally sparks fly off into the darkness.

Maybe our rescue from the white bombs was something that had to happen; maybe it was part of us changing destiny.

I just wish Aerithin would have told me about it.

He should have told me what would happen to Justin. I struggle to breathe every time I think about it, that look on his face that broke my heart.

Billy's betrayal was another sucker punch to all of us. Natalie hasn't been able to look me in the eye since we got here, as if she should have known. But how could she? Hunters are impossible to detect.

So are Leaders.

I have no idea when Billy got possessed or what his real endgame was. It really seemed like he was part of our team— right up until he pulled a gun on me.

Aerithin probably knows how it happened. He might even know which Xua possessed Justin and Billy.

Aerithin stands at the edge of the field, separated from our group. He looks injured, one arm held tight against his chest, and he limps when he walks.

I try to imagine his life, always traveling through a land of mirrors and corridors, where destiny is a game played for all of eternity. I can't understand it—the way time spirals and changes, how the universe shifts whenever someone travels through time, the fact that Aerithin can slice through the fabric of reality.

And the fact that he's so different from the other Xua.

There's an almost majestic quality to him, something about the way he holds his head and the expression on his face. I've always wondered if there was royalty in his blood. There must be a reason why he leads a band of rebels.

But it's all a mystery and I may never know. He may never tell me the answers I want to hear.

Gabe walks up to Noah, a scowl on his face. You'd think my brother would be happy that I'm safe or that his girlfriend, Ella, is here, but he's not. He's angry.

"Why did we get there so late?" Gabe demands. He pitches a stone into the distance, striking a nearby hillside with a *whumpf*. "They almost died! We were already traveling through time—couldn't you have chosen an earlier doorway? Look at them—they're burned. My sister's neck is covered with blisters, and have you seen Natalie's back? I think her first layer of skin must have peeled off." He shakes his head firmly. "We should have gotten there sooner; we could have saved Justin—"

Noah stills him by raising a hand.

"The Xua think your sister is dead," he says.

Gabe and I look at each other, then I glance at Natalie, who is obviously listening. I don't think any of us thought of that.

"I'm sorry," Noah says, and his gaze shifts away from me.

A minute earlier and Justin could have been rescued with

us. They exchanged his life for letting the Xua think I'm dead. In what world is that worth it?

A surge of panic thunders in my chest as the memory of Justin rushes through me—how he smells, the sound of his voice, the way his smile lifts my spirits—and I struggle to my feet. My heart feels like it's being ripped in half. That Xua poured down Justin's throat so fast, I couldn't have stopped it.

No. Letting him die was *definitely* not worth it. Nothing will ever be the same now.

I need to be alone.

I push my way through the long grass, down a slope, and into the forest, away from everyone else. Here, amid a covering of black oaks and willows, I fall to my knees, mourning everything I've lost. My parents, all the people in the abandoned building, Earth as we knew it.

And Justin.

I'm so in love with him. I always will be.

He's here, somewhere. I know it.

And he and Billy are both hunting for Gabe.

I shudder as I think about what Justin is now, a flesh-and-blood disguise for the Xua inside him.

The next time we see each other, he won't be the boy I fell in love with. He'll be my enemy.

Maybe it's his destiny to kill me.

No. I refuse to accept that it's over, that there's no hope.

There *must* be a way to bring Justin back. If I were possessed by a Xua, he'd do whatever he could to save me.

"I'll always love you," I whisper, hoping that some part of him knows I'm still alive and that I'll be looking for him.

I stay in the woods for a long time. A cool wind blows through the trees, stirring leaves and branches. I stand, planning to rejoin the others, but a shadow has crept into the forest behind me and has been waiting.

My brother.

He looks older now, like he's been here a year instead of a few days. He's got a *V* tattoo on his chest, his hair has grown long and wild, and he's as dirty as the other boys. He's thinner and taller, and his lip trembles as I draw near.

"I thought I would lose you," he confesses, his words soft. "I thought the Xua would get you. And then, I saw the white bombs dropping and I thought we were too late—"

Tears trace paths down his cheeks. Down mine, too.

"If we hadn't gotten there in time, I would have turned that fire-beast around and gone back to another doorway," he says with a sniff, wiping his nose with the back of his hand. "I don't care what Noah or any of the others say. I would have gone back for you."

I slide my arms around his waist and rest my head on his chest. "I would have done the same for you," I whisper.

For a long time, I listen to his heartbeat, the soft drum that says, *He's alive, he's alive, he's alive*, over and over again. His heartbeat gives me hope that somehow we'll all survive. Even Justin.

But, as much as I want it to be enough, it isn't.

I need answers and I need them now.

Gabe and I find Aerithin sitting beside his fire-beast, as if he's waiting for us, as if he's known all along that it would come down to this moment when I would confront him. Up until now, we've only had brief, frantic moments together, when he saved me from certain death and then transported me back in time.

This time, I'm not going anywhere and neither is he.

"I thought you were dead," I ask Aerithin. "What happened?"

He breathes slowly and deeply, his gaze fixed upon the distant horizon of broken buildings. "Exactly what should have happened."

I bristle. I'm tired of his circular logic and his cascading events. "If this was how it was supposed to happen, why didn't you save Gabe yourself in the first place? I obviously couldn't. I failed every single time!"

"You did not fail. You succeeded." He looks at me, his eyes flickering and dimming for a moment. "You did exactly what I told you to do. You kept your brother alive until morning."

"But you lied about the rest. You said saving him would save the world, and clearly *that* didn't happen." I gesture to the crumbling city I used to call home. "We lost everything."

Aerithin glances away. In that moment, I'm sure I'll never get the answers I need, something that will keep me going. For the first time, I notice all the battle scars on his silver skin, as if he's been fighting this war for a thousand years.

It feels like forever passes before he finally speaks.

"I did not lie when we met," Aerithin says. "You saved your brother. And now, Gabe will save your world."

Gabe takes a step backward, his eyes wide. "What?" he gasps. *"How?"*

"You will destroy the Xua."

In one horrifying rush, I know exactly what we're up against. I know why every Xua has been after him, and I know it isn't going to stop. We're on their territory now. There's nowhere left for us to hide. Nowhere left for us to run.

And now two people from my crew are after us, too. People who know all my secrets and weaknesses. Justin and Billy.

I take my brother's hand. "I'm going to help him."

"So will I," Natalie says behind me.

I jump, startled by her voice, and glance behind us and realize that everyone has moved closer.

"Me too," Noah says.

We all know what we're facing now.

One by one, each person on my team and Noah's team takes a vow. I don't know how Gabe is supposed to destroy an entire alien race, but I'll stand at my brother's side for the rest of my life, no matter how long it takes.

And when I find Justin—I know I will; our paths are destined to cross again and again—I'll find a way to save him, too.

No matter what happens next, I'm not going to be afraid.

This time we're going to win.

ACKNOWLEDGMENTS

Valiant was a book of my heart. It took me four months to write this story about a time-traveling girl who has to save the world. It then took years to edit and find it a proper home. I never gave up on this book, however. I always loved the idea of an average girl being given the task of saving everyone she knows—but most specifically, her younger brother.

For me, the essence of the story is this: Who would you be willing to save the world for?

Sara's younger brother, Gabriel, is a geeky, science-fiction-loving, comic-book-reading fourteen-year-old boy who's enchanted by the one thing that will end the world—the launch of the Valiant rocket ship. In many ways, Gabe is modeled after my son, Jesse. So, I can definitely understand why Sara would be willing to try so hard to save him. I would, too.

I never lost faith in this book, even though I injured my hands from typing it so quickly and, even though, as a result six years later, I still can't use my thumbs when I type. I never lost faith even though it took a long time for this story to make its way into print. One reason I didn't give up was because so many people helped and encouraged me along the way. First, I want to thank my agent, Natalie Lakosil, because she loved this book way back in the beginning, when it was still an untamed wild creature. Next, I want to thank my editor, Heather Howland, because she loved, nurtured, and polished it until it became a lovely, dark apocalyptic tale with a hint of romance. I also want to thank my beta readers, Kristian Kim, Teddi Deppner, Jane Wells, Carol Collett, Becca Johnson, Mac Wheeler, Cheri Williams, Eddie Clark, and Melanie Noelle Bernard, who patiently read this story and then gave me their input.

As always, I'm indebted to my writers' group for supporting me throughout Valiant's publishing journey. Rachel Marks, Rebecca Luella Miller, Paul Regnier, and Mike Duran—you'll always be my heroes!

A very special thank-you to my husband, Tom. Thank you for loving and supporting me when I work crazy hours staring at a computer screen, when I get emotionally attached to imaginary people, when I cry if I kill off one of my characters, and when I occasionally allow a bad guy to survive at the end of a story because there might be a sequel.

And, of course, I must say thank you to my son, Jesse, for giving me a reason to write this book. You are beautiful, intelligent, creative, and talented, and you have an incredibly gentle spirit. I will always love you. You are definitely the person I would save the world for—over and over again.

GRAB THE ENTANGLED TEEN RELEASES READERS ARE TALKING ABOUT!

PAPER GIRL
BY CINDY R. WILSON

I haven't left my house in over a year. The doctors say it's social anxiety. All I know is that when I'm inside, I feel safe. Then my mom hires a tutor. This boy…he makes me want to be brave again. I can almost taste the outside world. But so many things could go wrong, and it would only take one spark for my world made of paper to burst into flames.

KEEPER OF THE BEES
A BLACK BIRD OF THE GALLOWS NOVEL
BY MEG KASSEL

When the cursed Dresden arrives in a Midwest town marked for death, he encounters Essie, a girl who suffers from debilitating delusions and hallucinations. But Essie doesn't see a monster when she looks at Dresden.

Risking his own life, Dresden holds back his curse and spares her. What starts out as a simple act of mercy ends up unraveling Dresden's solitary life and Essie's tormented one. Their impossible romance might even be powerful enough to unravel a centuries-old curse.

STAR-CROSSED
BY PINTIP DUNN

Princess Vela's people are starving. She makes the ultimate sacrifice and accepts a genetic modification that takes sixty years off her life, allowing her to feed her colony via nutrition pills. But now the king is dying, too. When the boy she's had a crush on since childhood volunteers to give his life for her father's, secrets and sabotage begin to threaten the future of the colony itself. Unless Vela is brave enough to save them all...

SEVENTH BORN
A WITCHLING ACADEMY NOVEL
BY MONICA SANZ

Sera dreams of becoming a detective and finding her family. When the brooding yet handsome Professor Barrington offers to assist her if she becomes his assistant, Sera is thrust into a world where someone is raising the dead and burning seventhborns alive. As Sera and Barrington work together to find the killer, she'll discover that some secrets are best left buried...and fire isn't the only thing that makes a witch burn.

KEEP READING FOR AN EXCERPT FROM MERRIE DESTEFANO'S LOST GIRLS...

Yesterday, Rachel went to sleep listening to Taylor Swift, curled up in her grammy's quilt, worrying about geometry. Today, she woke up in a ditch, bloodied, bruised, and missing a year of her life.

She doesn't recognize the person she's become: she's popular. She wears nothing but black.

Black to cover the blood.

And she can fight.

Tell no one.

She's not the only girl to go missing within the last year...but she's the only girl to come back. She desperately wants to unravel what happened to her, to try and recover the rest of the Lost Girls.

But the more she discovers, the more her memories return. And as much as her new life scares her, it calls to her. Seductively. The good girl gone bad: sex, drugs, and raves, and something darker... something she still craves. The rush of the fight, the thrill of the win—something she can't resist, that might still get her killed...

Excerpt from *Lost Girls*
by Merrie Destefano

I didn't recognize myself.

When I went to sleep last night, my hair had been dark brown and shoulder-length. Now it was cropped short and dyed platinum blond. My face looked longer and thinner, my cheekbones more pronounced. I looked away from the mirrored wall on my left and focused on the man sitting across from me instead.

FBI agent Ryan Bennet.

Any other time I would have thought it was cool to be alone with a guy like this. About ten years older than me, he looked like a stunt double for Channing Tatum. Cool green eyes studied me, a pensive expression on his face. He glanced down at his notes, tapping his pen on the table between us.

"You don't remember anything about where you were for the past two weeks?"

He'd asked this before. I'd already answered it.

I sighed. I wanted to go home.

"There was a smell. Like a forest, maybe. Pine and cedar. That's all."

"Could that smell have been a man's cologne?"

I shrugged. "Maybe."

"The last thing you remember is…"

"Going to bed and listening to music."

"And your current class schedule is..." He began naming all my sophomore classes, reading a list I had written down a few minutes ago.

I nodded.

"You don't remember taking chemistry or Algebra II?"

"Are you kidding?" There's no way I was in Algebra II. I hadn't even mastered geometry yet. I was still worried Miss Wallace was going to flunk me.

He shifted in his chair, then shot a quick glance at the mirror, maybe wishing he could talk to whoever was on the other side. "There's one other thing we haven't discussed yet."

An unwelcome shudder raced over me. I already knew that I hadn't been raped. I'd spent hours with a doctor while she gently poked and prodded me, asking me questions. When she was drawing my blood, both of us had been puzzled by the marks on my inner arms.

Needle marks.

Either I was a druggie, which just couldn't be true, or someone had been injecting something into me. The tricky thing was, some of those track marks looked a lot older than two weeks. Now I had a possible threat of withdrawal hanging over my head, with symptoms that could range from headaches to night terrors to tremors.

Across from me, Agent Bennet opened a large manila envelope, one that had been sitting conspicuously beside him throughout our interview. He slid out several photographs, all eight-by-ten glossies—each one catching his attention for a moment and causing his brow to lower—and then he slapped them down on the table, lining them up in a row so they faced me. They were all shots of girls about my age, each one with different hair and eye and skin color, each one smiling into the camera, like they were expecting something wonderful to happen. These had to be yearbook photos, because every hair was perfect, every girl was staring right at me.

All of them waiting for something.

I glanced up at Agent Bennet, wondering what he wanted. "Do you know any of these girls?" he asked.

I ran a gaze over them again, imagining them stretching on the barre, wearing one-piece black leotards, or running down the hall at Lincoln High, wearing jeans and T-shirts, backpacks slung over their shoulders. Six girls looked up at me, wanting me to know their names, but I was lucky to remember my own name right now.

I shook my head. "Who are they?"

He started listing them off as if they were his younger sisters; every time he touched a photo he would say the girl's name and his jaw would shift, just a fraction, as if the muscle was working too hard. As I expected, he said six names I didn't recognize—Emily, Hannah, Madison, Nicole, Haley, and Brooke—then he spoke again, still staring down at their faces.

"All these girls have gone missing within the past three months. Two of them disappeared after school, like you did. Three left home for sporting events but never came back. One girl told her mother she was spending the weekend with a friend, but the friend waited and waited. The girl never showed up."

He paused, then looked directly into my eyes, watching me so closely that a trickle of sweat began to run down my neck. "You're the only girl who has come back," he said, leaning forward. "How did you get away?"

How was I supposed to know? My skin started to heat up, a feeling of being trapped started to overwhelm me, and my breathing turned ragged and raw. I needed to get out of here.

I shook my head, my stomach roiling. "I don't remember."

"There were pine needles stuck to your clothes, Rachel, and seedpods that can only be found in the San Gabriel Mountains. Could someone have been holding you captive in the mountains?"

That smell of cedar and pine came back, as if he had conjured it. It wafted around me, oozing out of the floorboards and the seams where the walls met. It curled like smoke away from the mirror until foggy clouds covered the floor. I fought a gag reflex, holding my right hand over my mouth. Without realizing it, I pushed my chair backward, accidentally knocking it to the floor with a loud crash. I struggled to my feet.

At the same time, the door behind me clicked and swung open. A woman dressed in a navy blue suit looked in at us, a stern expression on her face as she glanced from me to Agent Bennet. "That's enough for today, Bennet. In fact, it's enough, period. Miss Evans can go home now. Her parents have been waiting for more than an hour."

One hand still over my mouth and nose, trying to block out the stench of pine and cedar, I stumbled past her, heading down the hallway. But no matter how fast I walked, I could still hear the two of them arguing.

"You will not follow this line of questioning any further, do you understand, Bennet?" the woman was saying. "This girl has been traumatized enough."

"But there's something here that connects these cases. I'm sure of it. Something we're overlooking—"

"Half of these girls are probably runaways. There's not enough evidence to prove they fall into the category of Violent Crimes Against Children, or that these cases are related—"

The farther I walked away from them, the more their voices faded, which was what I wanted. I could see Mom and Dad and Kyle through a large glass window up ahead, all of them waving at me, big smiles on their faces like we were going to Disneyland.

The two agents behind me probably hadn't realized that I could still hear them. It was like I was invisible. I tried to ignore them and forget about what might have happened during that two-week period when I was lost.

Except now, after talking to that FBI agent, I knew that I wasn't the only one. There were other girls out there who had gone missing, too.

And they were still lost.

entangled teen

an imprint of Entangled Publishing LLC